CREATED BY Jay Faerber & Scott Godl[...]

COPPERHE[...]

writer **JAY FAERBER**   **SCOTT GODLEWSKI** artist
colorist **RON RILEY**   **THOMAS MAUER** letterer
book design **SASHA HEAD**   **VINCENT KUKUA** book production

Image Comics, Inc.

Robert Kirkman — Chief Operating Officer
Erik Larsen — Chief Financial Officer
Todd McFarlane — President
Marc Silvestri — Chief Executive Officer
Jim Valentino — Vice President

Eric Stephenson — Publisher
Ron Richards — Director of Business Development
Jennifer de Guzman — Director of Trade Book Sales
Kat Salazar — Director of PR & Marketing
Corey Murphy — Director of Retail Sales
Jeremy Sullivan — Director of Digital Sales
Emilio Bautista — Sales Assistant

Branwyn Bigglestone — Senior Accounts Manager
Emily Miller — Accounts Manager
Jessica Ambriz — Administrative Assistant
Tyler Shainline — Events Coordinator
David Brothers — Content Manager
Jonathan Chan — Production Manager
Drew Gill — Art Director
Meredith Wallace — Print Manager
Addison Duke — Production Artist
Tricia Ramos — Production Assistant

COPPERHEAD, VOL 1. First printing. March 2015. Published by Image Comics, Inc. Office of publication: 2001 Center Street, 6th Floor, Berkeley, CA 94704. Originally published in single issue format as COPPERHEAD #1-5. Copyright © 2015 Jay Faerber & Scott Godlewski. All rights reserved. COPPERHEAD™ (including all prominent characters featured herein), its logo and all character likenesses are trademarks of Jay Faerber & Scott Godlewski, unless otherwise noted. Image Comics® and its logos are registered trademarks of Image Comics, Inc. No part of this publication may be reproduced or transmitted, in any form or by any means (except for short excerpts for review purposes) without the express written permission of Image Comics, Inc. All names, characters, events and locales in this publication are entirely fictional. Any resemblance to actual persons (living or dead), events or places, without satiric intent, is coincidental. Printed in the USA. For information regarding the CPSIA on this printed material call: 203-595-3636 and provide reference #RICH–608093. For international rights, contact: foreignlicensing@imagecomics.com. ISBN: 978-1-63215-221-3

01

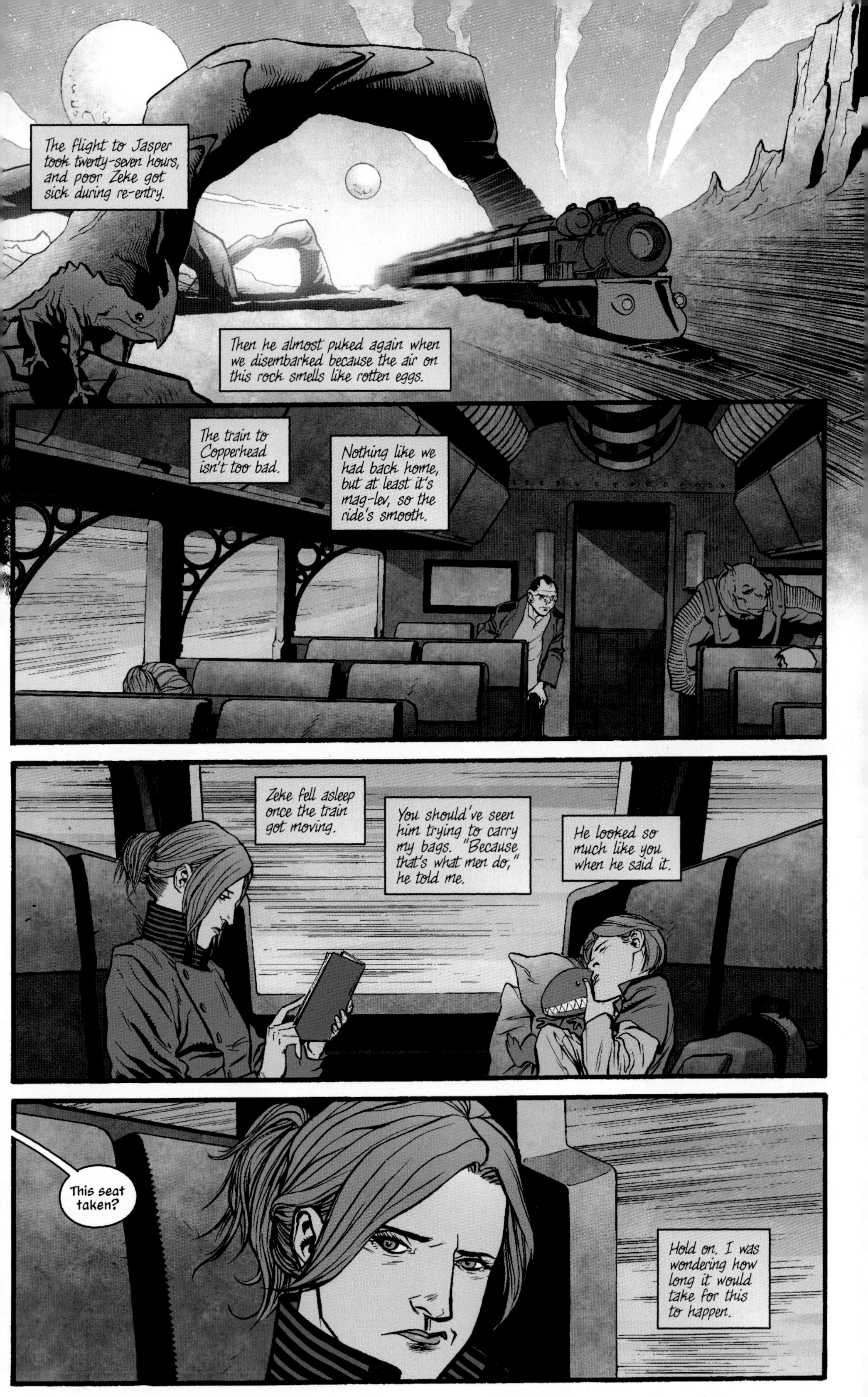
The flight to Jasper took twenty-seven hours, and poor Zeke got sick during re-entry.
Then he almost puked again when we disembarked because the air on this rock smells like rotten eggs.
The train to Copperhead isn't too bad.
Nothing like we had back home, but at least it's mag-lev, so the ride's smooth.
Zeke fell asleep once the train got moving.
You should've seen him trying to carry my bags. "Because that's what men do," he told me.
He looked so much like you when he said it.
This seat taken?
Hold on. I was wondering how long it would take for this to happen.

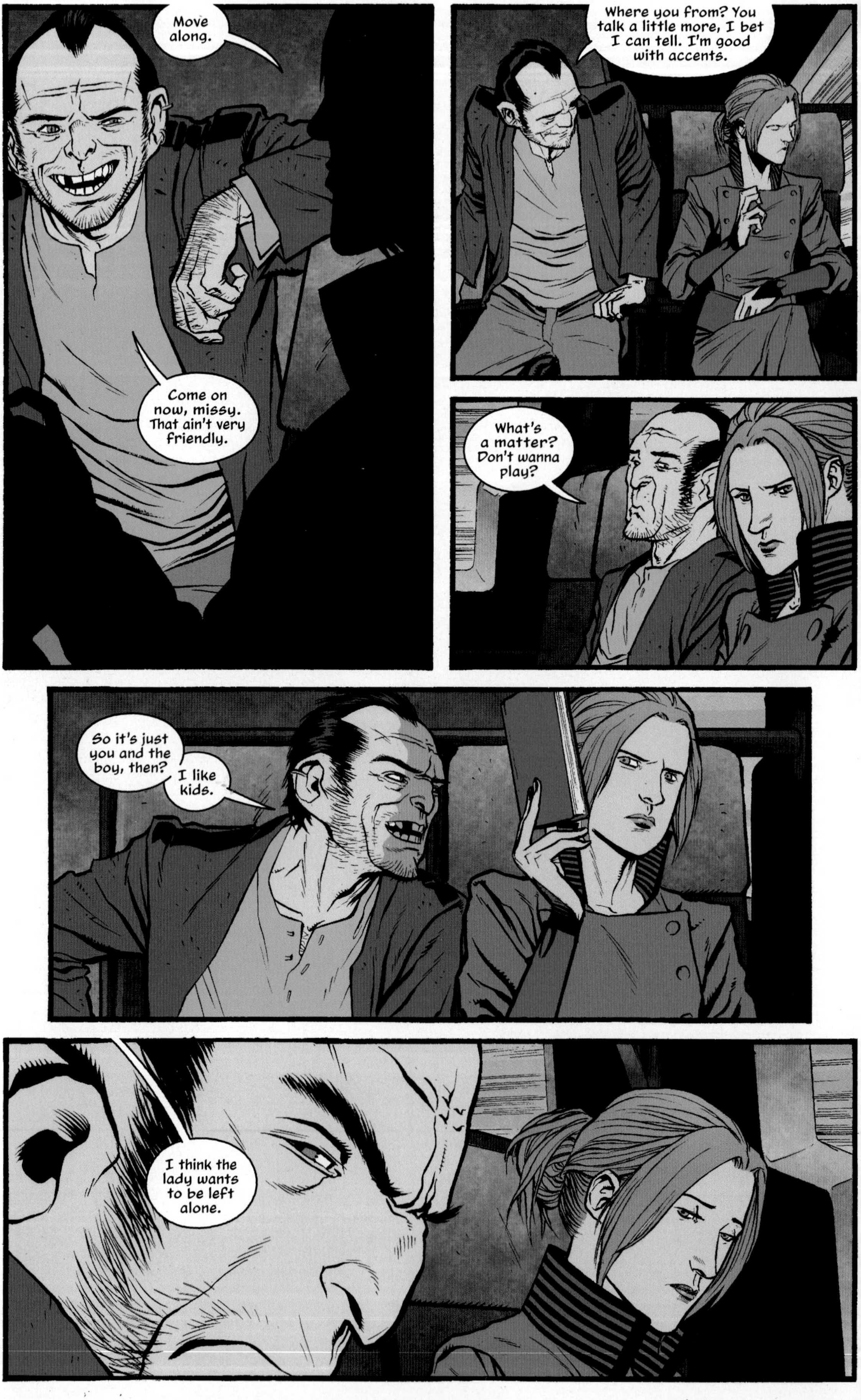
Move along.
Come on now, missy. That ain't very friendly.
Where you from? You talk a little more, I bet I can tell. I'm good with accents.
What's a matter? Don't wanna play?
So it's just you and the boy, then?
I like kids.
I think the lady wants to be left alone.

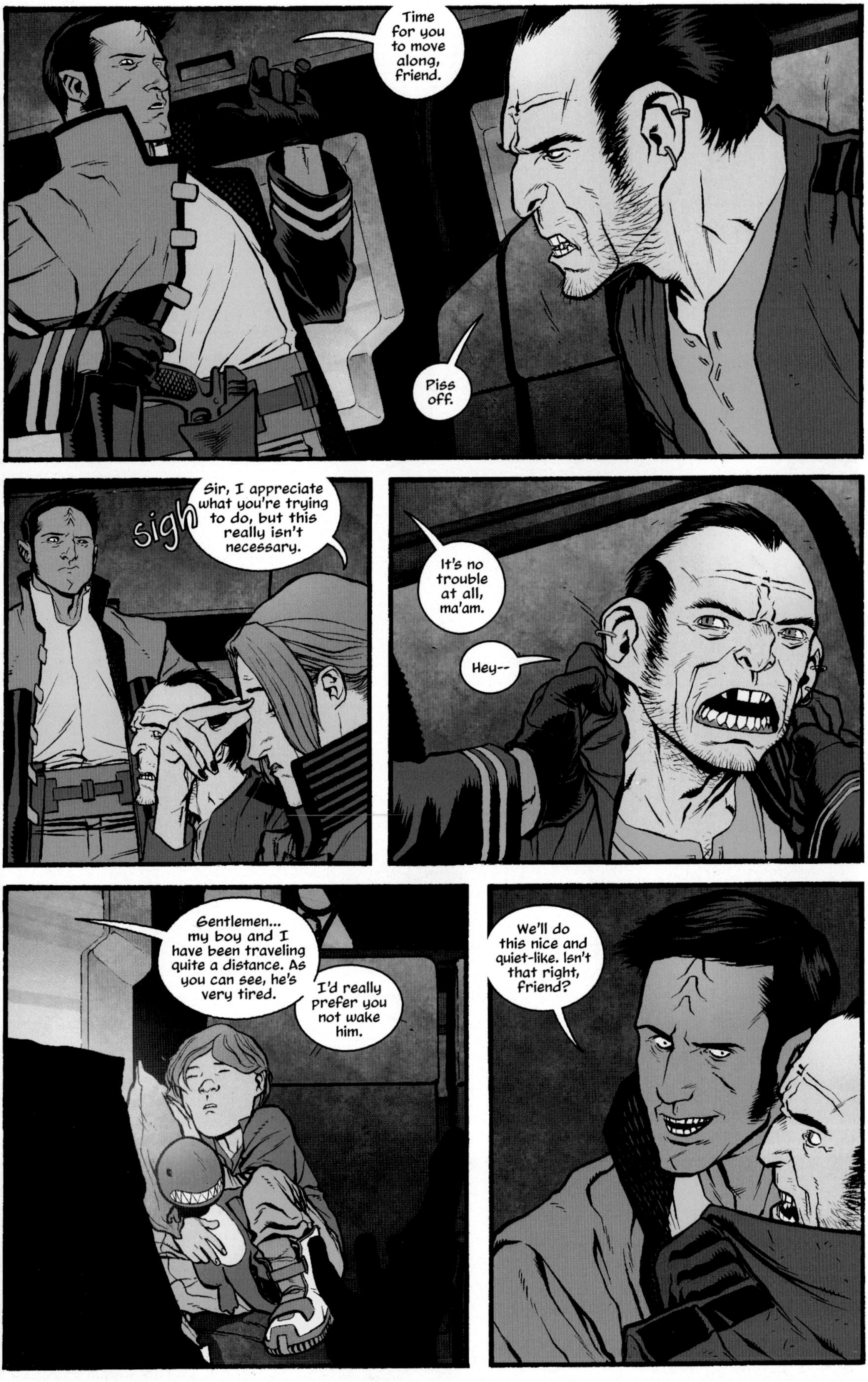
Time for you to move along, friend.
Piss off.
Sir, I appreciate what you're trying to do, but this really isn't necessary.
sigh
It's no trouble at all, ma'am.
Hey--
Gentlemen... my boy and I have been traveling quite a distance. As you can see, he's very tired.
I'd really prefer you not wake him.
We'll do this nice and quiet-like. Isn't that right, friend?

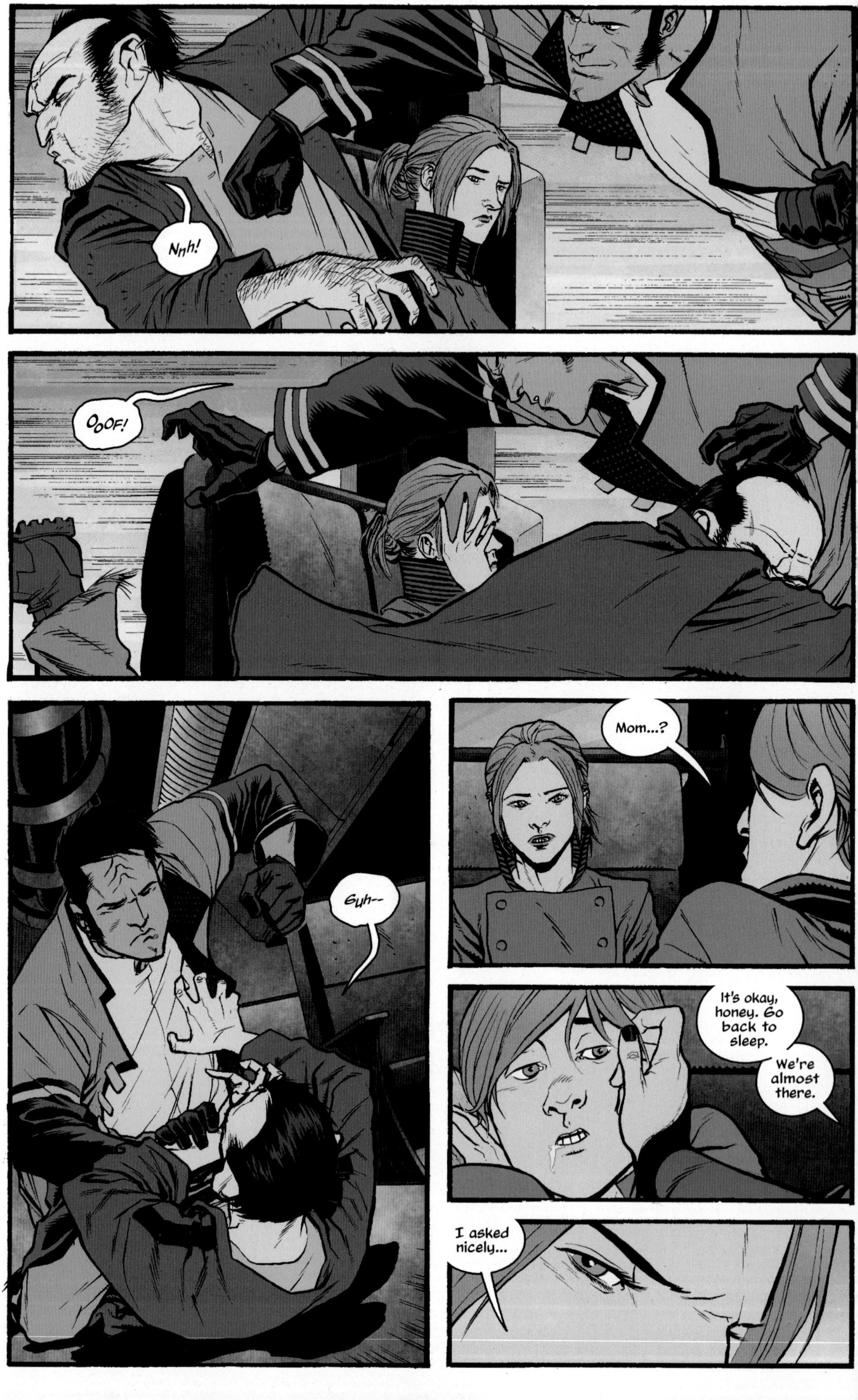
Nnh!
OOOF!
Guh--
Mom...?
It's okay, honey. Go back to sleep.
We're almost there.
I asked nicely...

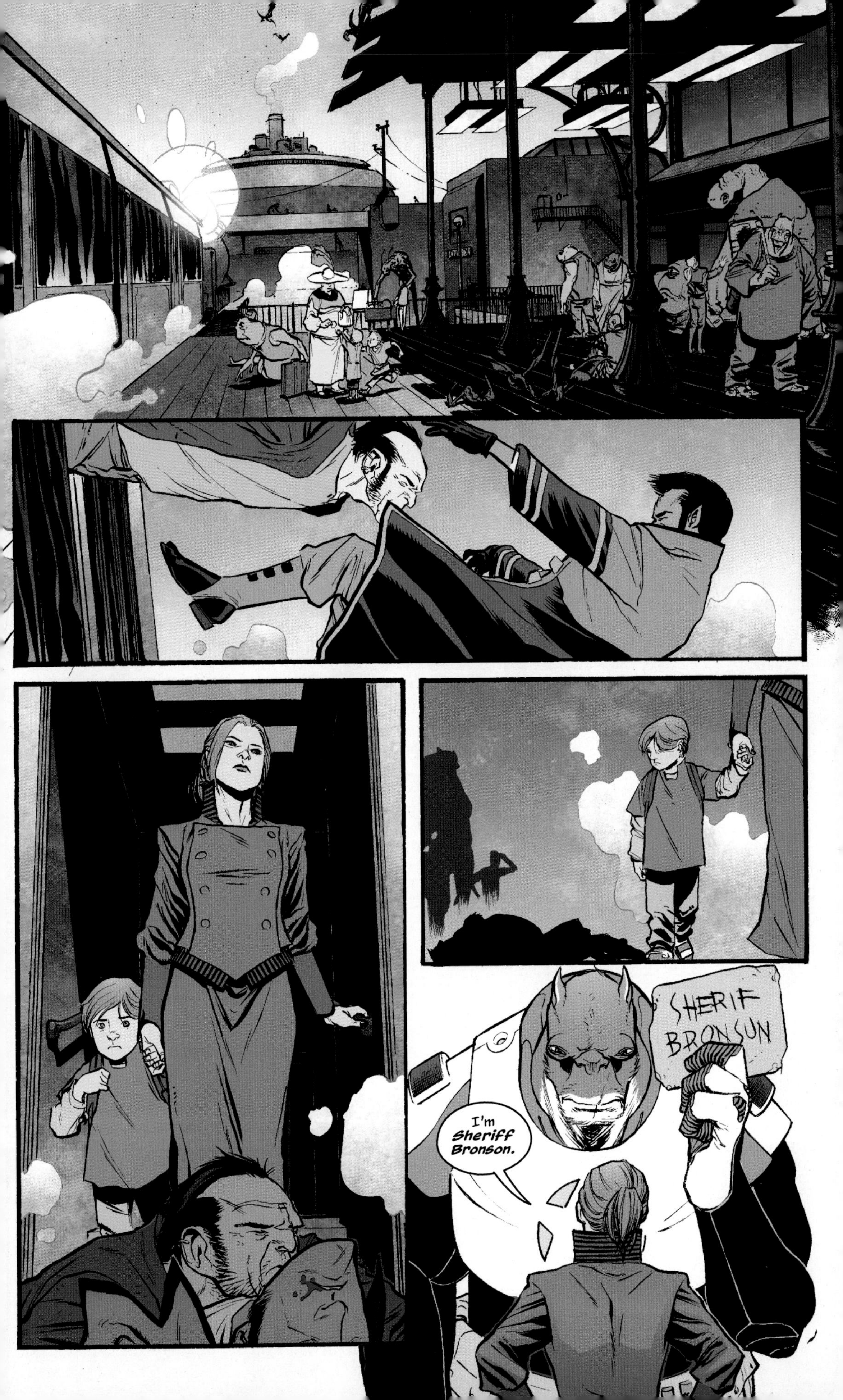
SHERIF BRONSUN
I'm Sheriff Bronson.

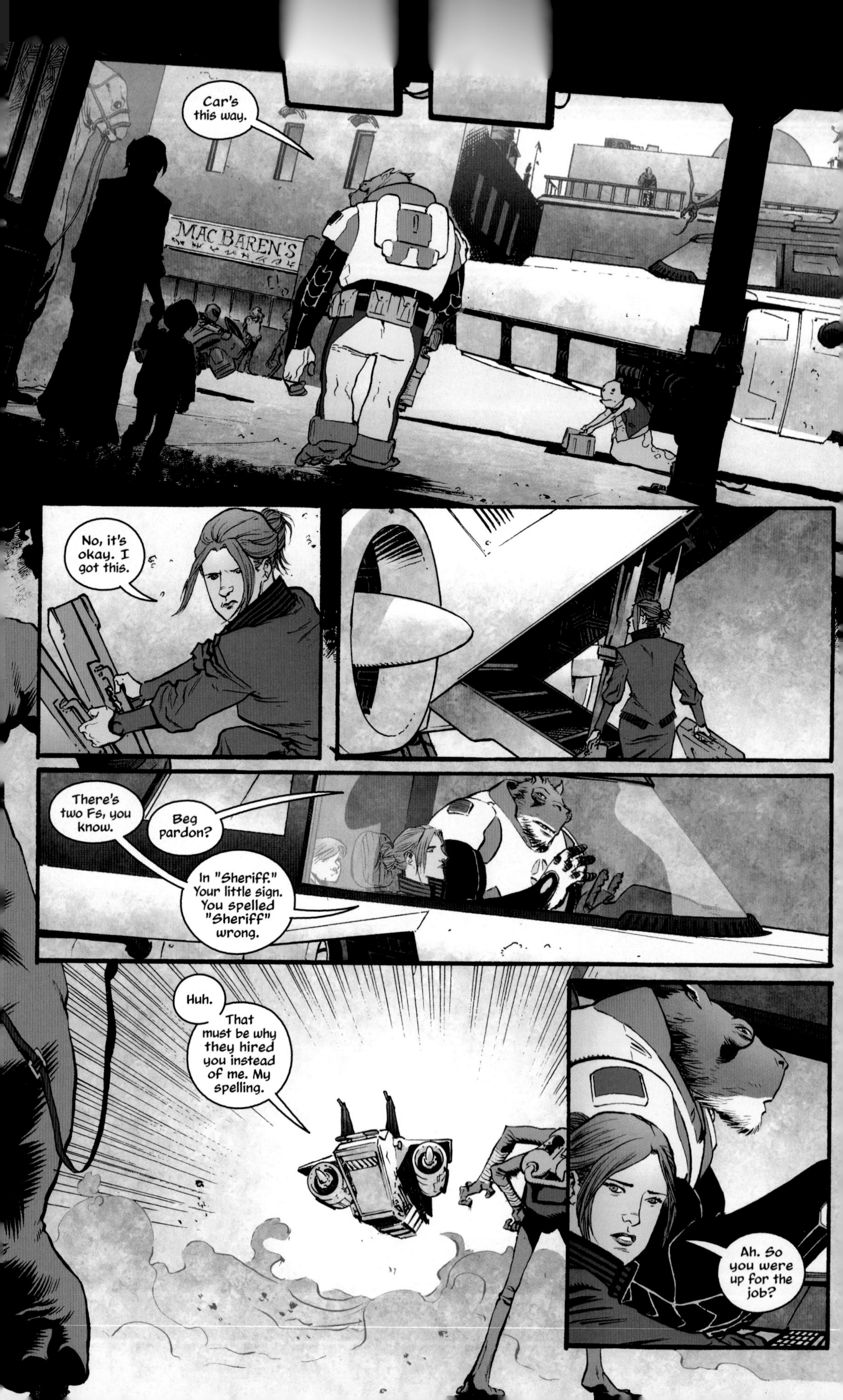
Car's this way.
MAC BAREN'S
No, it's okay. I got this.
There's two Fs, you know.
Beg pardon?
In "Sheriff." Your little sign. You spelled "Sheriff" wrong.
Huh.
That must be why they hired you instead of me. My spelling.
Ah. So you were up for the job?

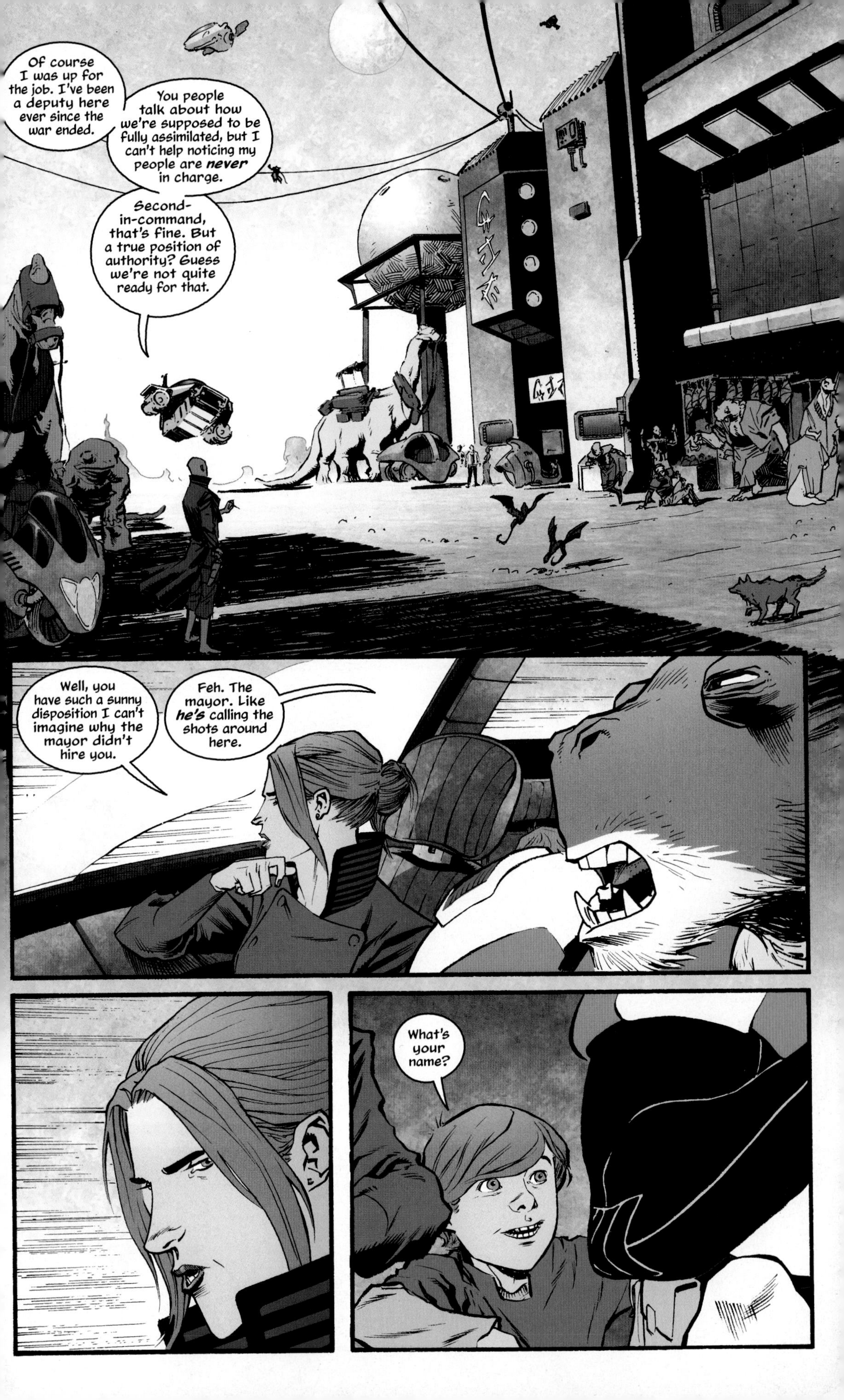

Of course I was up for the job. I've been a deputy here ever since the war ended.
You people talk about how we're supposed to be fully assimilated, but I can't help noticing my people are *never* in charge.
Second-in-command, that's fine. But a true position of authority? Guess we're not quite ready for that.
Well, you have such a sunny disposition I can't imagine why the mayor didn't hire you.
Feh. The mayor. Like *he's* calling the shots around here.
What's your name?

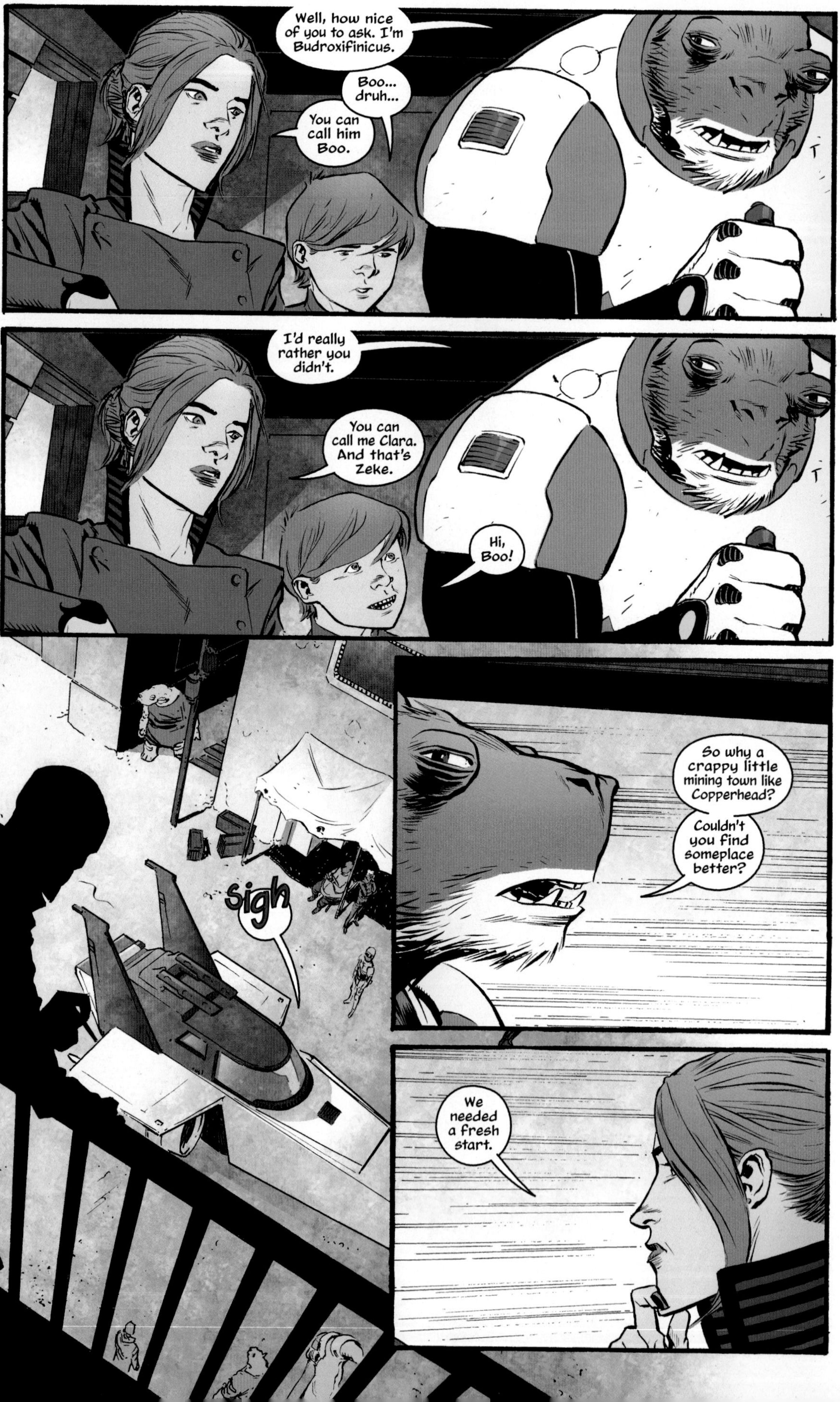
Well, how nice of you to ask. I'm Budroxifinicus.
Boo... druh...
You can call him Boo.
I'd really rather you didn't.
You can call me Clara. And that's Zeke.
Hi, Boo!
SIGH
So why a crappy little mining town like Copperhead?
Couldn't you find someplace better?
We needed a fresh start.

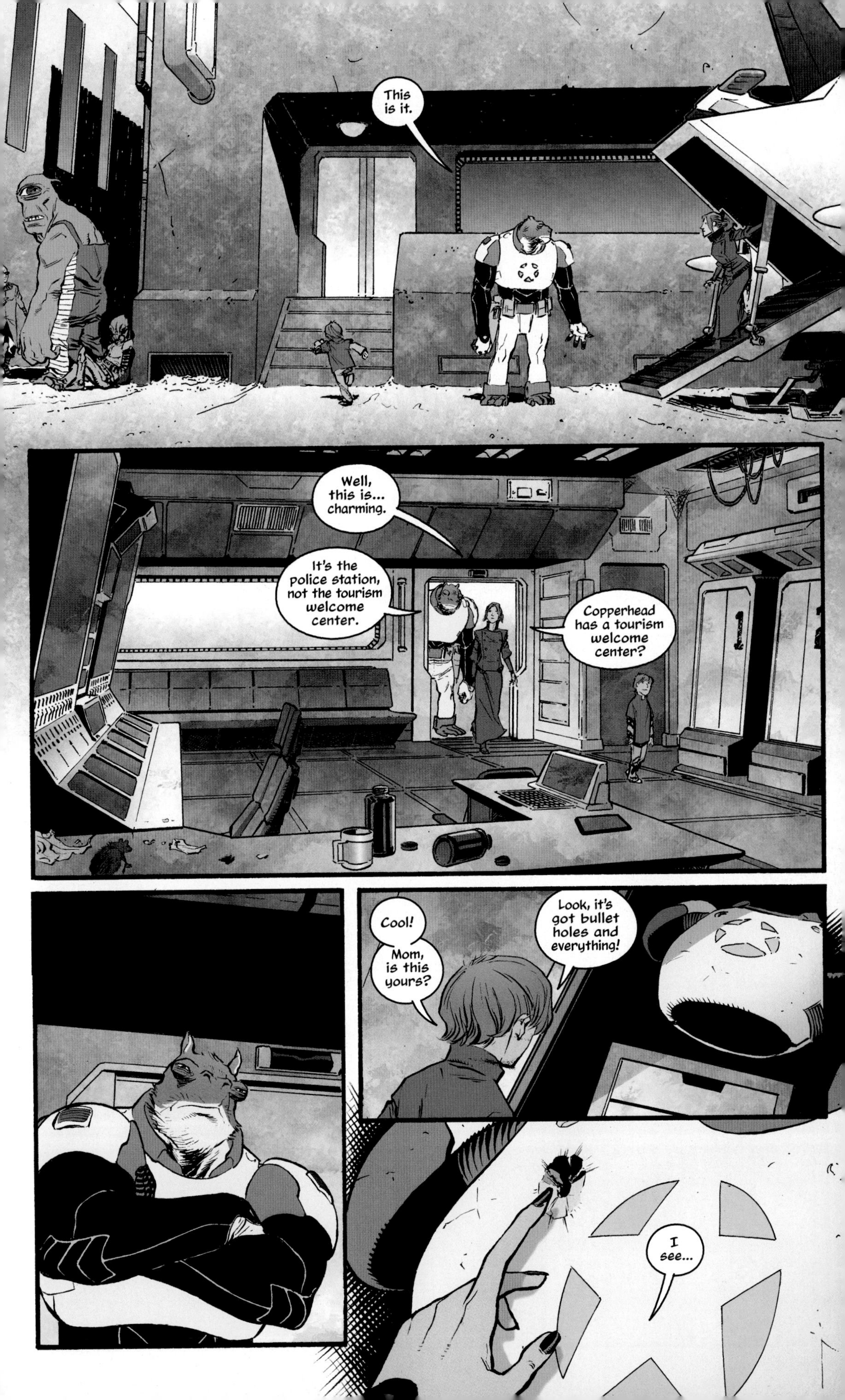
This is it.
Well, this is... charming.
It's the police station, not the tourism welcome center.
Copperhead has a tourism welcome center?
Cool!
Mom, is this yours?
Look, it's got bullet holes and everything!
I see...

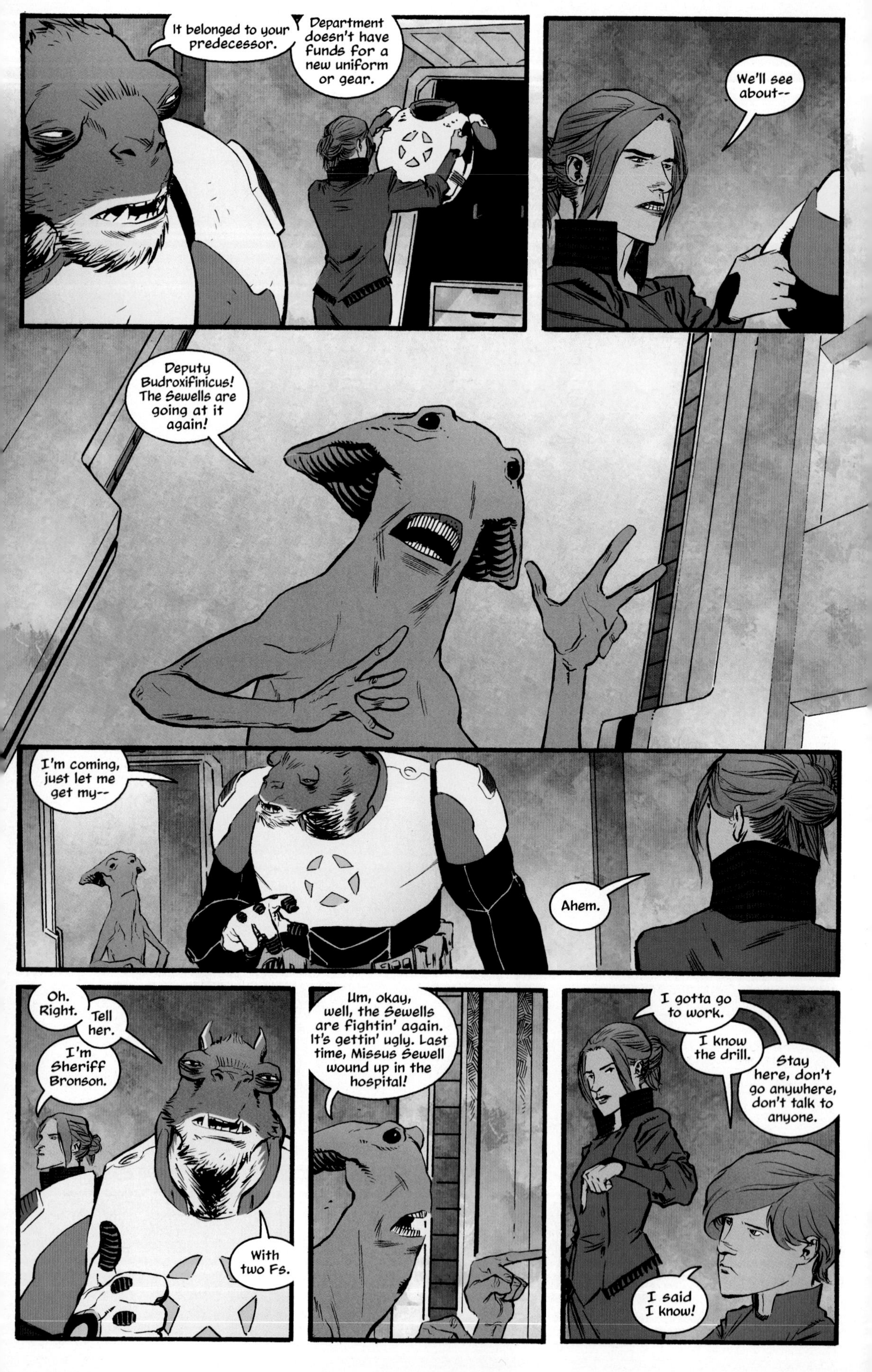

It belonged to your predecessor.
Department doesn't have funds for a new uniform or gear.
We'll see about--
Deputy Budroxifinicus! The Sewells are going at it again!
I'm coming, just let me get my--
Ahem.
Oh. Right.
Tell her.
I'm Sheriff Bronson.
With two Fs.
Um, okay, well, the Sewells are fightin' again. It's gettin' ugly. Last time, Missus Sewell wound up in the hospital!
I gotta go to work.
I know the drill.
Stay here, don't go anywhere, don't talk to anyone.
I said I know!

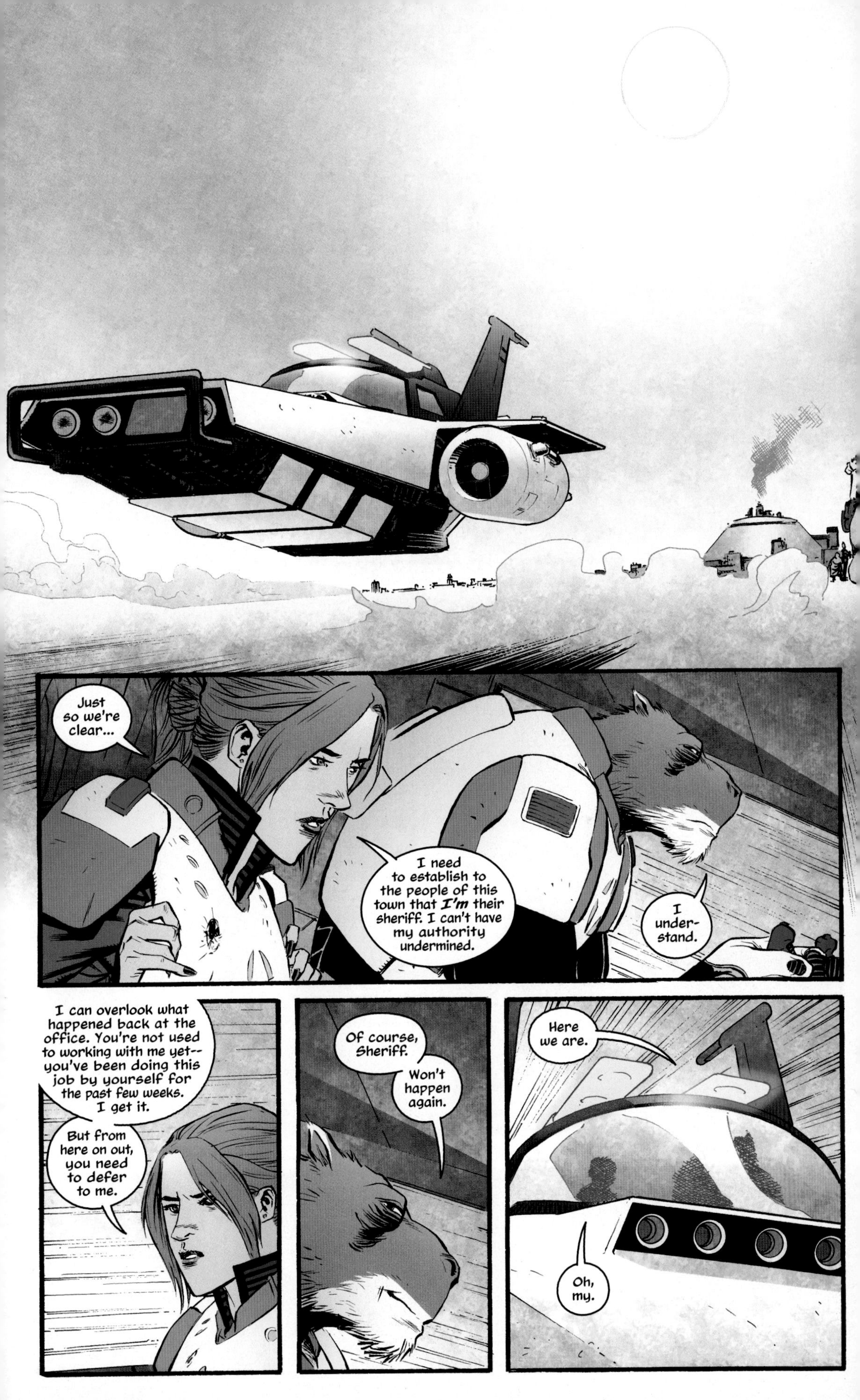

Just so we're clear...
I need to establish to the people of this town that *I'm* their sheriff. I can't have my authority undermined.
I under-stand.
I can overlook what happened back at the office. You're not used to working with me yet-- you've been doing this job by yourself for the past few weeks. I get it.
But from here on out, you need to defer to me.
Of course, Sheriff.
Won't happen again.
Here we are.
Oh, my.

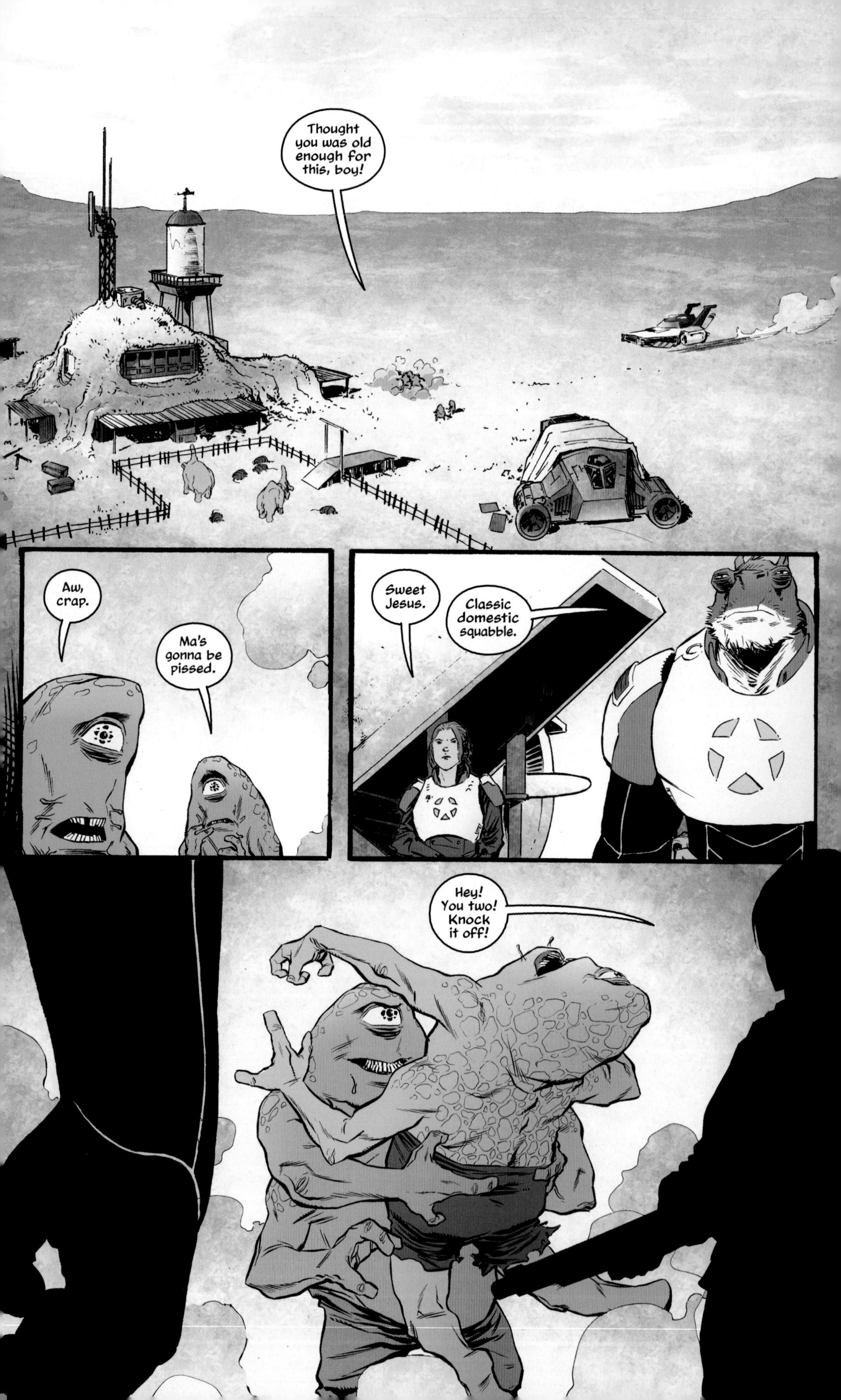
Thought you was old enough for this, boy!
Aw, crap.
Ma's gonna be pissed.
Sweet Jesus.
Classic domestic squabble.
Hey! You two! Knock it off!

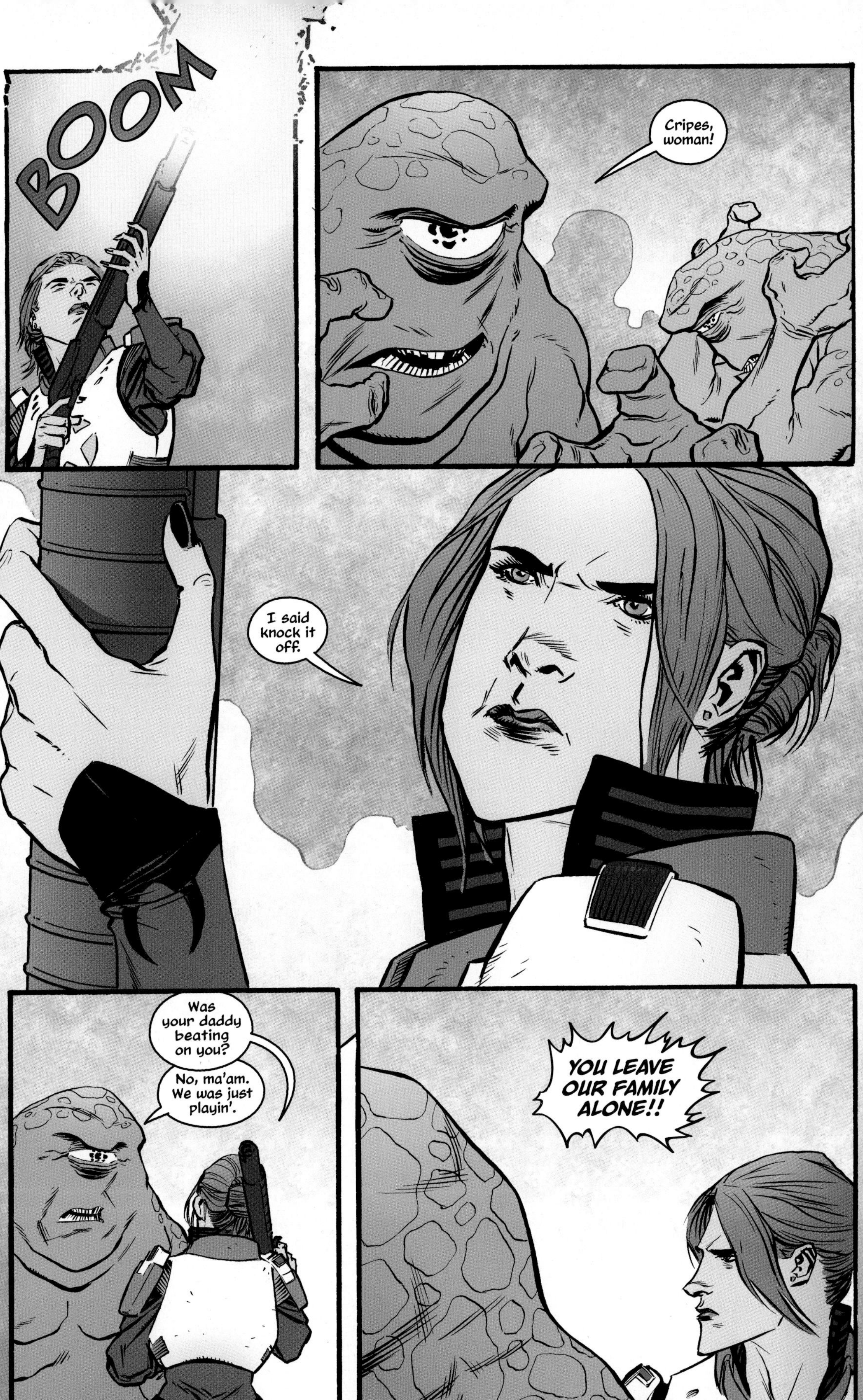
BOOM
Cripes, woman!
I said knock it off.
Was your daddy beating on you?
No, ma'am. We was just playin'.
YOU LEAVE OUR FAMILY ALONE!!

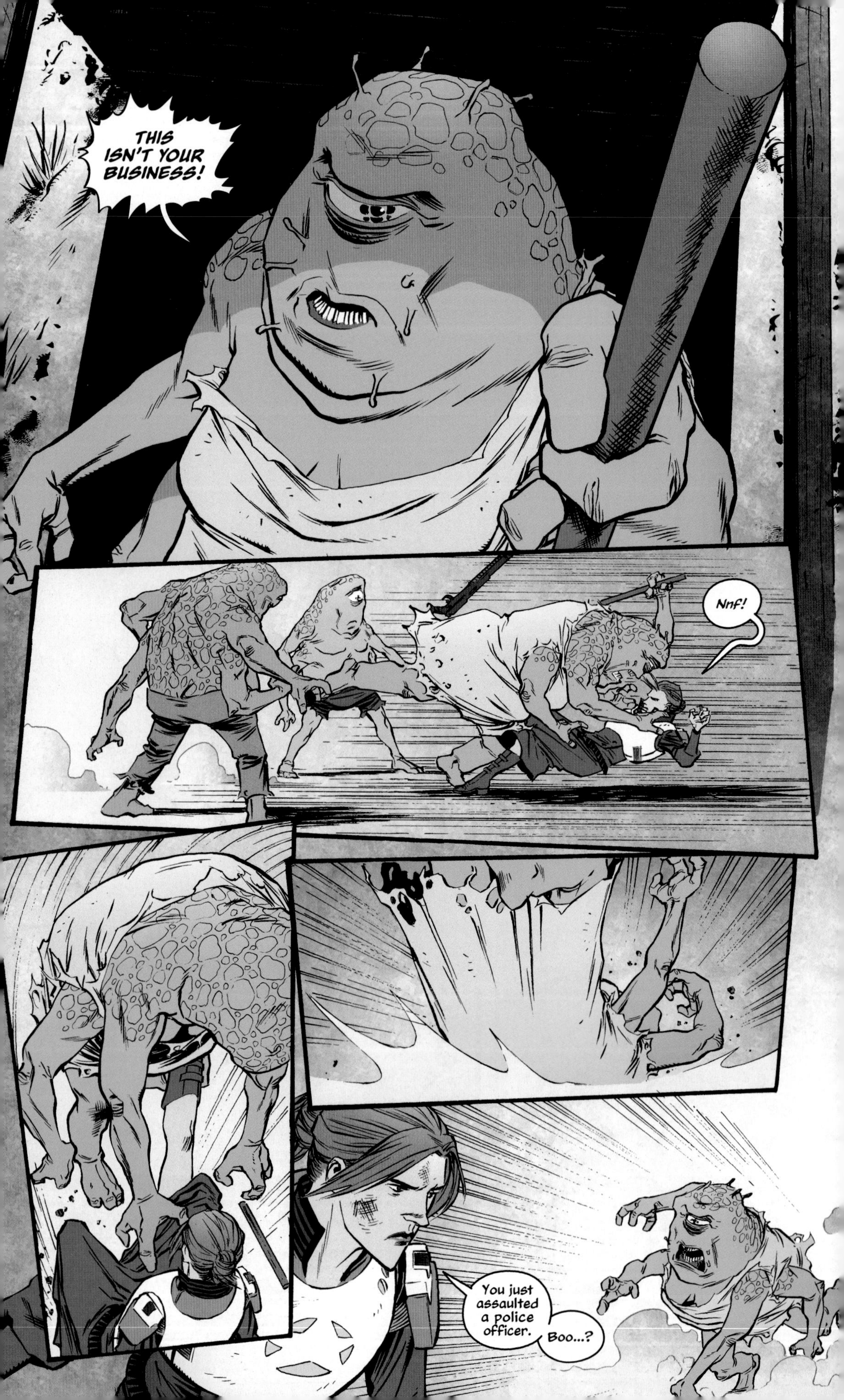
THIS ISN'T YOUR BUSINESS!
Nnf!
You just assaulted a police officer.
Boo...?

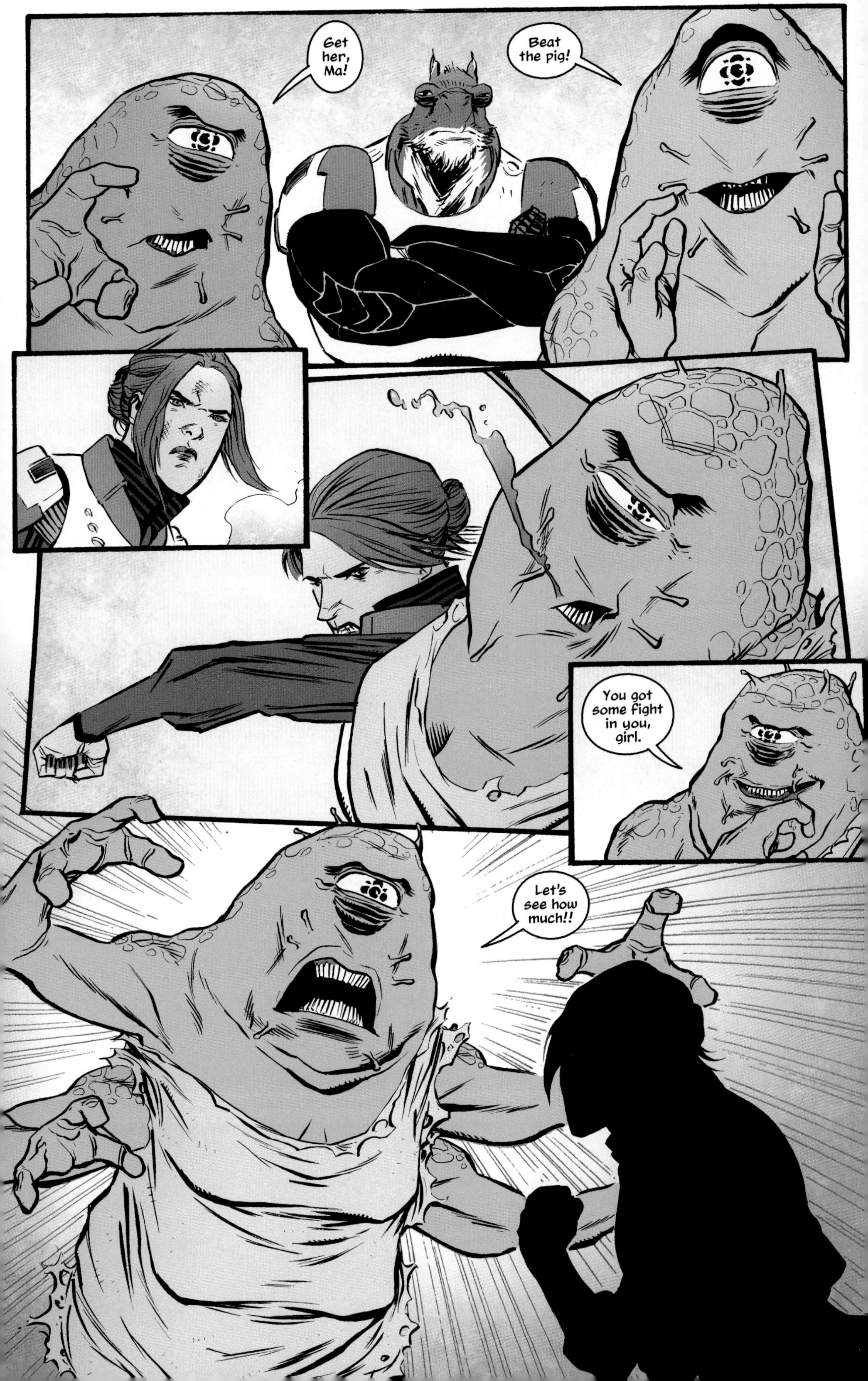
Get her, Ma!
Beat the pig!
You got some fight in you, girl.
Let's see how much!!

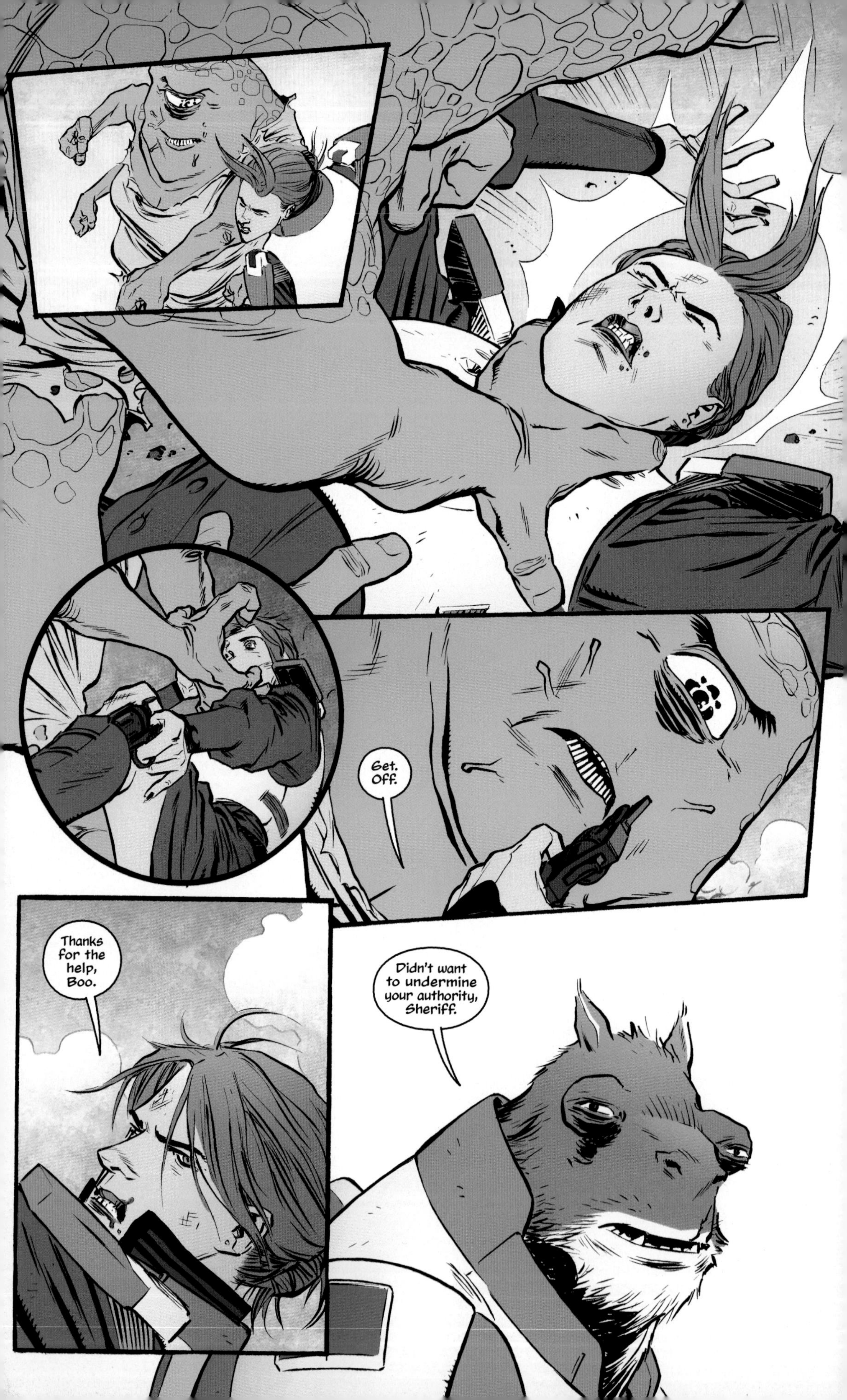
Get. Off.
Thanks for the help, Boo.
Didn't want to undermine your authority, Sheriff.

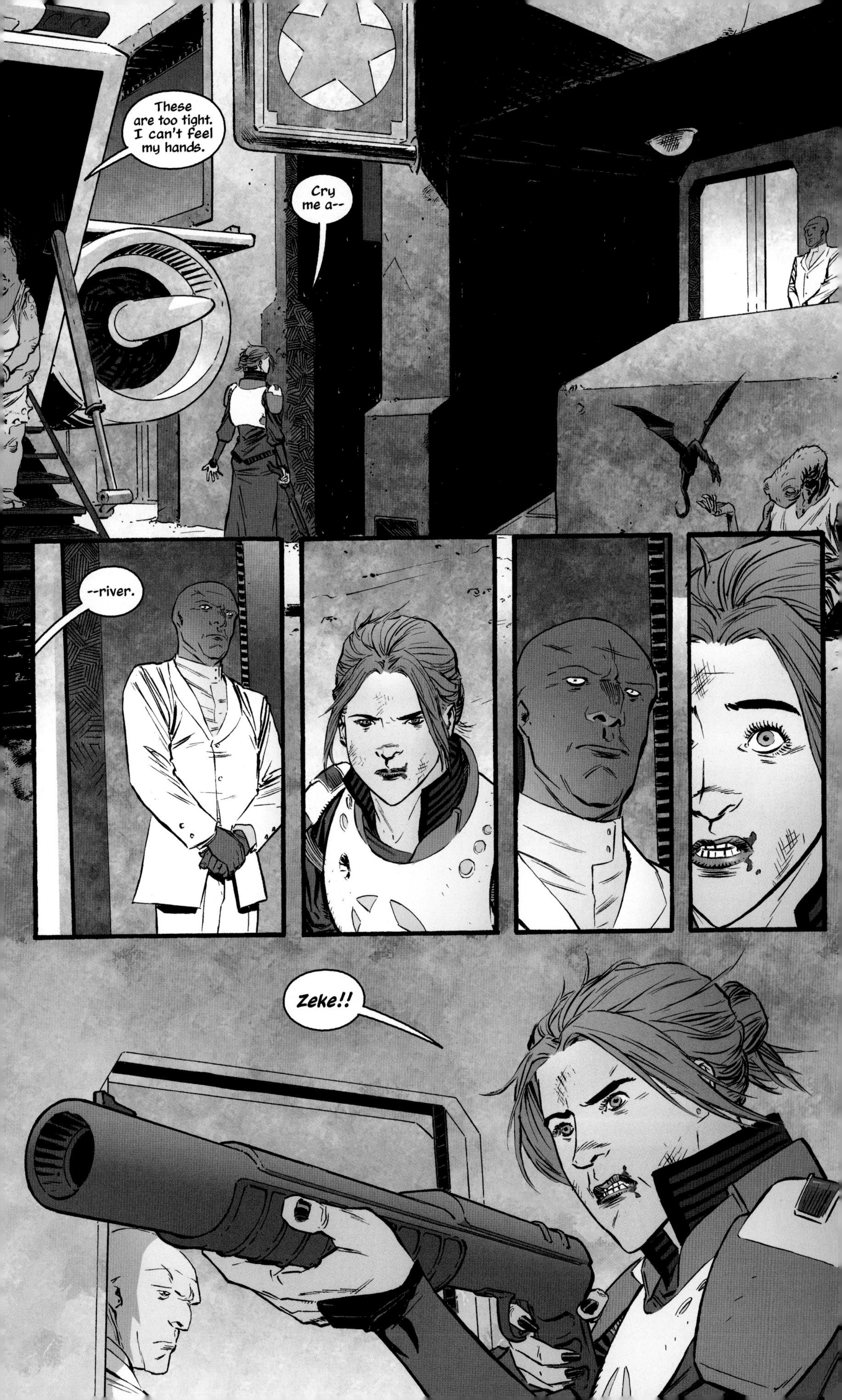
These are too tight. I can't feel my hands.
Cry me a--
--river.
Zeke!!

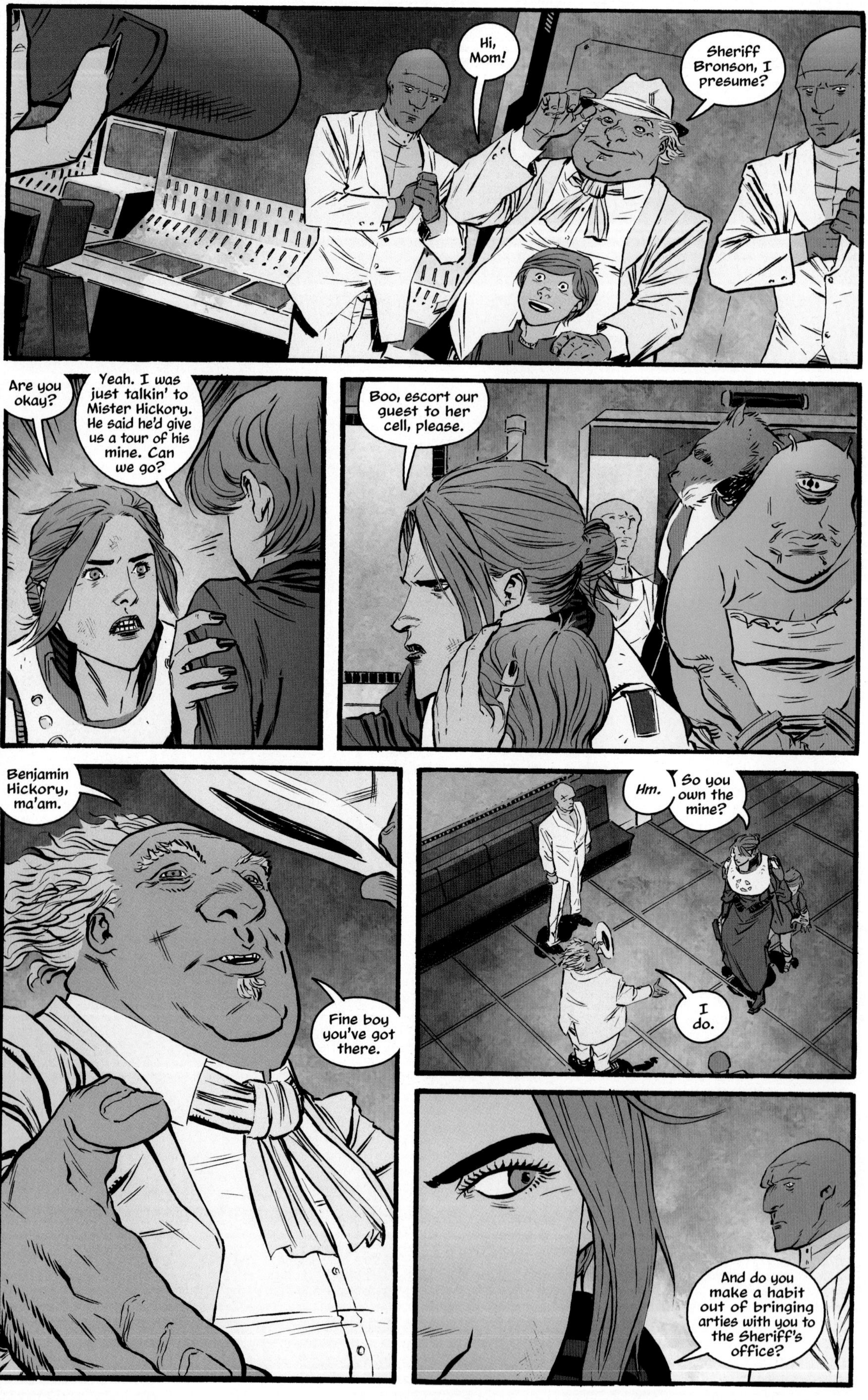
Hi, Mom!
Sheriff Bronson, I presume?
Are you okay?
Yeah. I was just talkin' to Mister Hickory. He said he'd give us a tour of his mine. Can we go?
Boo, escort our guest to her cell, please.
Benjamin Hickory, ma'am.
Fine boy you've got there.
Hm.
So you own the mine?
I do.
And do you make a habit out of bringing arties with you to the Sheriff's office?

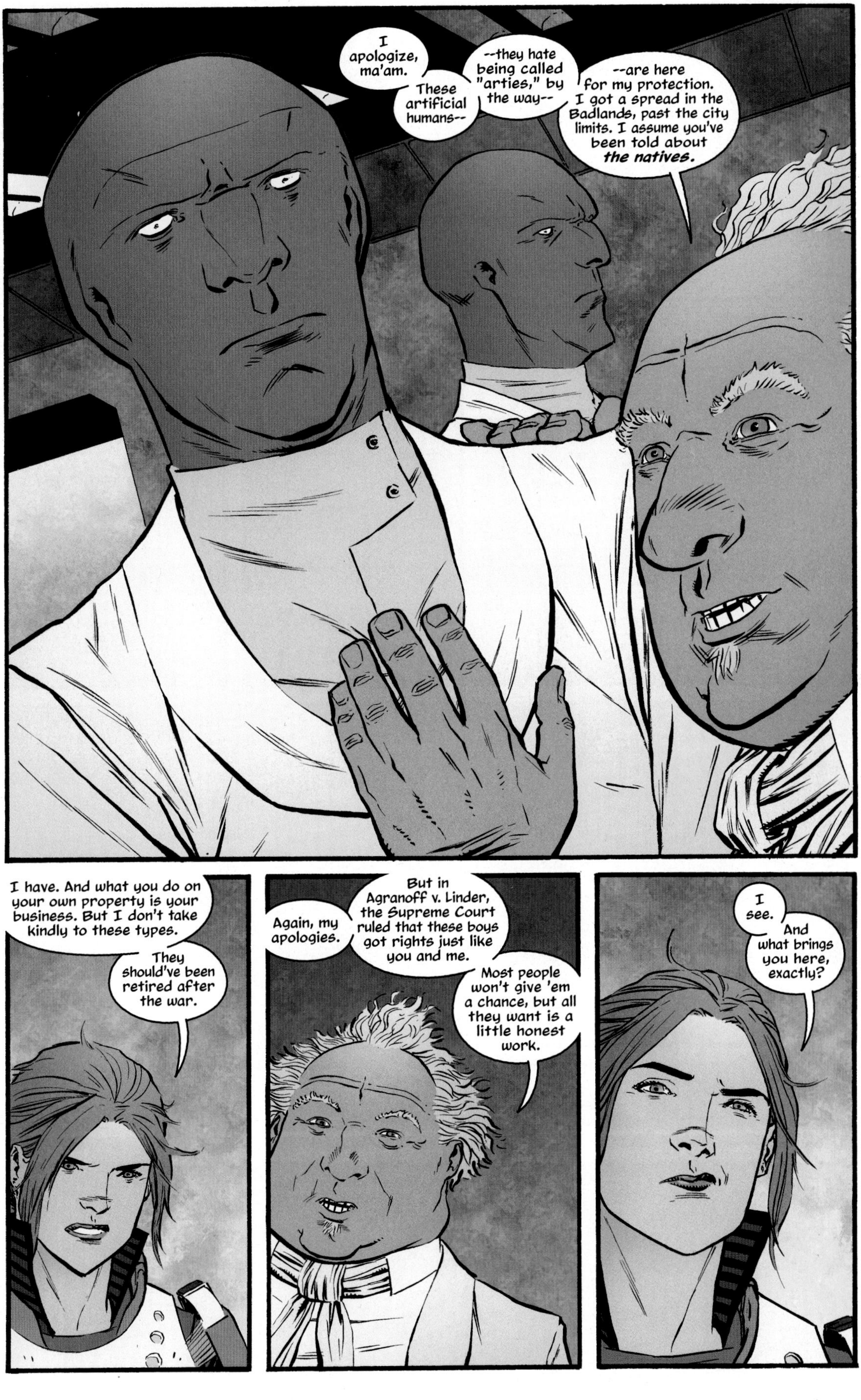
I apologize, ma'am.
These artificial humans--
--they hate being called "arties," by the way--
--are here for my protection. I got a spread in the Badlands, past the city limits. I assume you've been told about *the natives.*
I have. And what you do on your own property is your business. But I don't take kindly to these types.
They should've been retired after the war.
Again, my apologies.
But in Agranoff v. Linder, the Supreme Court ruled that these boys got rights just like you and me.
Most people won't give 'em a chance, but all they want is a little honest work.
I see.
And what brings you here, exactly?

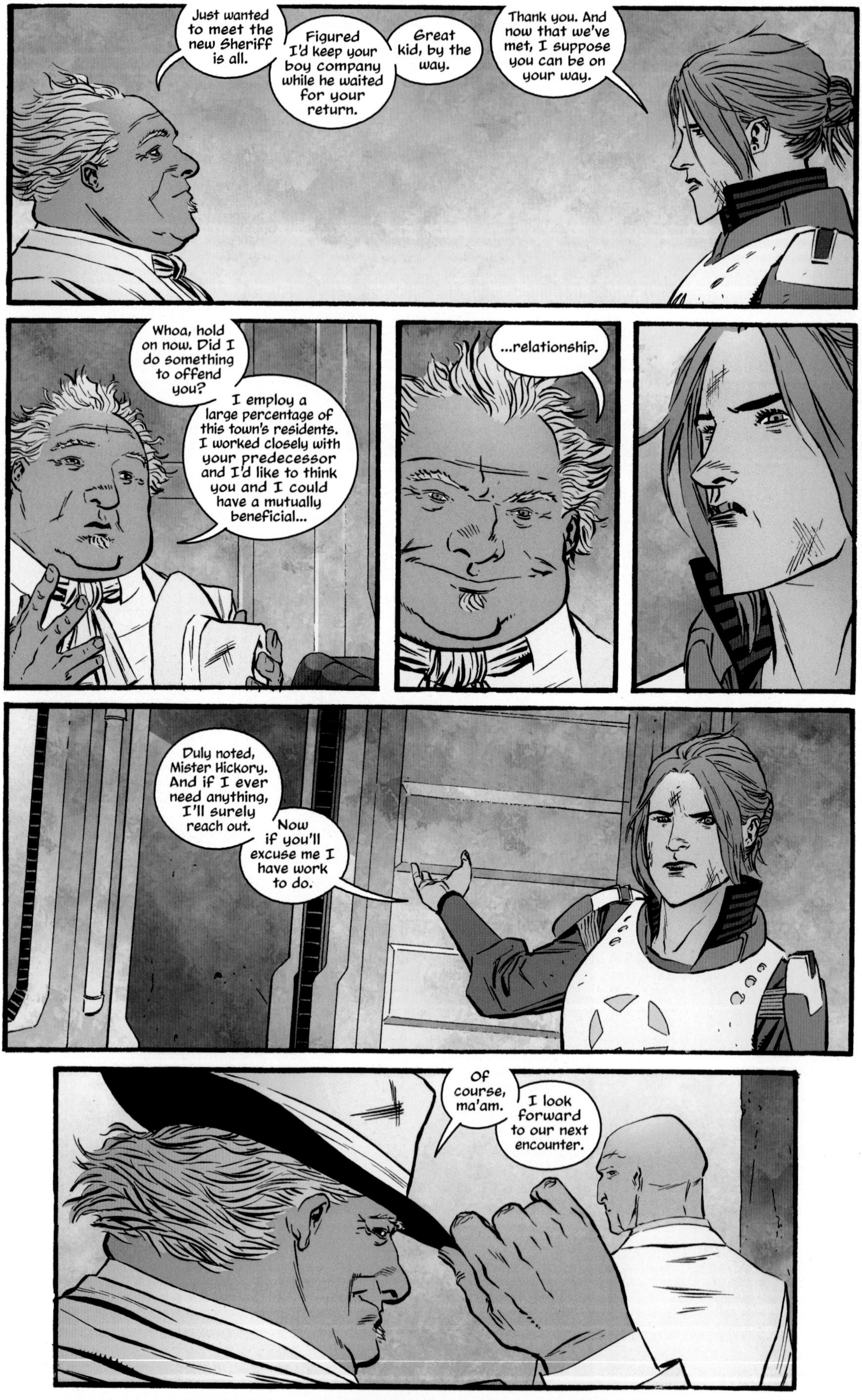
Just wanted to meet the new Sheriff is all.
Figured I'd keep your boy company while he waited for your return.
Great kid, by the way.
Thank you. And now that we've met, I suppose you can be on your way.
Whoa, hold on now. Did I do something to offend you?
I employ a large percentage of this town's residents. I worked closely with your predecessor and I'd like to think you and I could have a mutually beneficial...
...relationship.
Duly noted, Mister Hickory. And if I ever need anything, I'll surely reach out.
Now if you'll excuse me I have work to do.
Of course, ma'am.
I look forward to our next encounter.

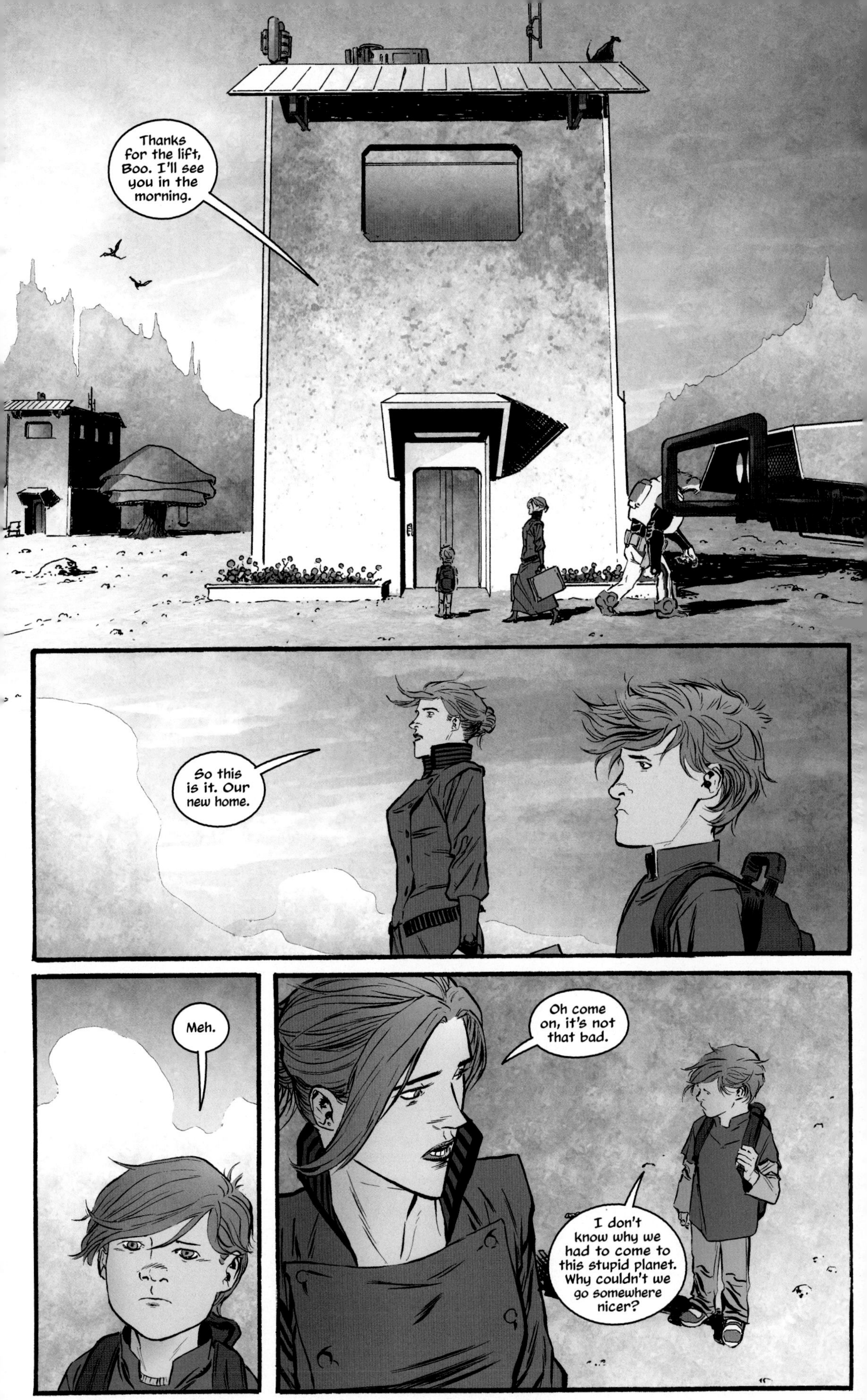
Thanks for the lift, Boo. I'll see you in the morning.
So this is it. Our new home.
Meh.
Oh come on, it's not that bad.
I don't know why we had to come to this stupid planet. Why couldn't we go somewhere nicer?

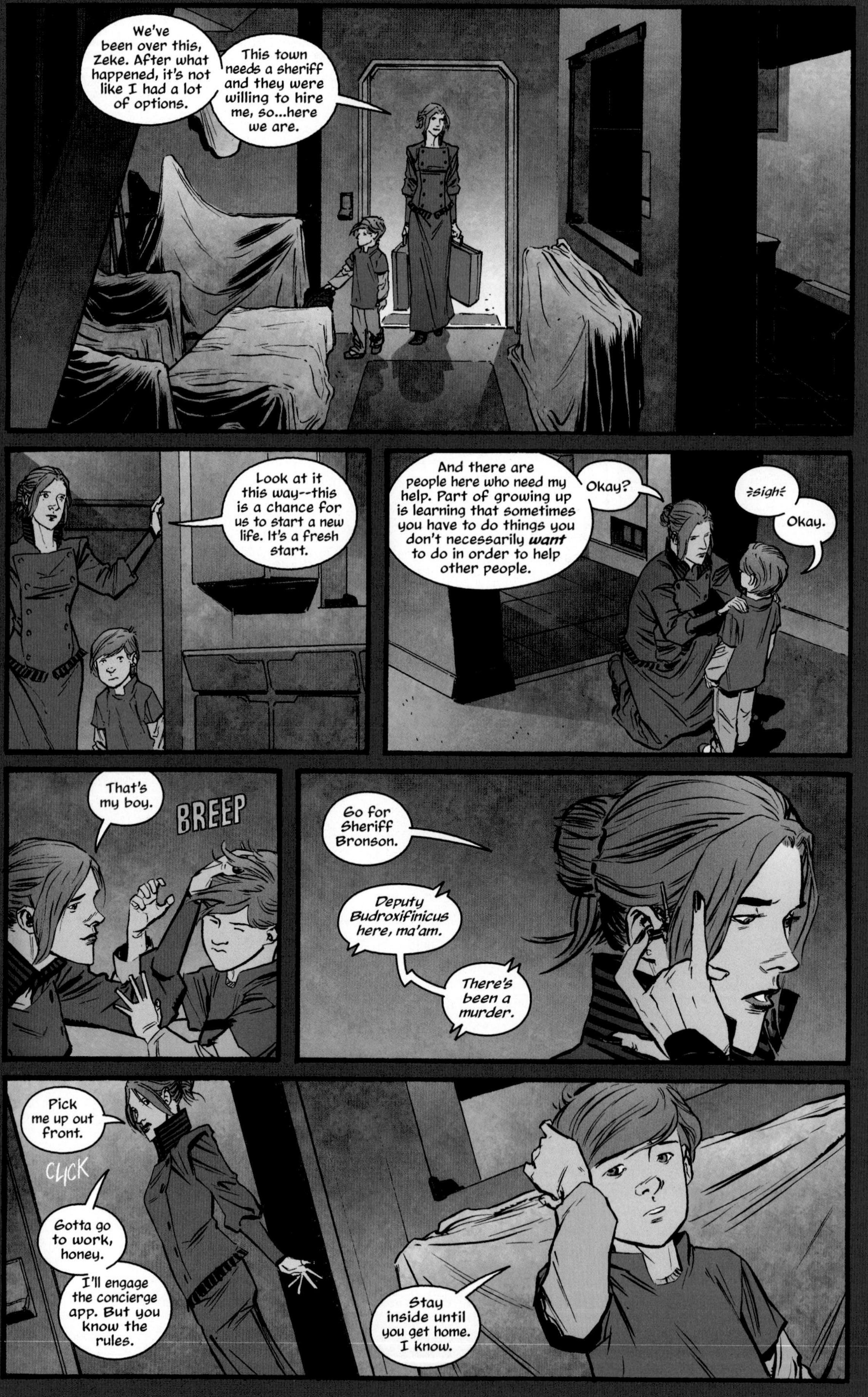
We've been over this, Zeke. After what happened, it's not like I had a lot of options.
This town needs a sheriff and they were willing to hire me, so...here we are.
Look at it this way--this is a chance for us to start a new life. It's a fresh start.
And there are people here who need my help. Part of growing up is learning that sometimes you have to do things you don't necessarily *want* to do in order to help other people.
Okay?
sigh
Okay.
That's my boy.
BREEP
Go for Sheriff Bronson.
Deputy Budroxifinicus here, ma'am.
There's been a murder.
Pick me up out front.
CLICK
Gotta go to work, honey.
I'll engage the concierge app. But you know the rules.
Stay inside until you get home. I know.

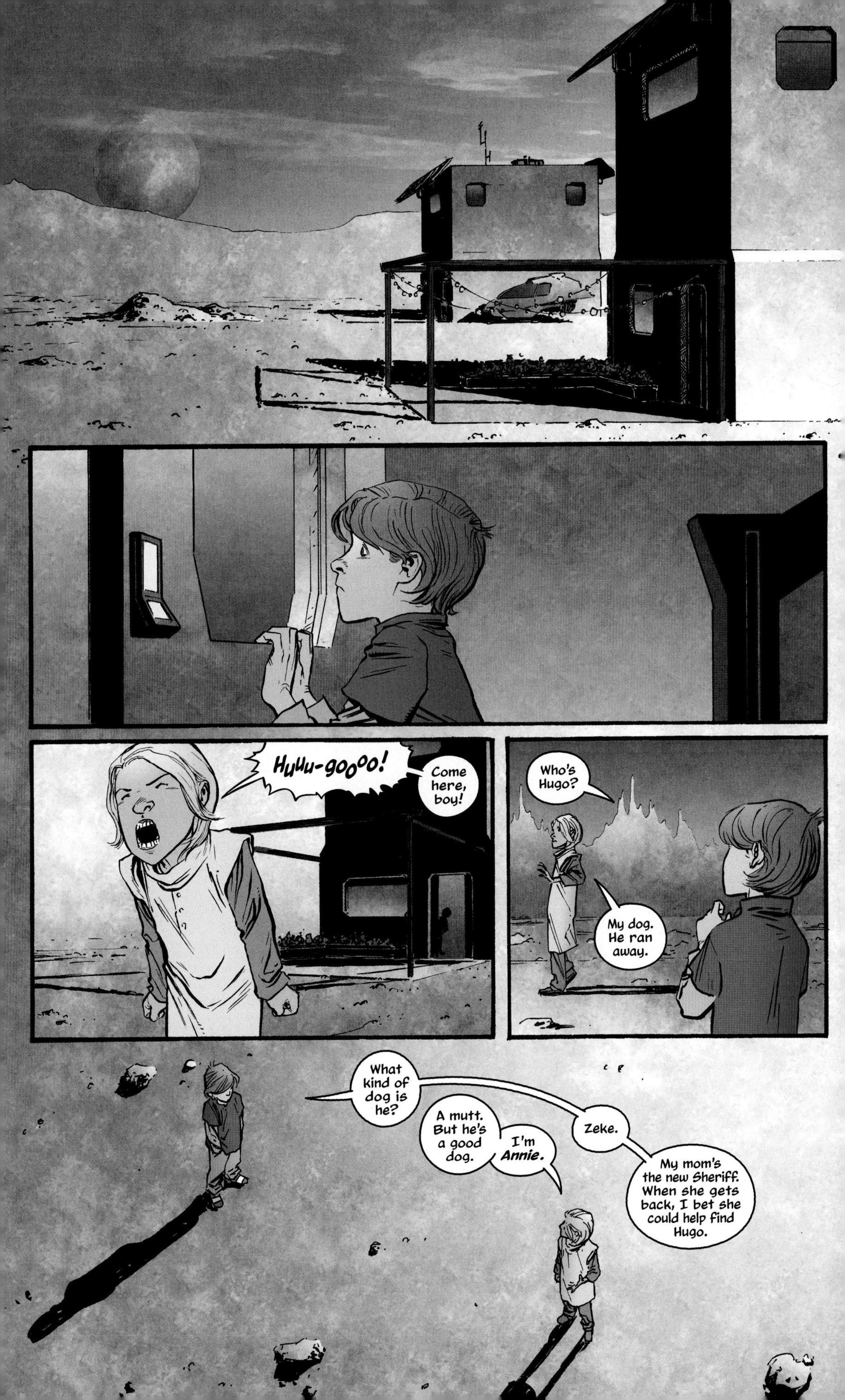
Huuu-goooo!
Come here, boy!
Who's Hugo?
My dog. He ran away.
What kind of dog is he?
A mutt. But he's a good dog.
I'm Annie.
Zeke.
My mom's the new Sheriff. When she gets back, I bet she could help find Hugo.

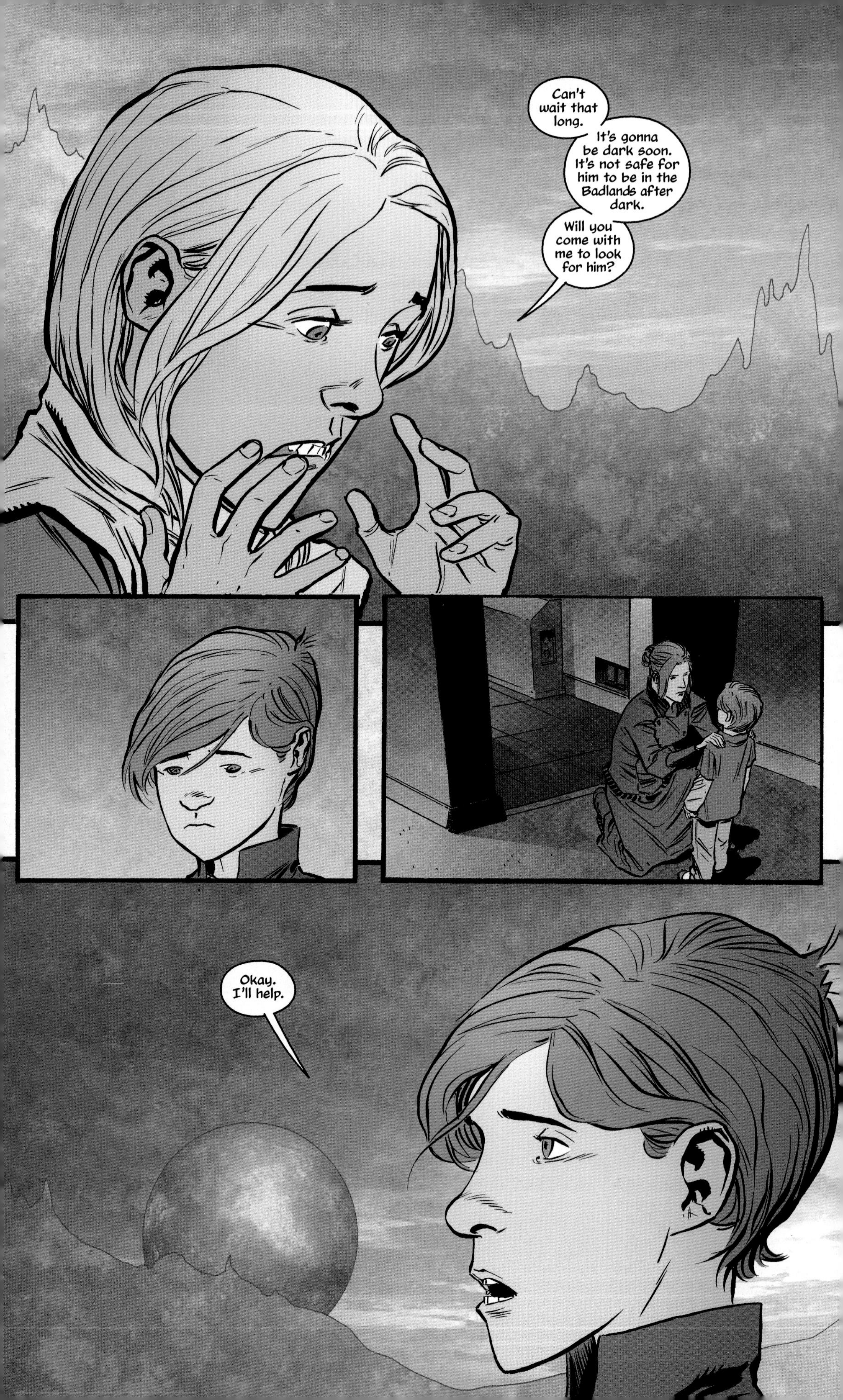
Can't wait that long.
It's gonna be dark soon. It's not safe for him to be in the Badlands after dark.
Will you come with me to look for him?
Okay. I'll help.

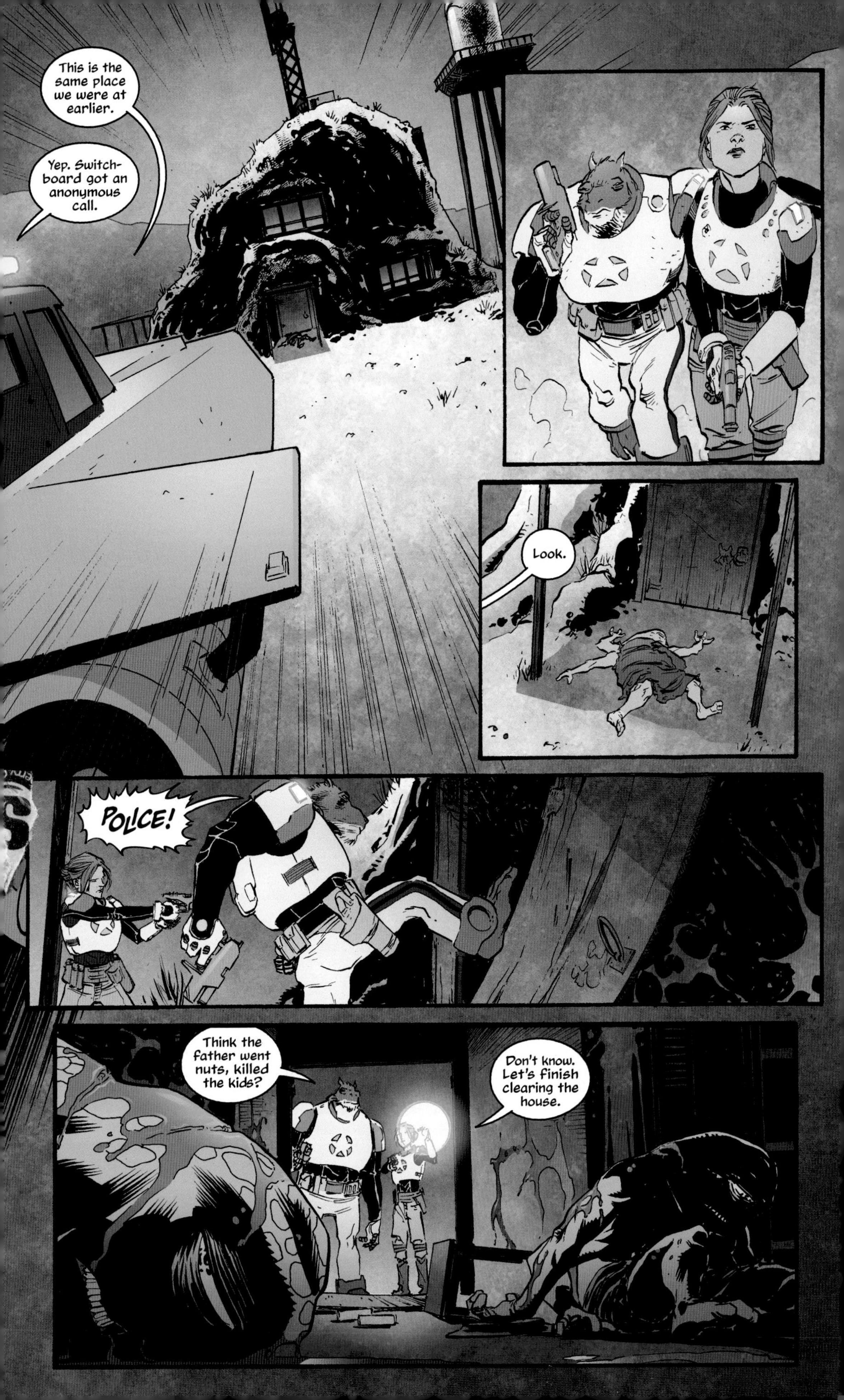
This is the same place we were at earlier.
Yep. Switch-board got an anonymous call.
Look.
POLICE!
Think the father went nuts, killed the kids?
Don't know. Let's finish clearing the house.

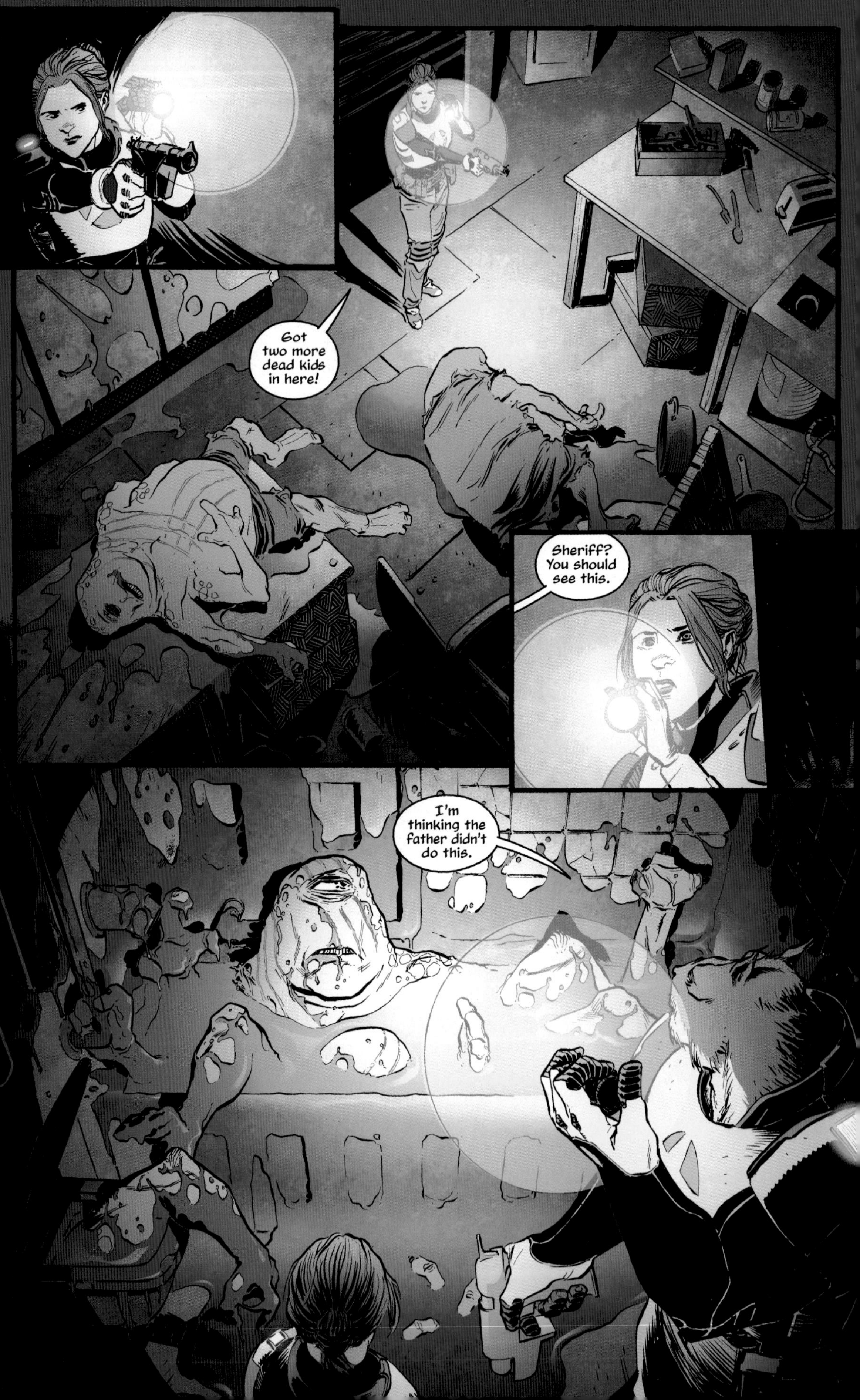
Got two more dead kids in here!
Sheriff? You should see this.
I'm thinking the father didn't do this.

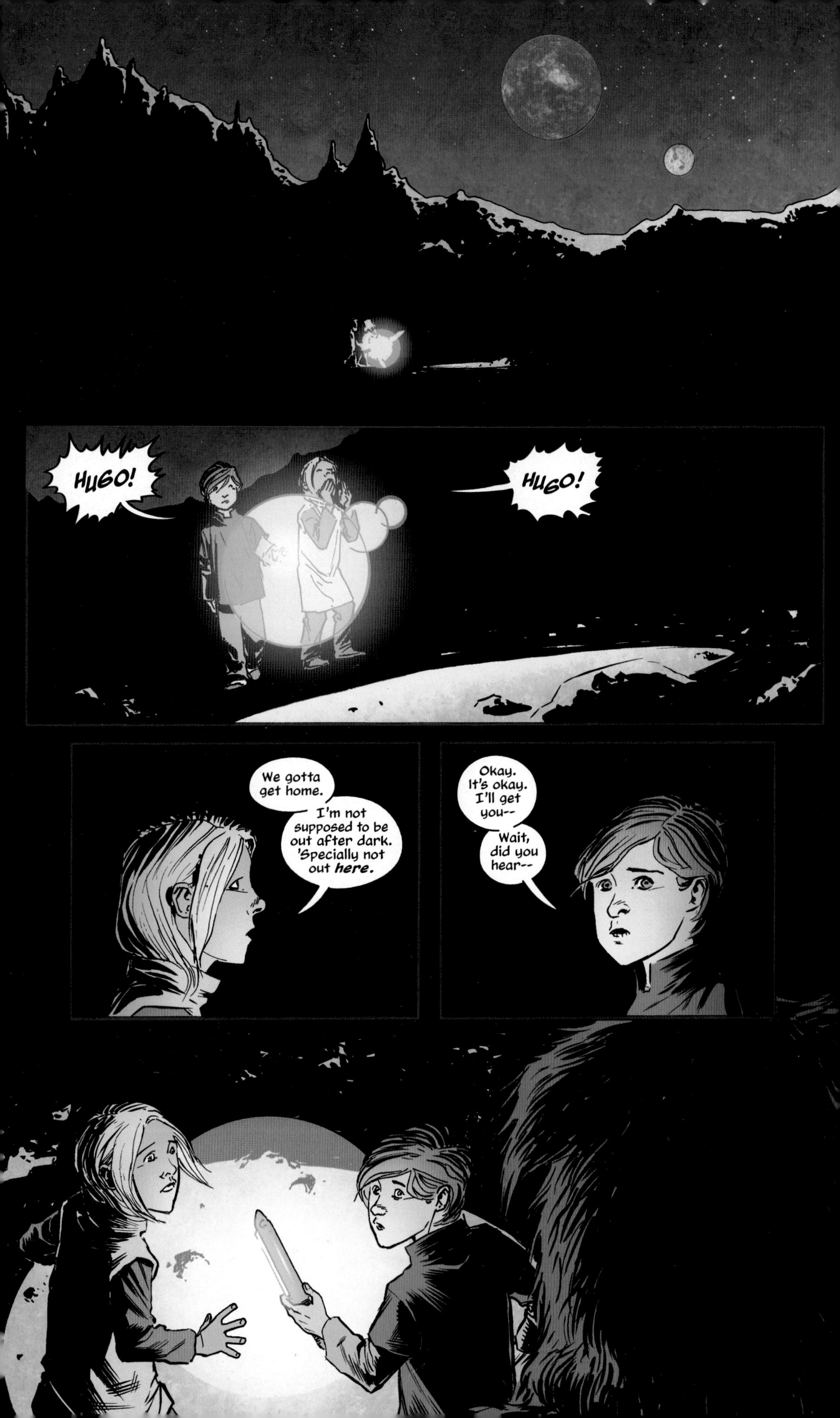
HUGO!
HUGO!
We gotta get home.
I'm not supposed to be out after dark. 'Specially not out *here*.
Okay. It's okay. I'll get you--
Wait, did you hear--

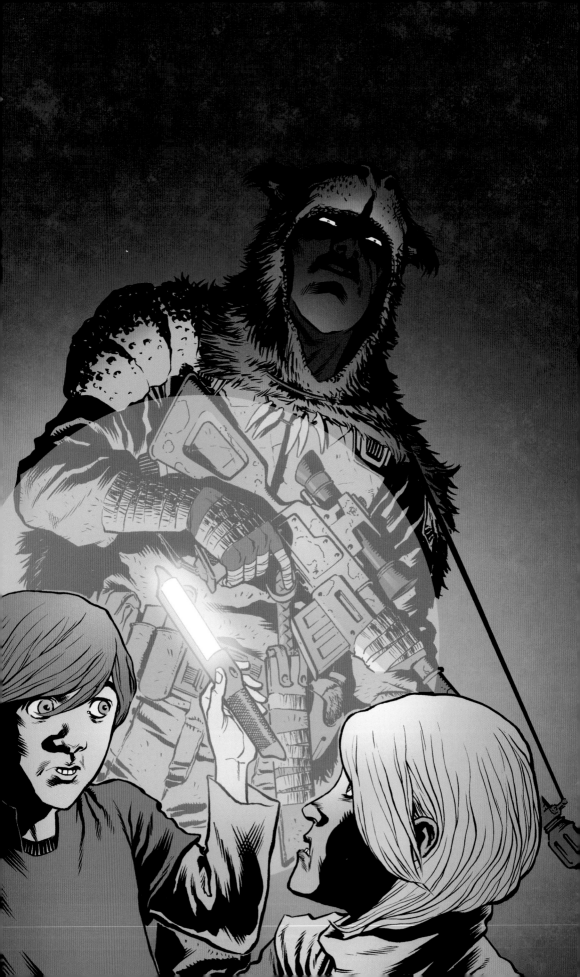

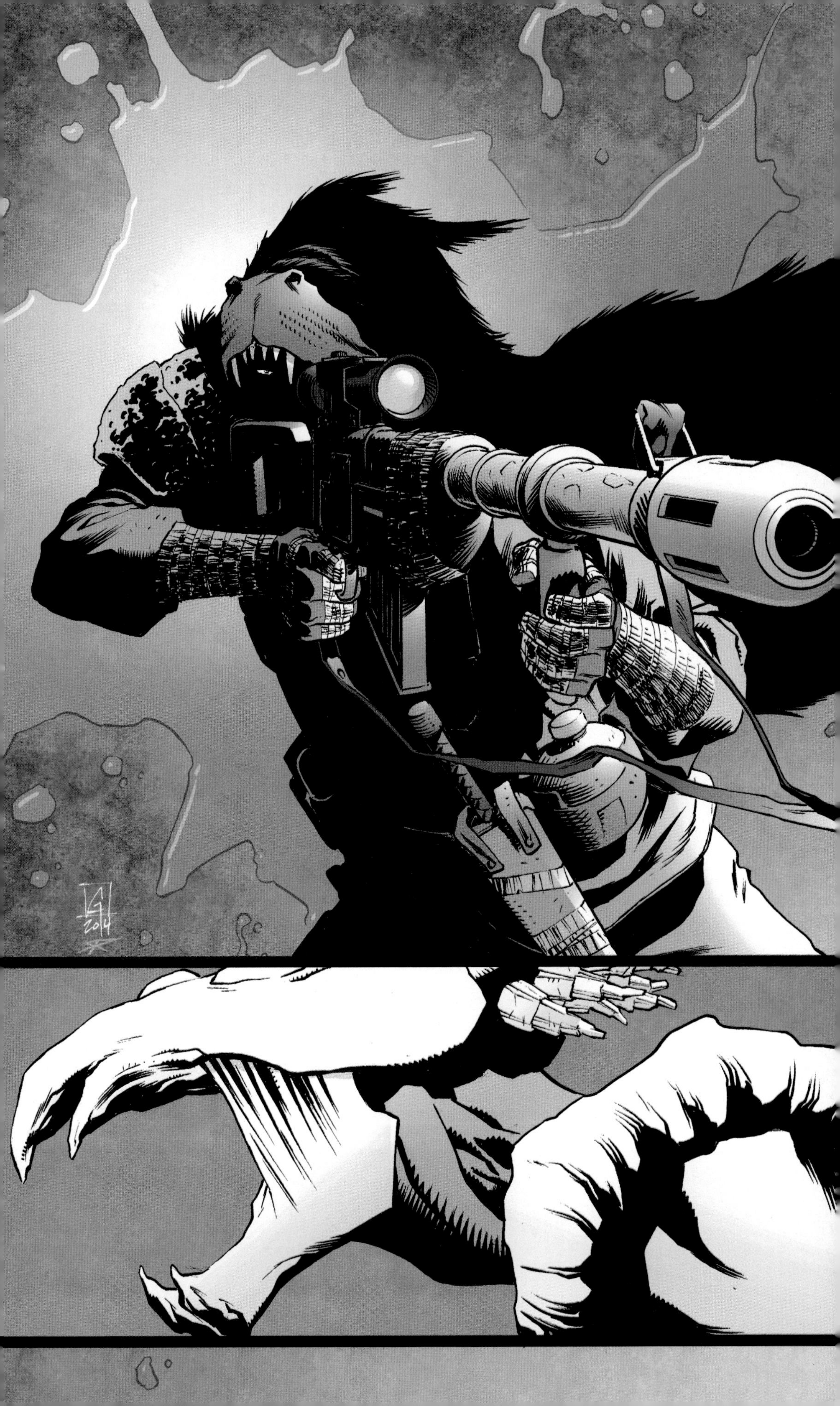

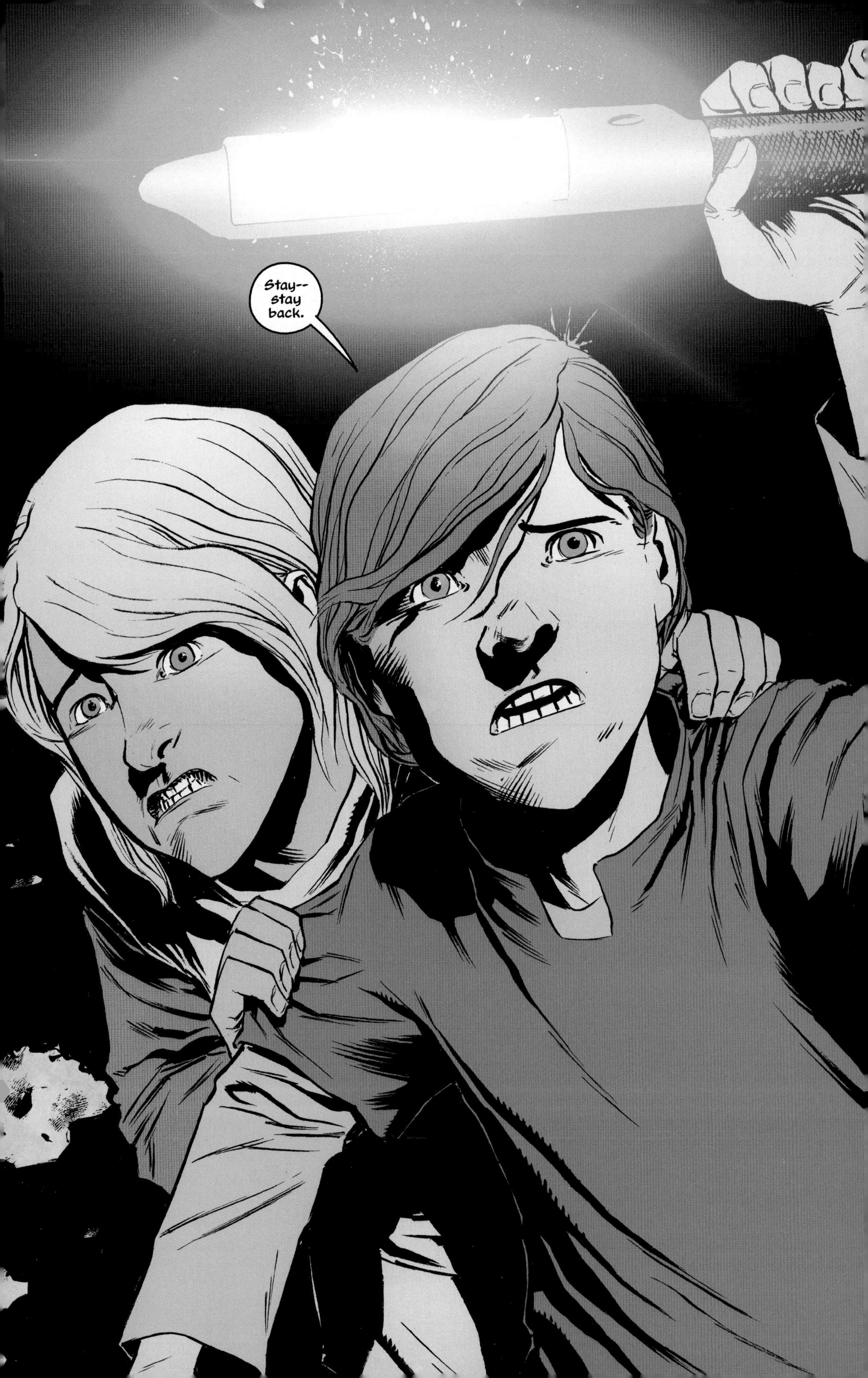
Stay--
stay
back.

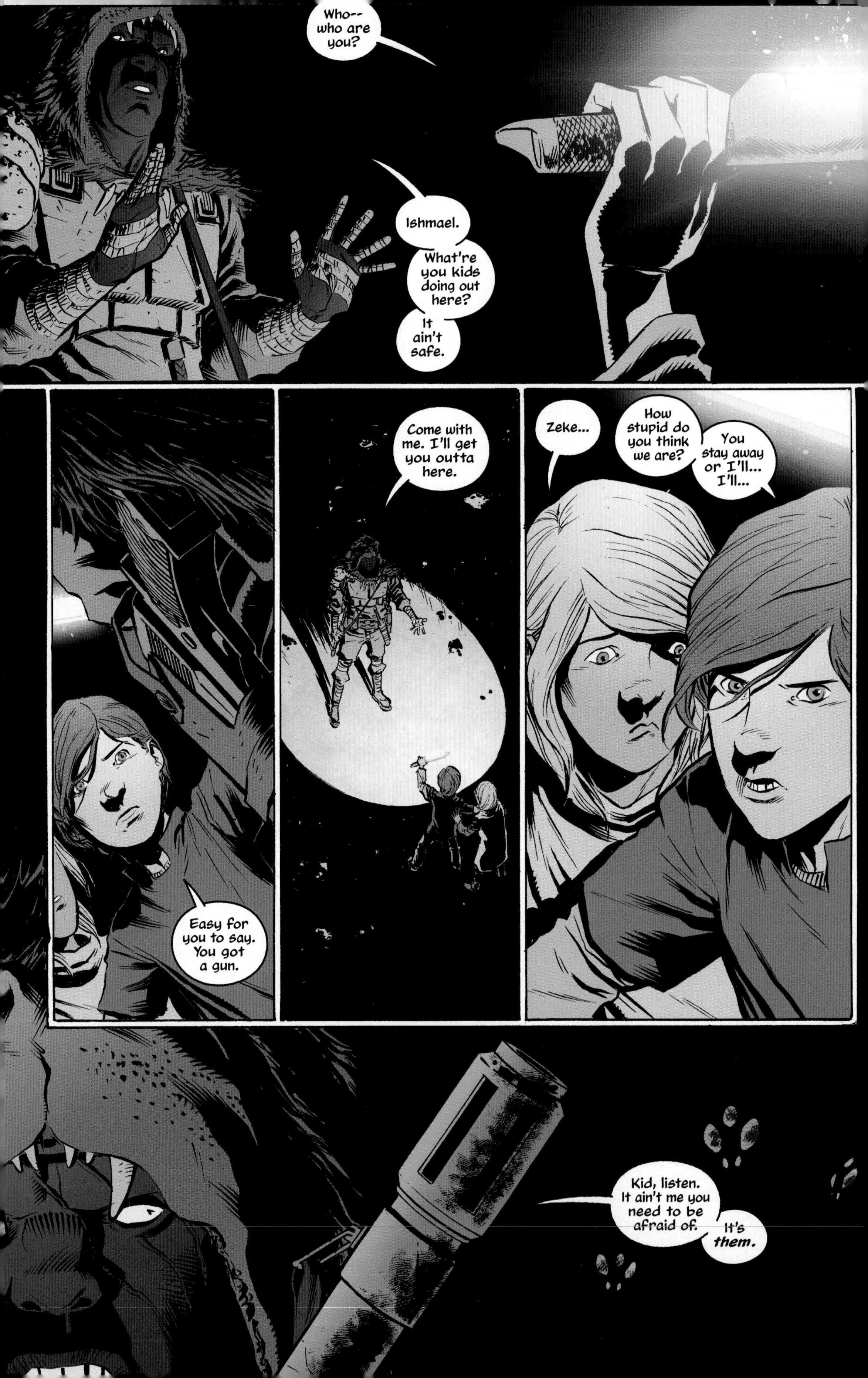
Who-- who are you?
Ishmael.
What're you kids doing out here?
It ain't safe.
Easy for you to say. You got a gun.
Come with me. I'll get you outta here.
Zeke...
How stupid do you think we are?
You stay away or I'll... I'll...
Kid, listen. It ain't me you need to be afraid of.
It's *them.*

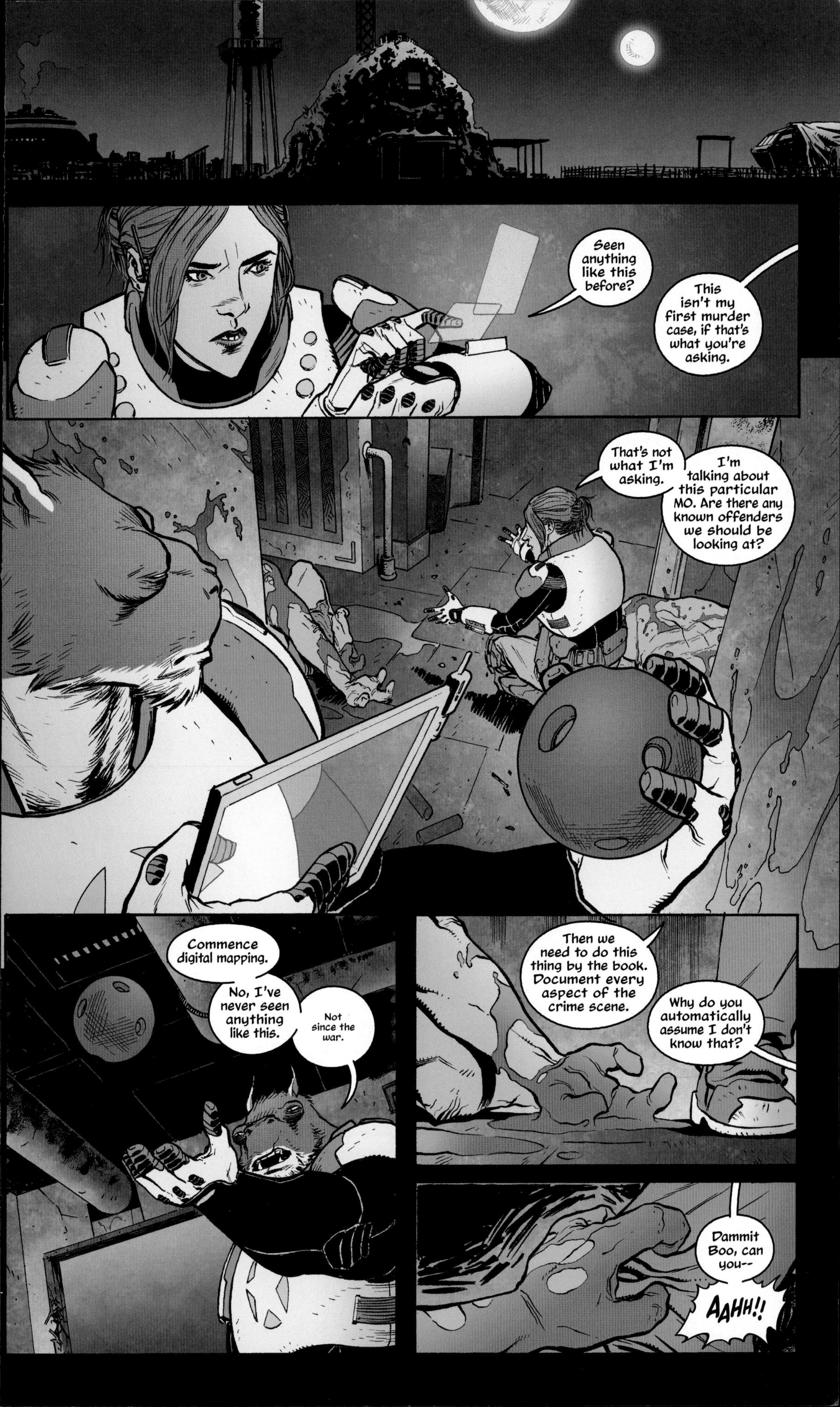
Seen anything like this before?
This isn't my first murder case, if that's what you're asking.
That's not what I'm asking.
I'm talking about this particular MO. Are there any known offenders we should be looking at?
Commence digital mapping.
No, I've never seen anything like this.
Not since the war.
Then we need to do this thing by the book. Document every aspect of the crime scene.
Why do you automatically assume I don't know that?
Dammit Boo, can you--
AAHH!!

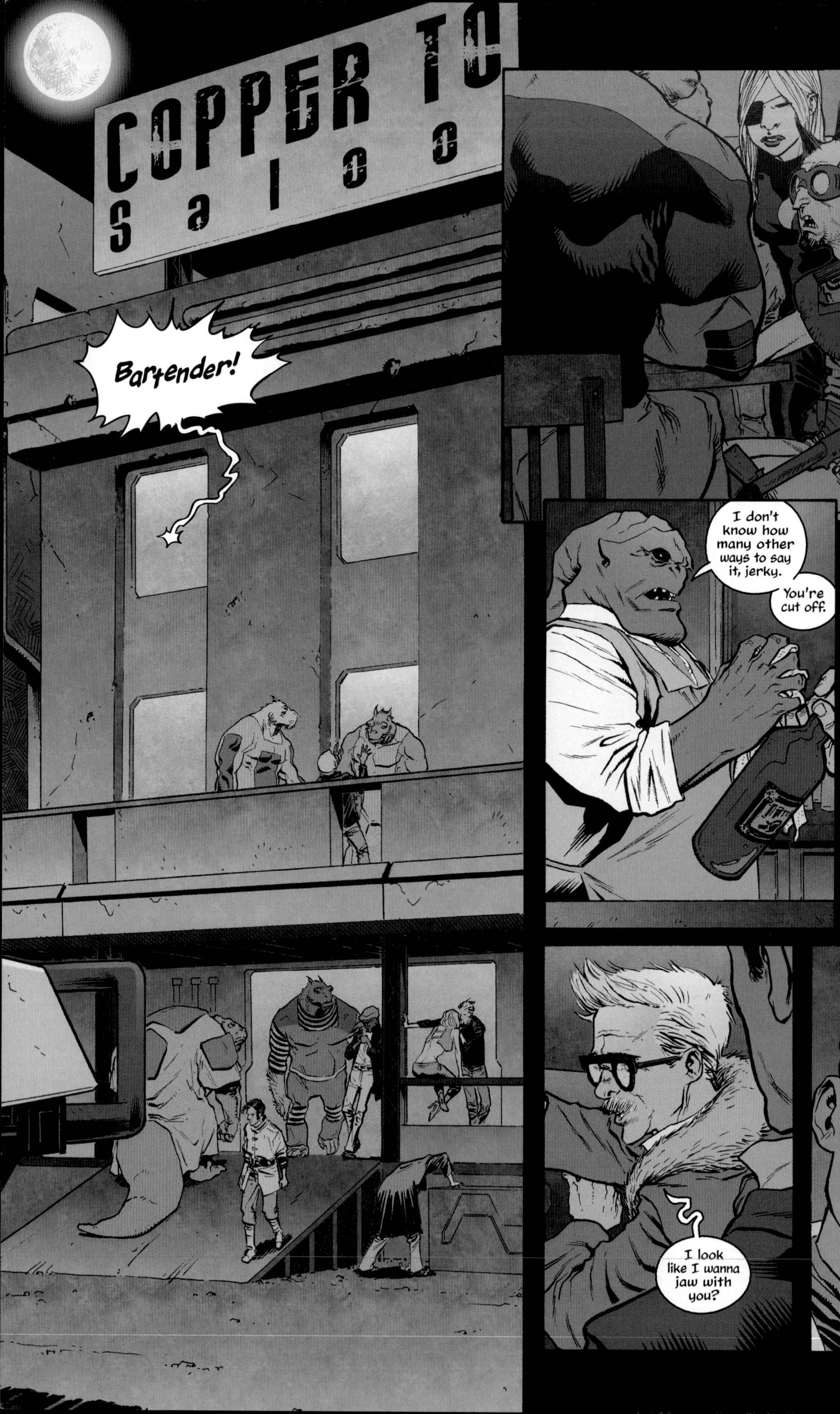
COPPER TO
Salo
Bartender!
I don't know how many other ways to say it, jerky.
You're cut off.
I look like I wanna jaw with you?

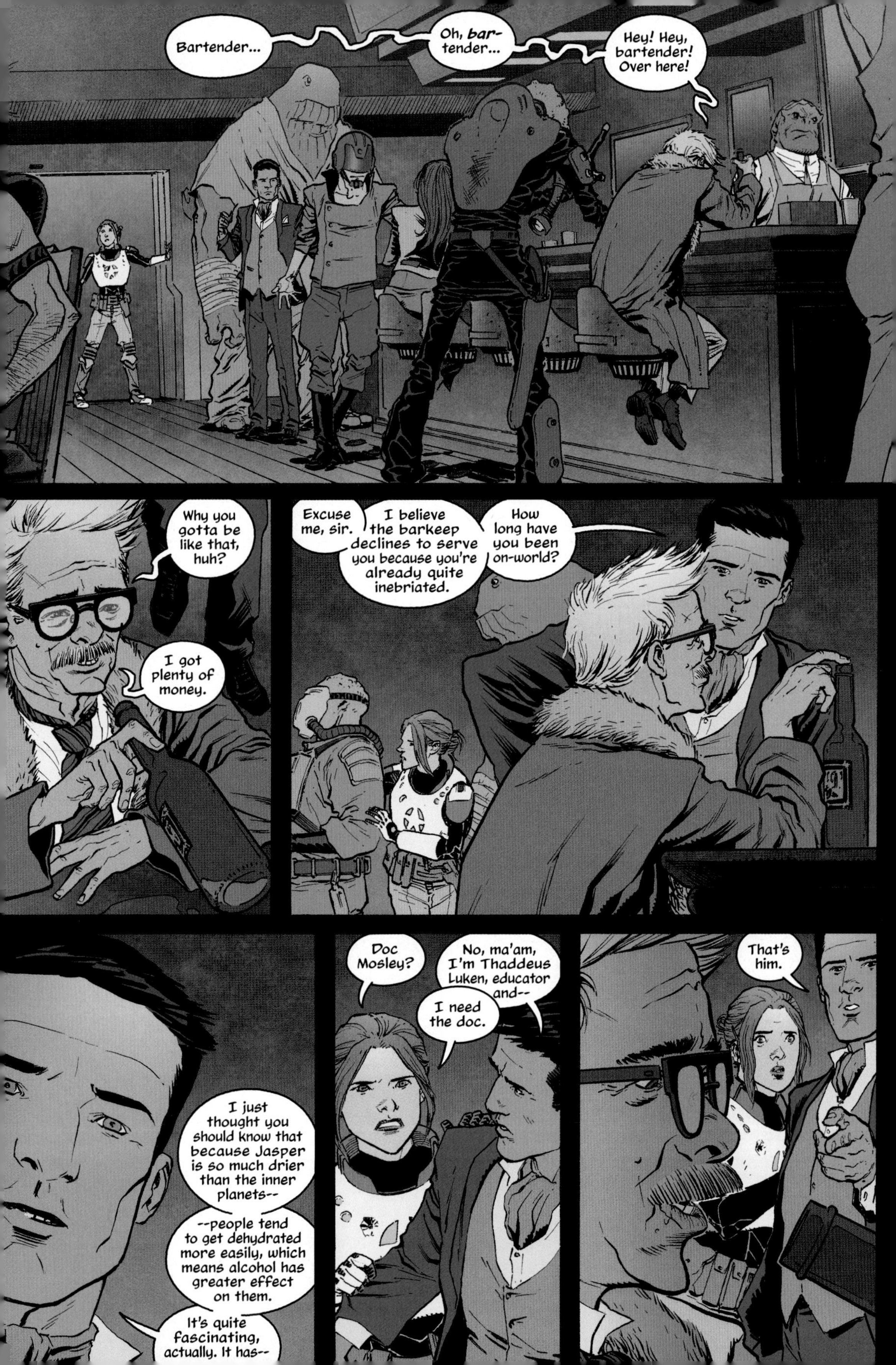
Bartender...
Oh, bar-tender...
Hey! Hey, bartender! Over here!
Why you gotta be like that, huh?
I got plenty of money.
Excuse me, sir.
I believe the barkeep declines to serve you because you're already quite inebriated.
How long have you been on-world?
I just thought you should know that because Jasper is so much drier than the inner planets--
--people tend to get dehydrated more easily, which means alcohol has greater effect on them.
It's quite fascinating, actually. It has--
Doc Mosley?
No, ma'am, I'm Thaddeus Luken, educator and--
I need the doc.
That's him.

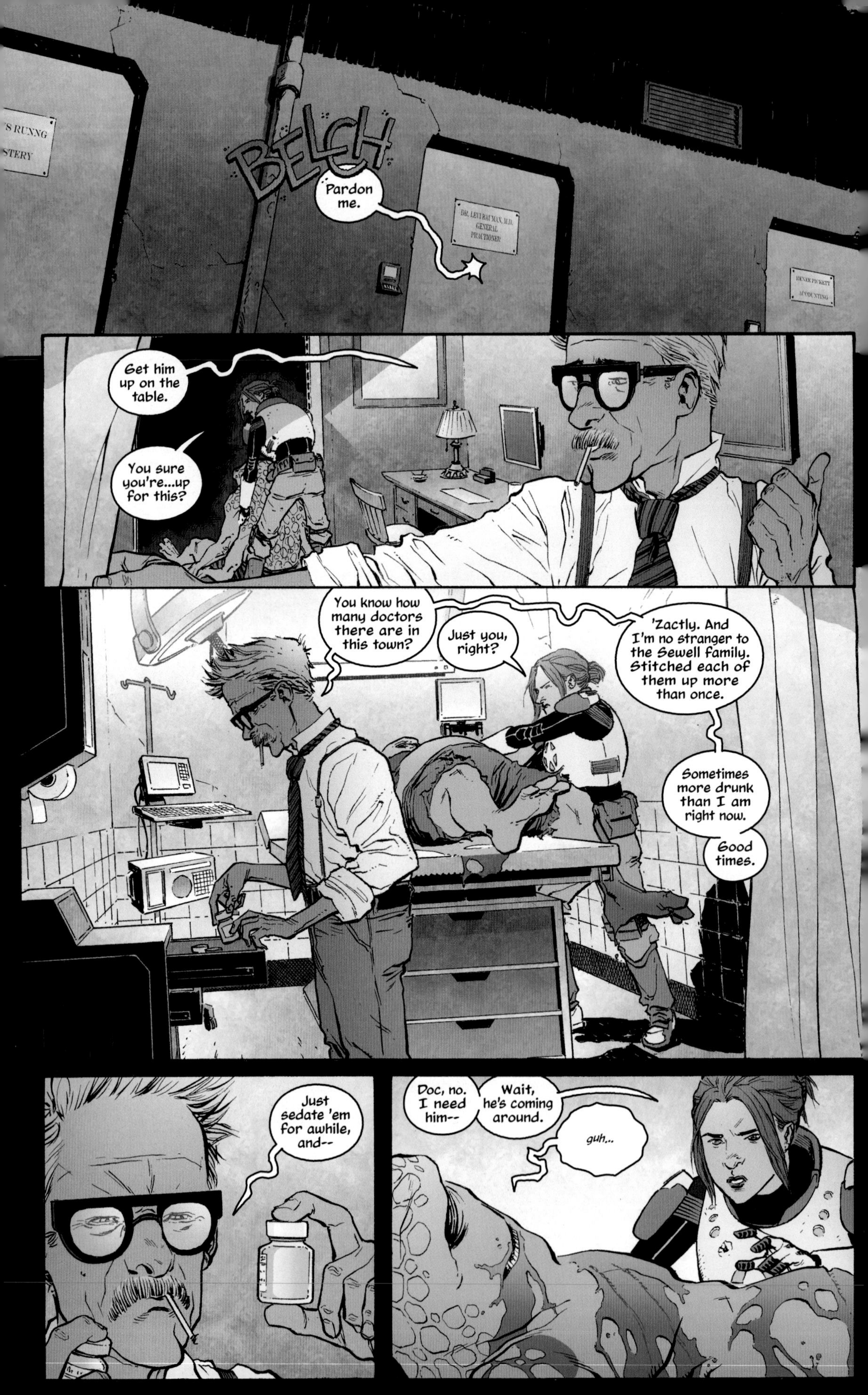
'S RUNNG
STERY
BELCH
Pardon me.
DR. LEVI BAUMAN, M.D.
GENERAL
PRACTIONER
RENEE PICKETT
ACCOUNTING
Get him up on the table.
You sure you're...up for this?
You know how many doctors there are in this town?
Just you, right?
'Zactly. And I'm no stranger to the Sewell family. Stitched each of them up more than once.
Sometimes more drunk than I am right now.
Good times.
Just sedate 'em for awhile, and--
Doc, no. I need him--
Wait, he's coming around.
guh...

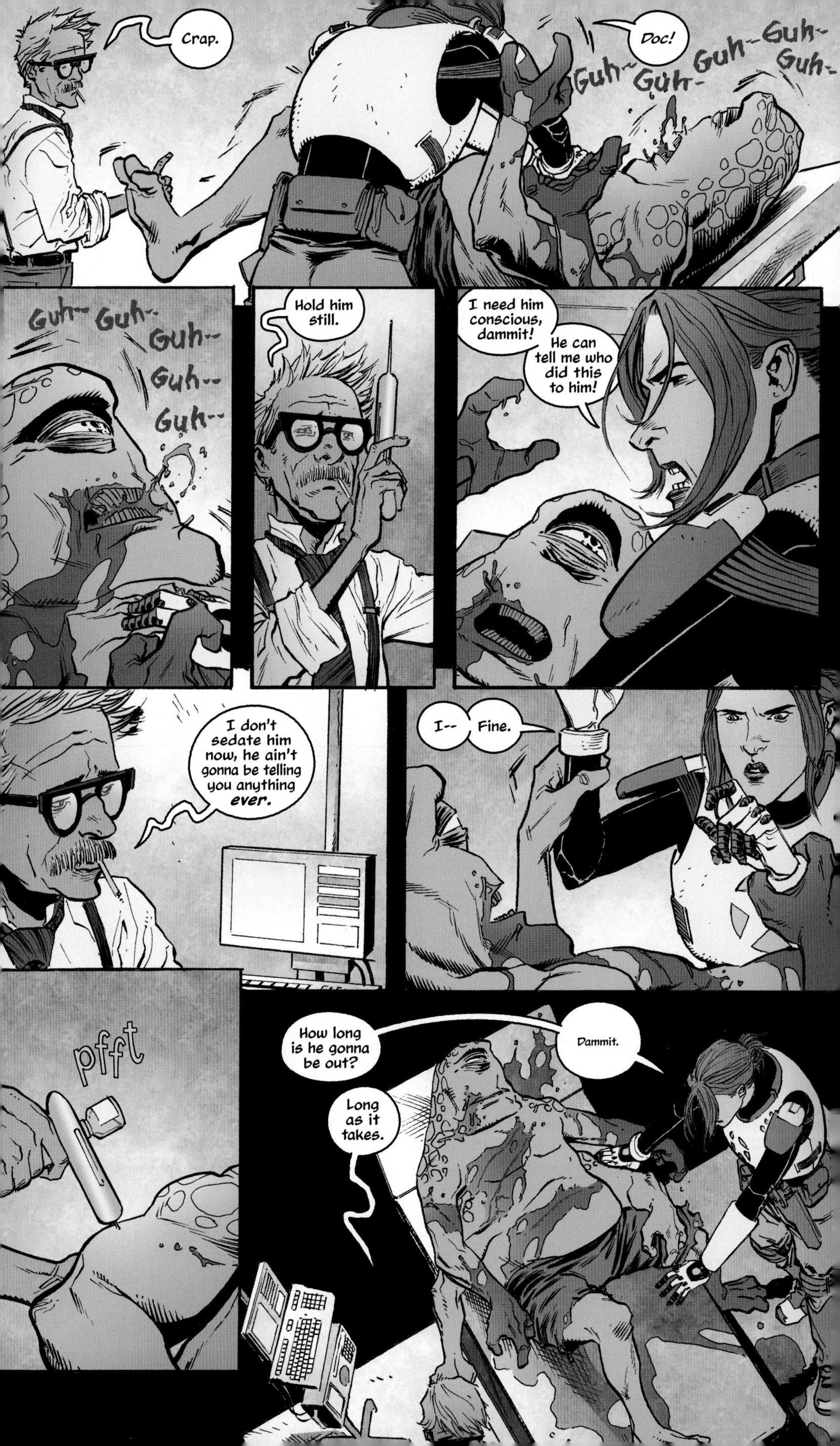
Crap.
Doc!
Guh-- Guh-- Guh-- Guh-- Guh--
Guh-- Guh-- Guh-- Guh-- Guh--
Hold him still.
I need him conscious, dammit!
He can tell me who did this to him!
I don't sedate him now, he ain't gonna be telling you anything *ever.*
I--
Fine.
pfft
How long is he gonna be out?
Long as it takes.
Dammit.

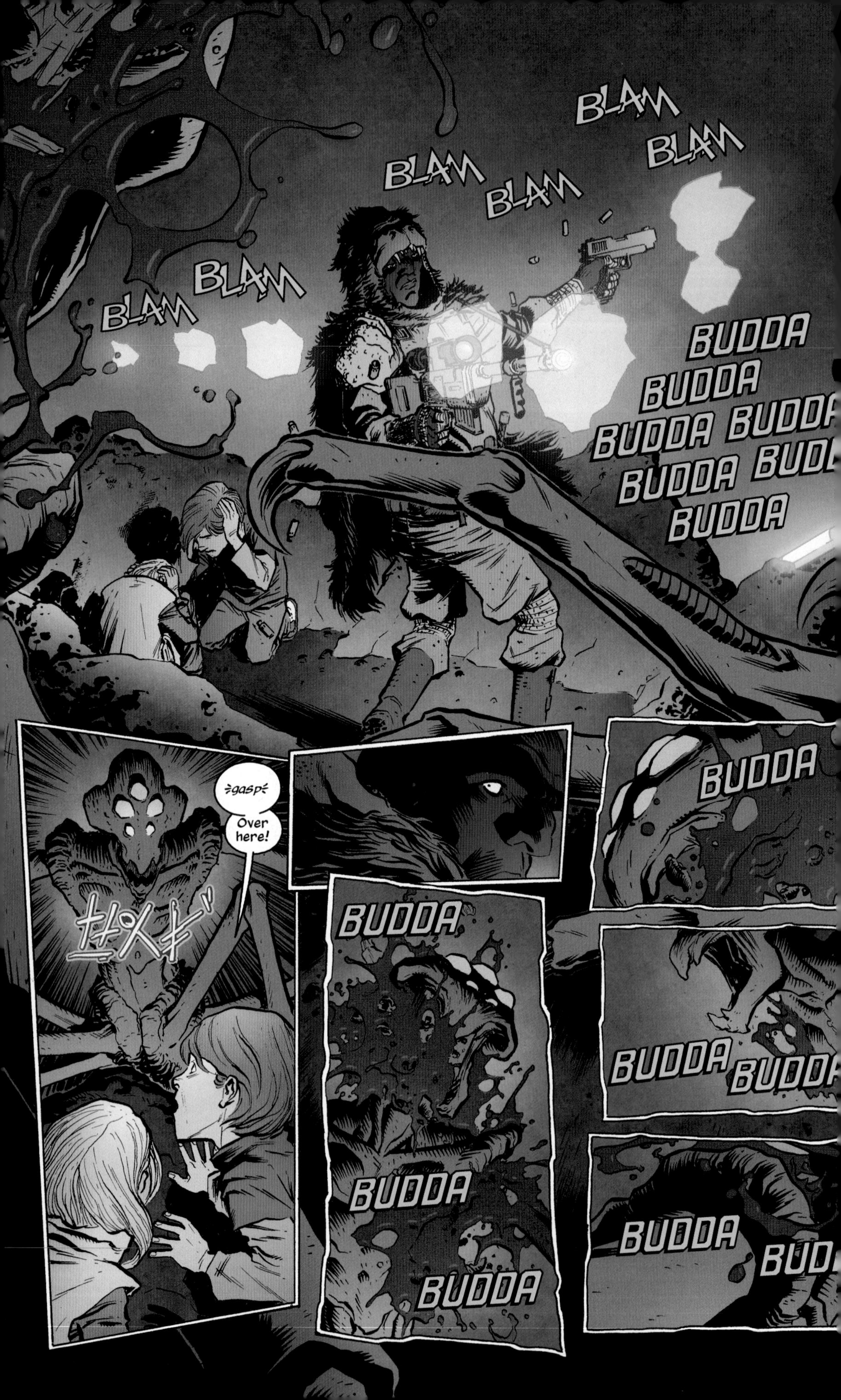
BLAM
BLAM
BLAM
BLAM
BLAM
BLAM
BUDDA
BUDDA
BUDDA BUDDA
BUDDA BUDD
BUDDA
gasp
Over here!
BUDDA
BUDDA
BUDDA
BUDDA
BUDDA BUDDA
BUDDA
BUD

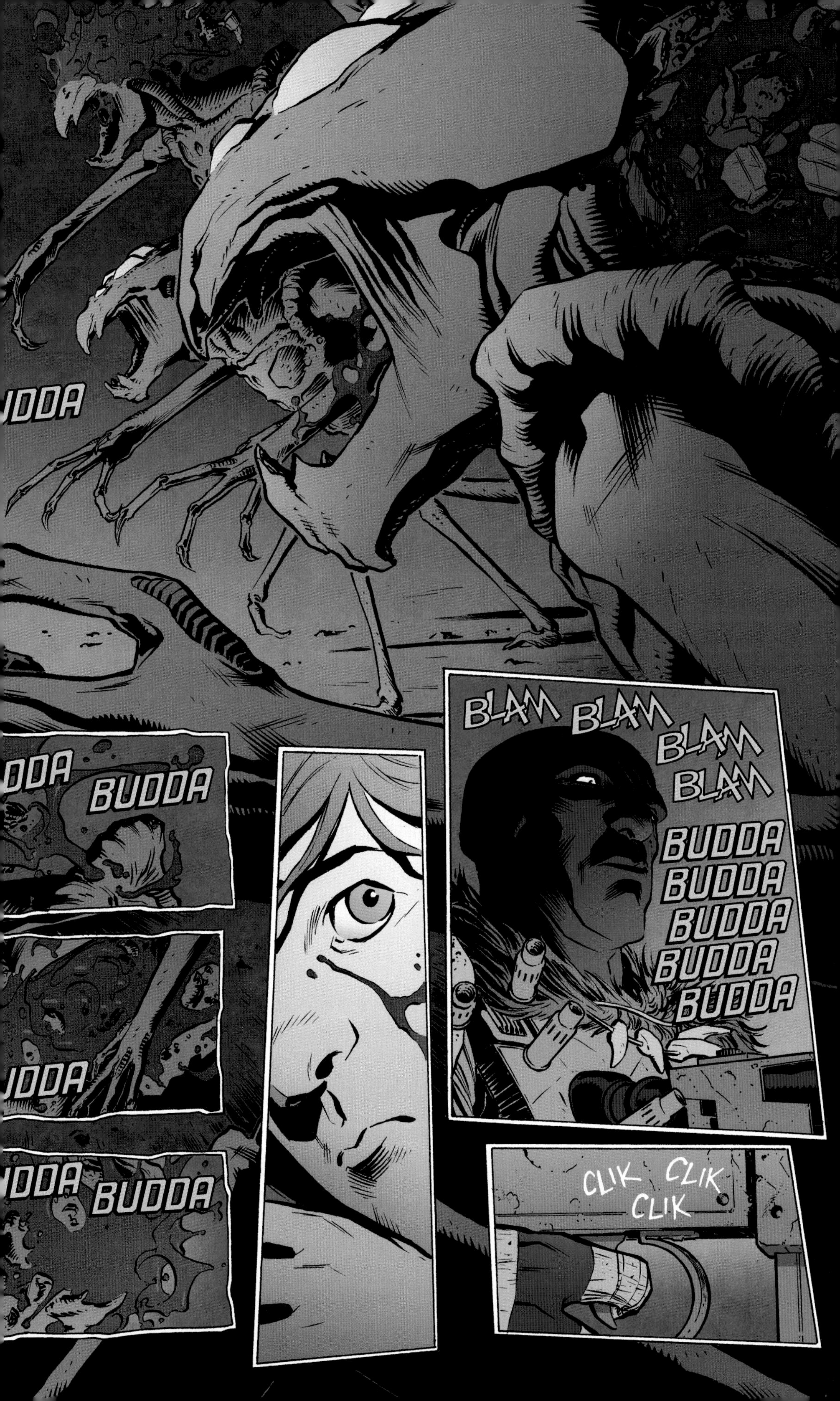

UDDA
UDDA BUDDA
UDDA
UDDA BUDDA
BLAM BLAM BLAM BLAM
BUDDA BUDDA BUDDA BUDDA BUDDA
CLIK CLIK CLIK

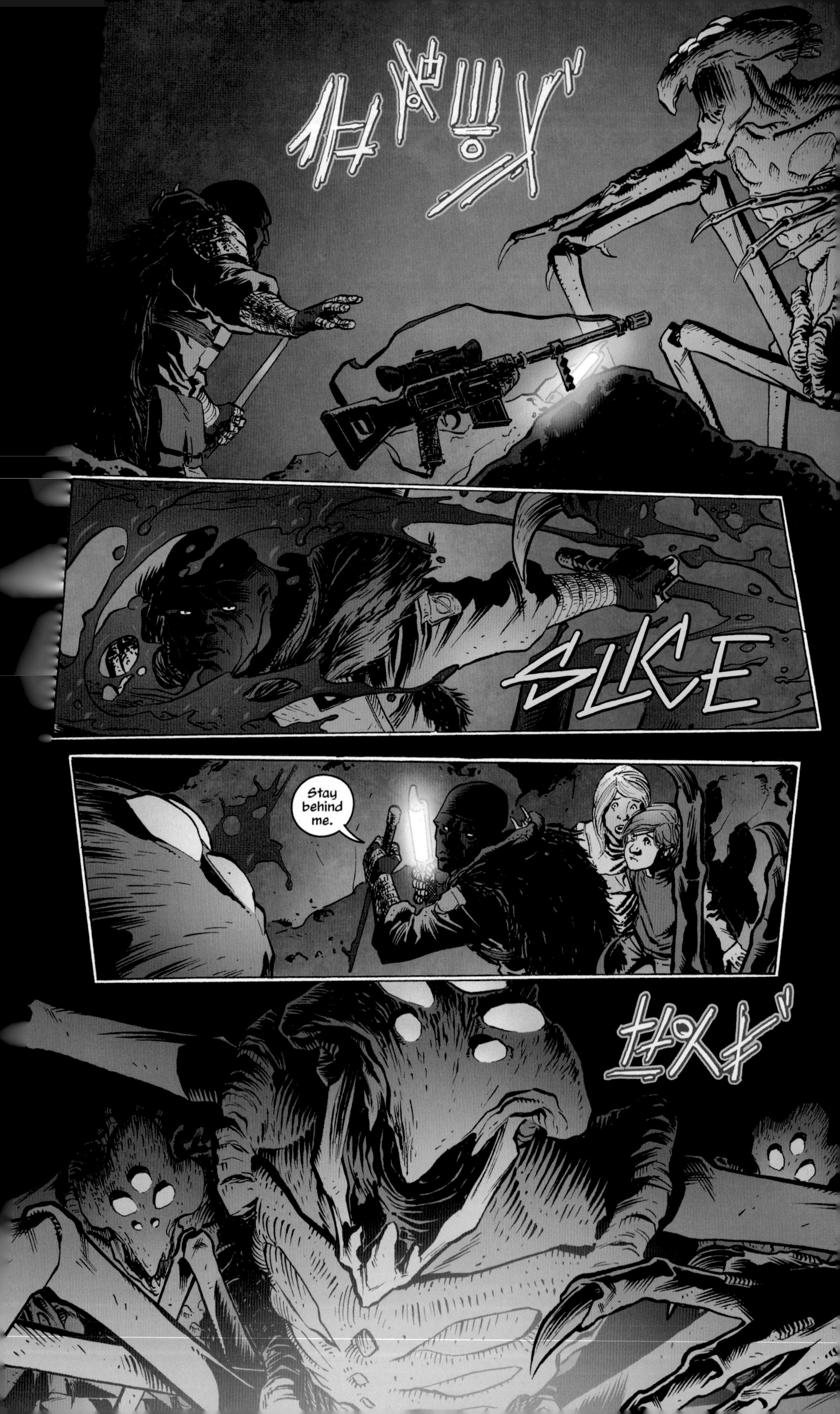
SLICE
Stay behind me.

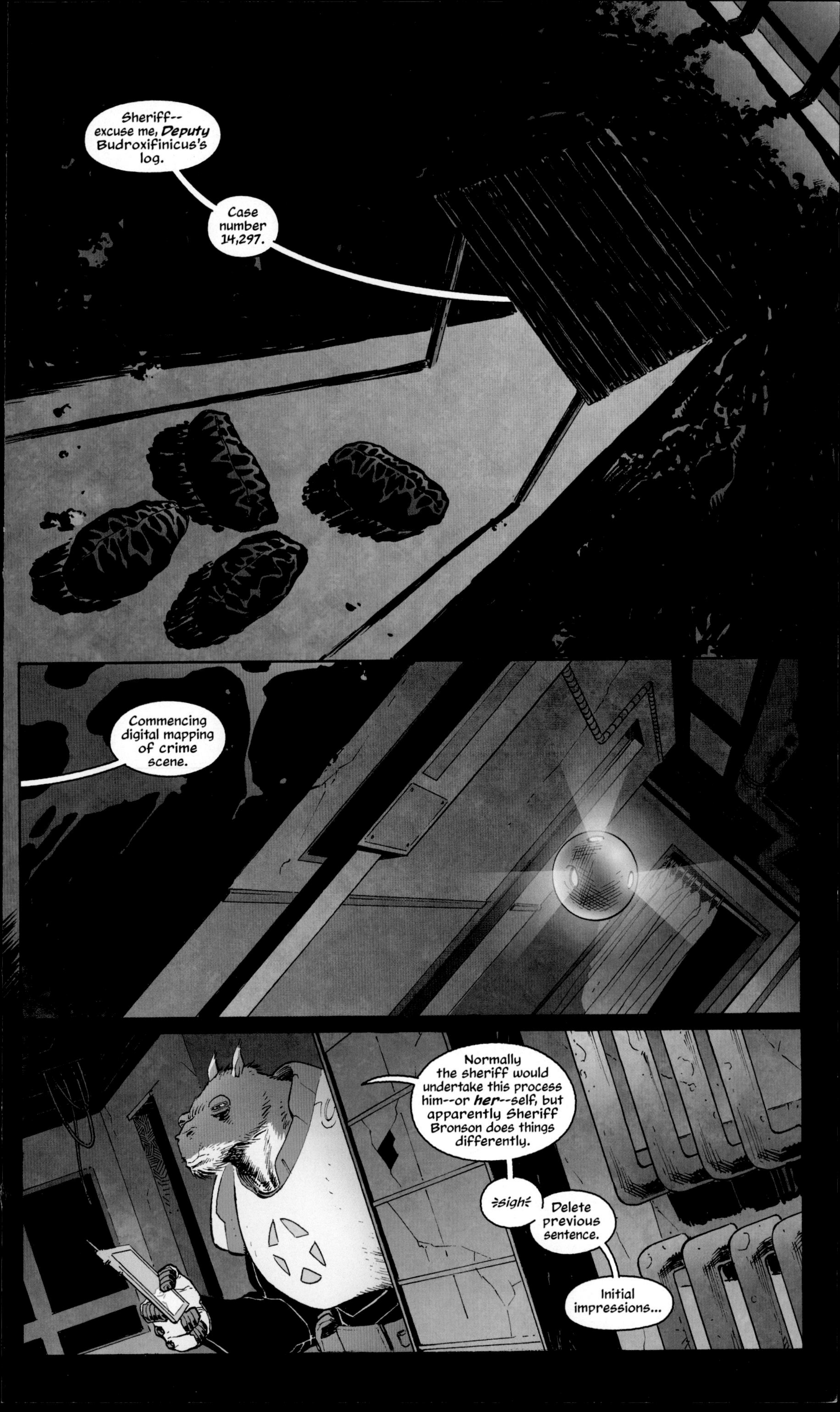
Sheriff-- excuse me, Deputy Budroxifinicus's log.
Case number 14,297.
Commencing digital mapping of crime scene.
Normally the sheriff would undertake this process him--or her--self, but apparently Sheriff Bronson does things differently.
sigh
Delete previous sentence.
Initial impressions...

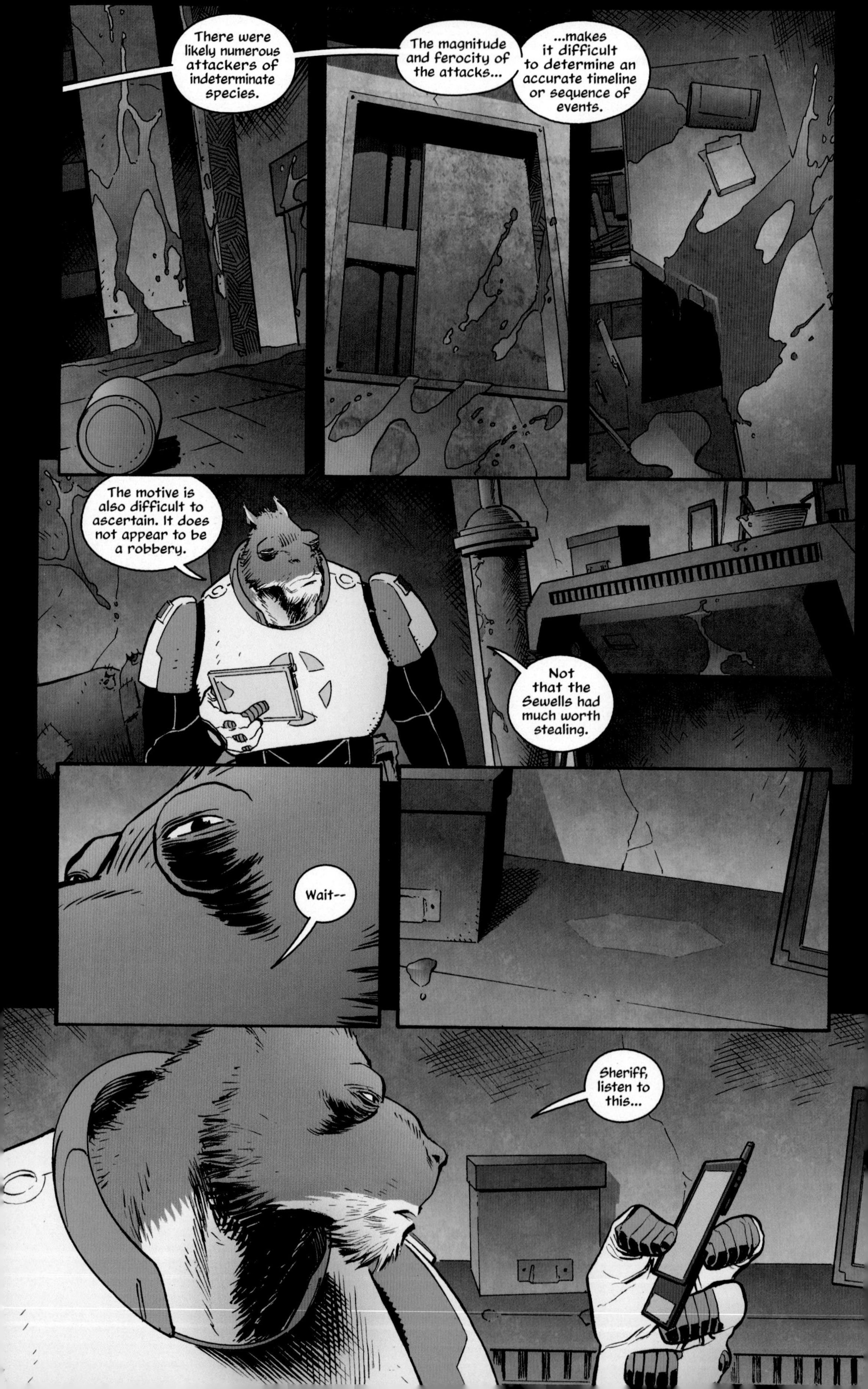
There were likely numerous attackers of indeterminate species.
The magnitude and ferocity of the attacks...
...makes it difficult to determine an accurate timeline or sequence of events.
The motive is also difficult to ascertain. It does not appear to be a robbery.
Not that the Sewells had much worth stealing.
Wait--
Sheriff, listen to this...

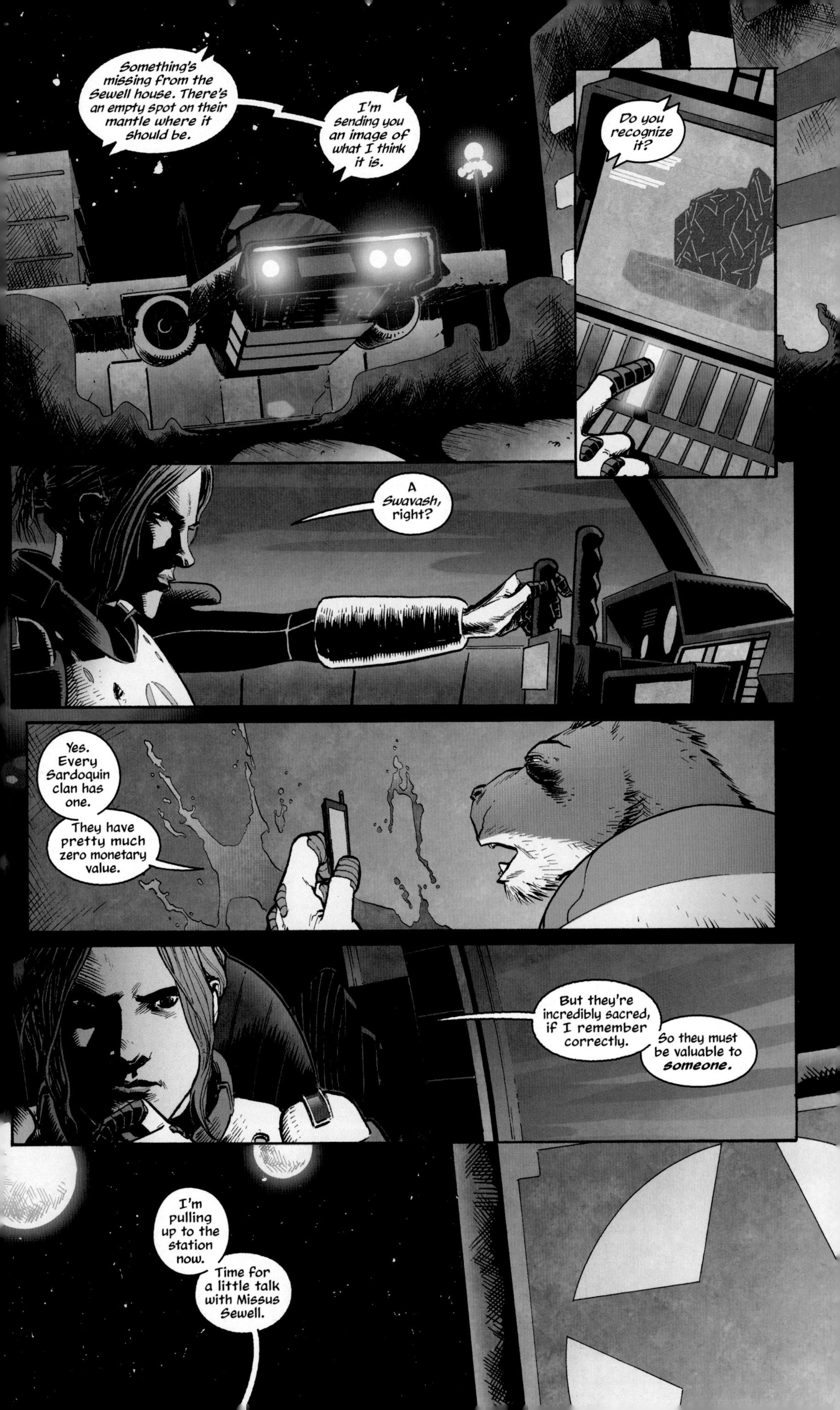

Something's missing from the Sewell house. There's an empty spot on their mantle where it should be.
I'm sending you an image of what I think it is.
Do you recognize it?
A Swavash, right?
Yes. Every Sardoquin clan has one.
They have pretty much zero monetary value.
But they're incredibly sacred, if I remember correctly.
So they must be valuable to *someone*.
I'm pulling up to the station now.
Time for a little talk with Missus Sewell.

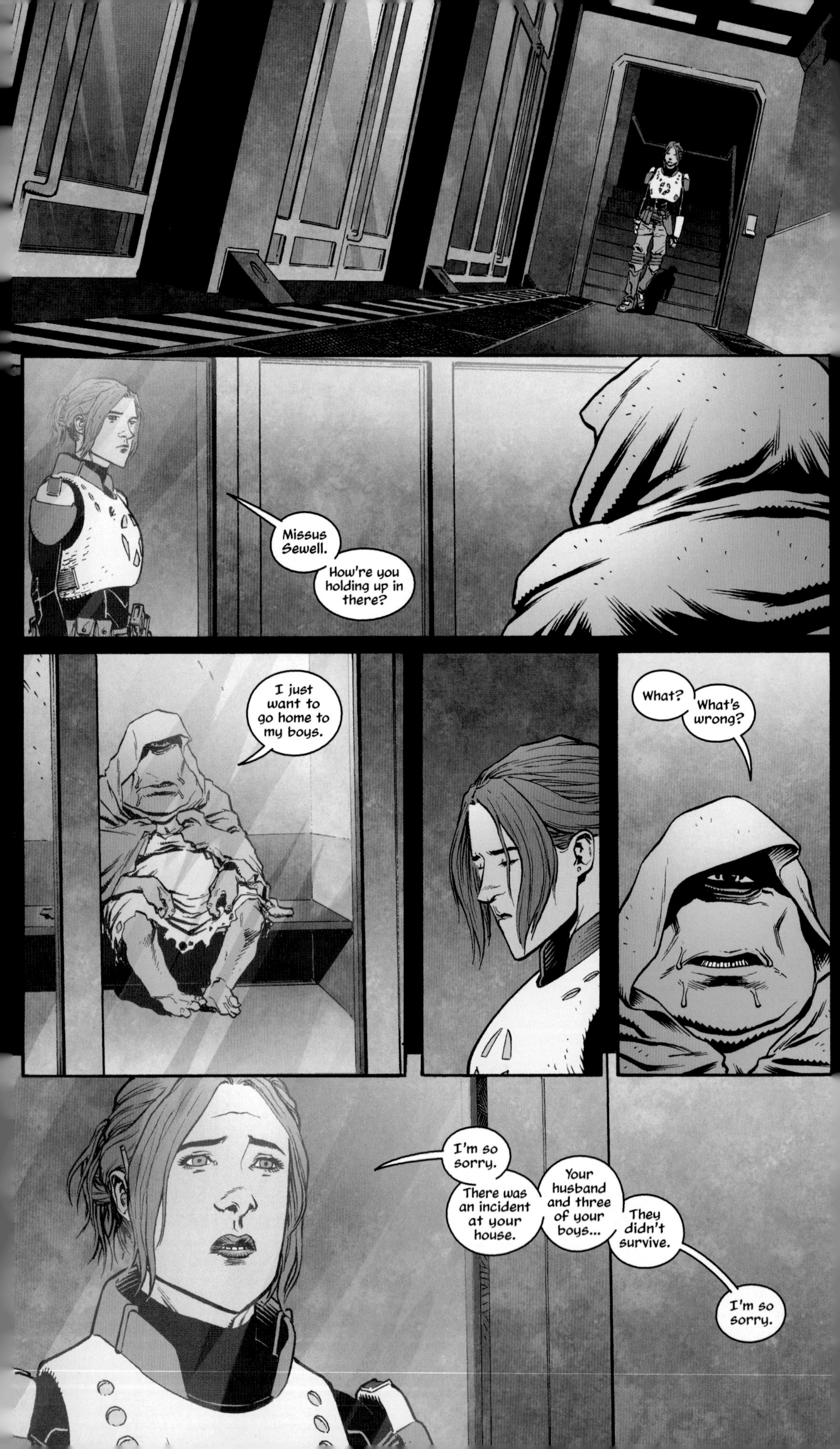
Missus Sewell.
How're you holding up in there?
I just want to go home to my boys.
What?
What's wrong?
I'm so sorry.
There was an incident at your house.
Your husband and three of your boys...
They didn't survive.
I'm so sorry.

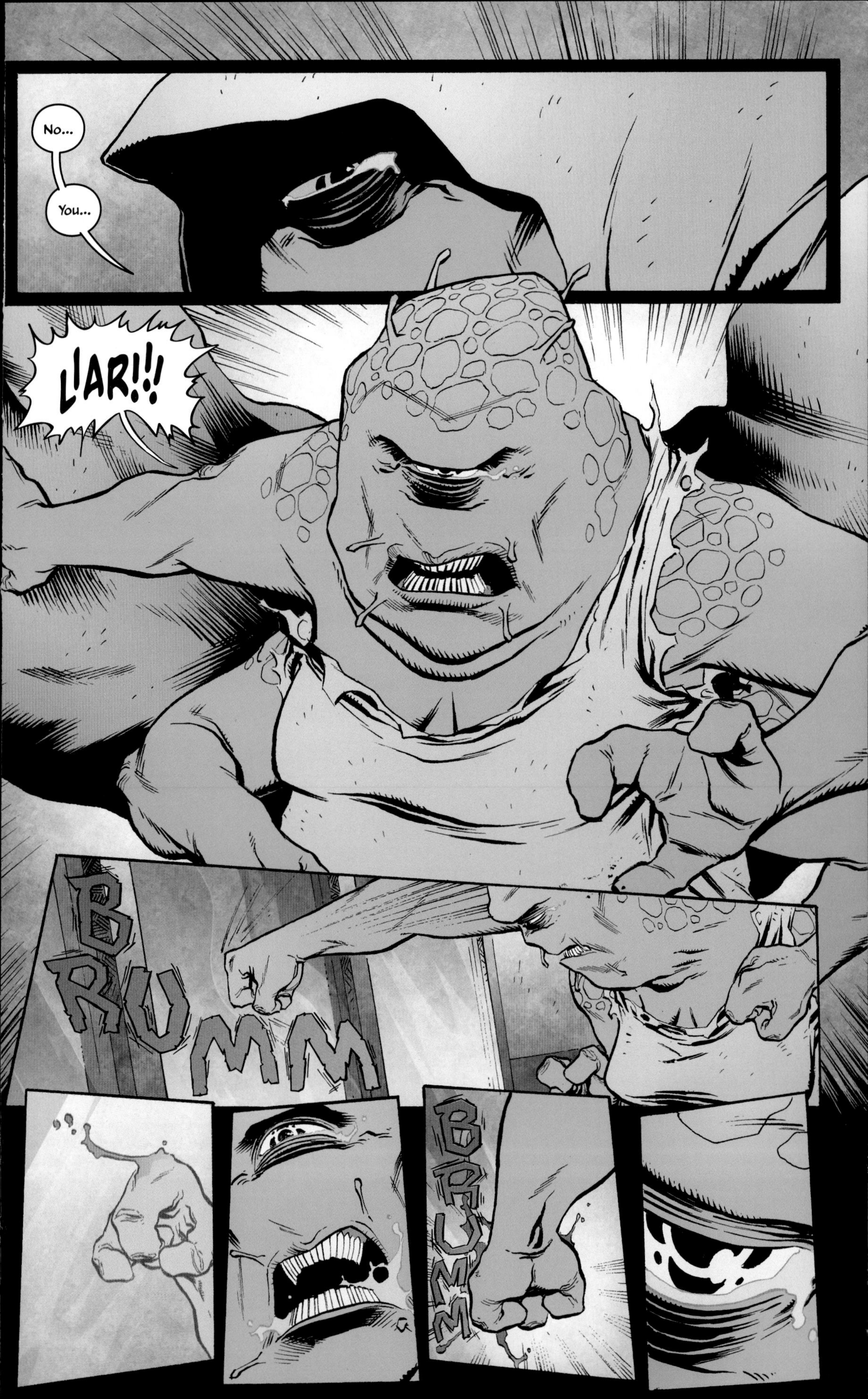
No...
You...
LIAR!!!
BRUMM
BRUMM

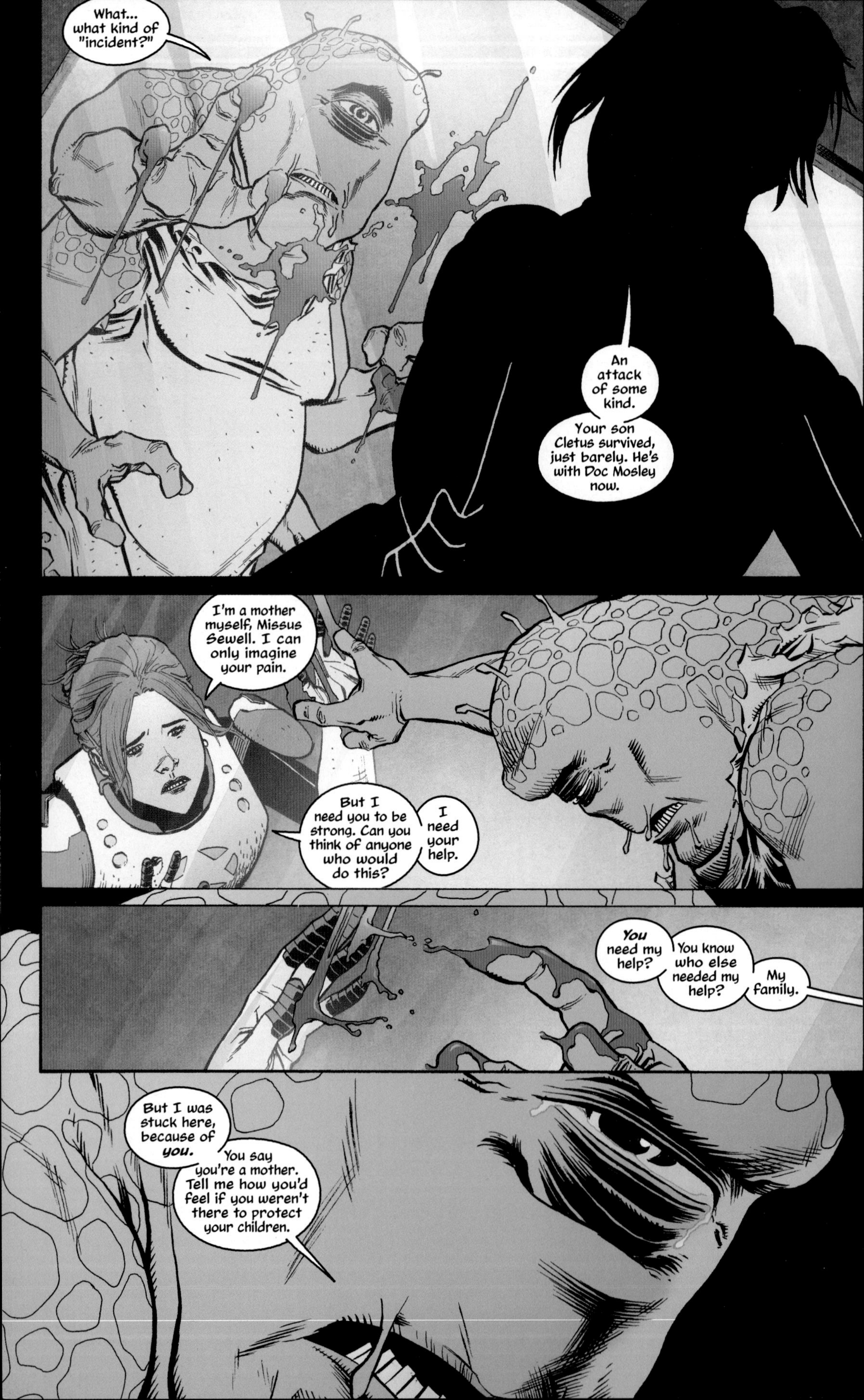
What... what kind of "incident?"
An attack of some kind.
Your son Cletus survived, just barely. He's with Doc Mosley now.
I'm a mother myself, Missus Sewell. I can only imagine your pain.
But I need you to be strong. Can you think of anyone who would do this?
I need your help.
You need my help?
You know who else needed my help?
My family.
But I was stuck here, because of you.
You say you're a mother. Tell me how you'd feel if you weren't there to protect your children.

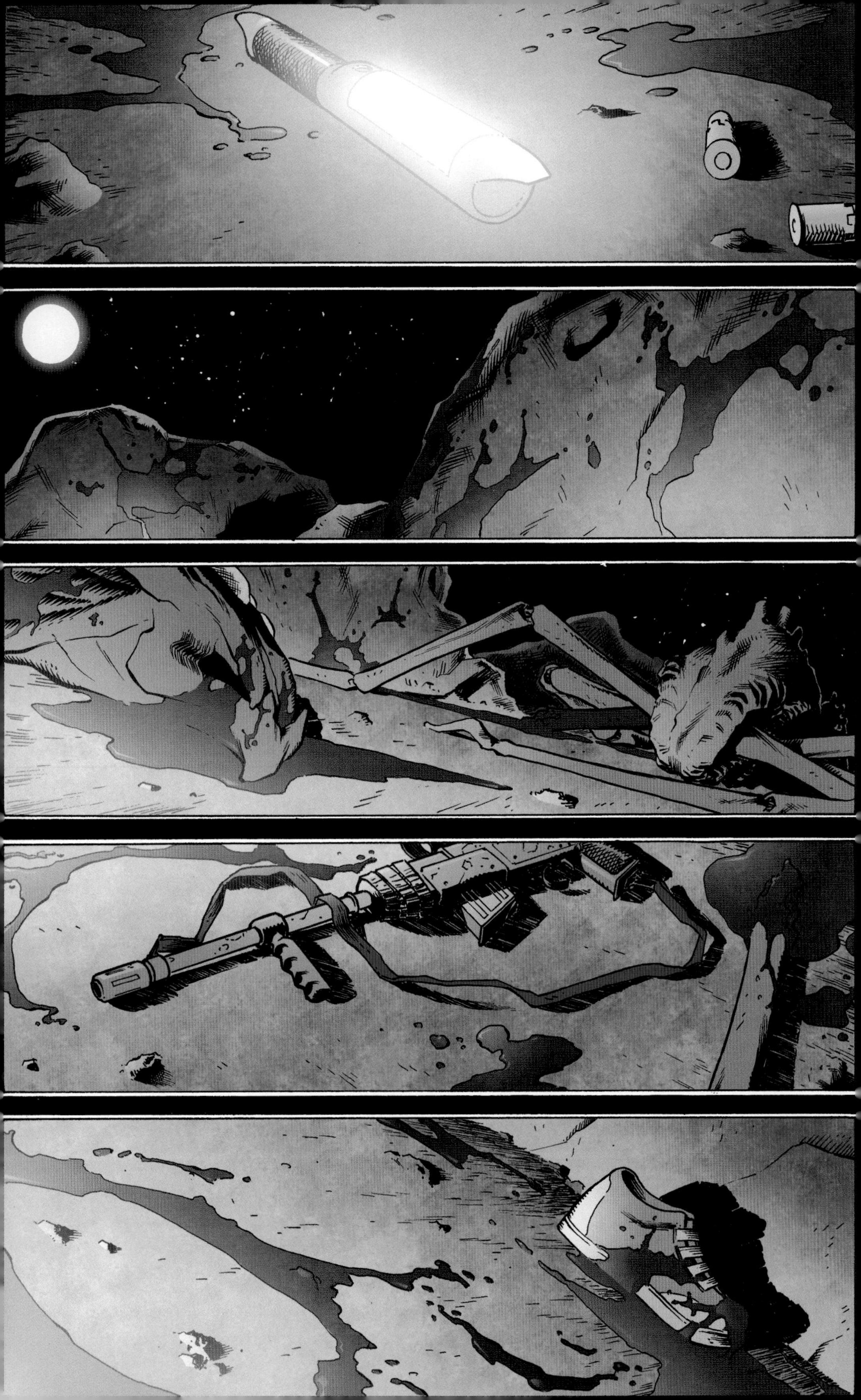

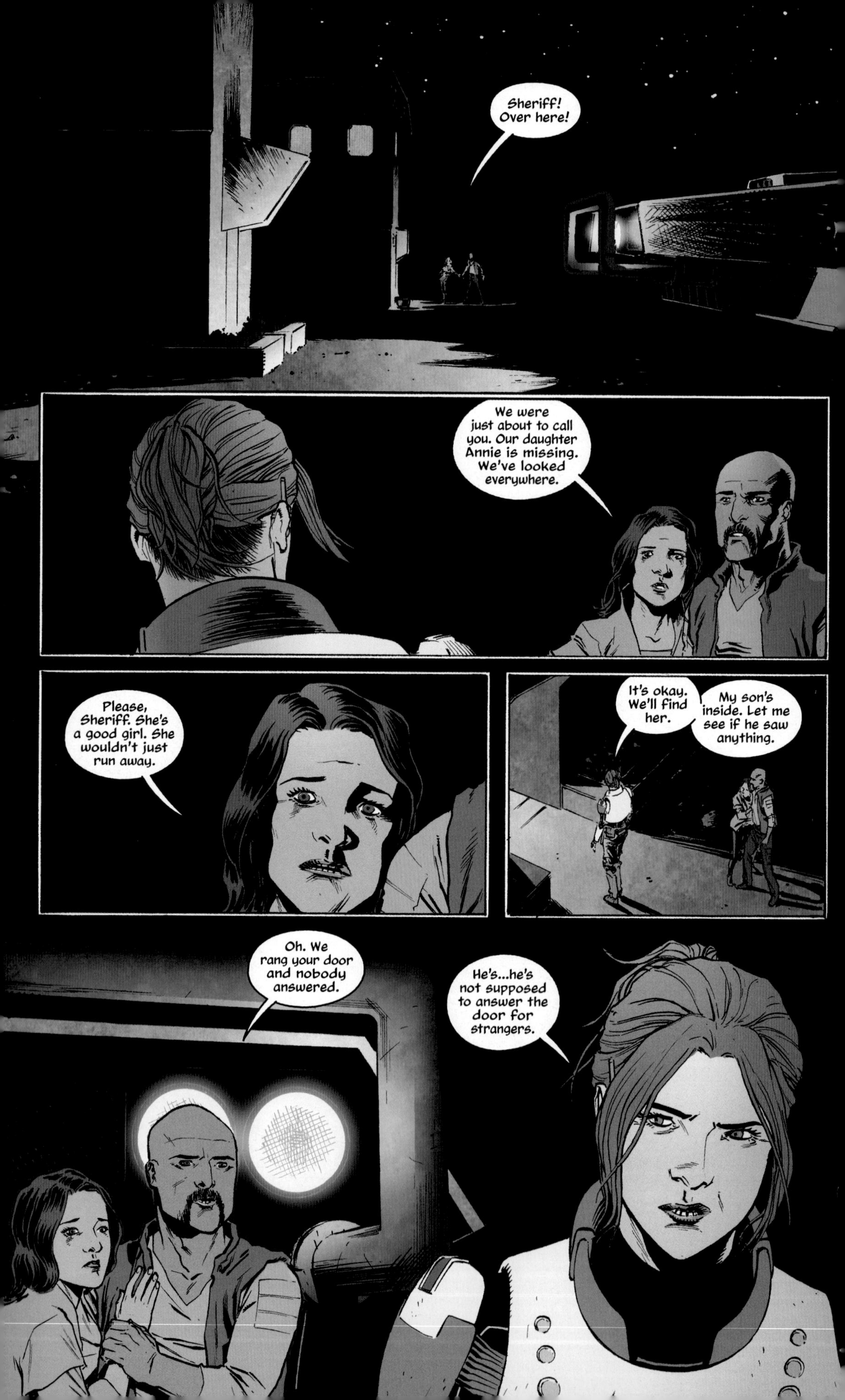
Sheriff! Over here!
We were just about to call you. Our daughter Annie is missing. We've looked everywhere.
Please, Sheriff. She's a good girl. She wouldn't just run away.
It's okay. We'll find her.
My son's inside. Let me see if he saw anything.
Oh. We rang your door and nobody answered.
He's...he's not supposed to answer the door for strangers.

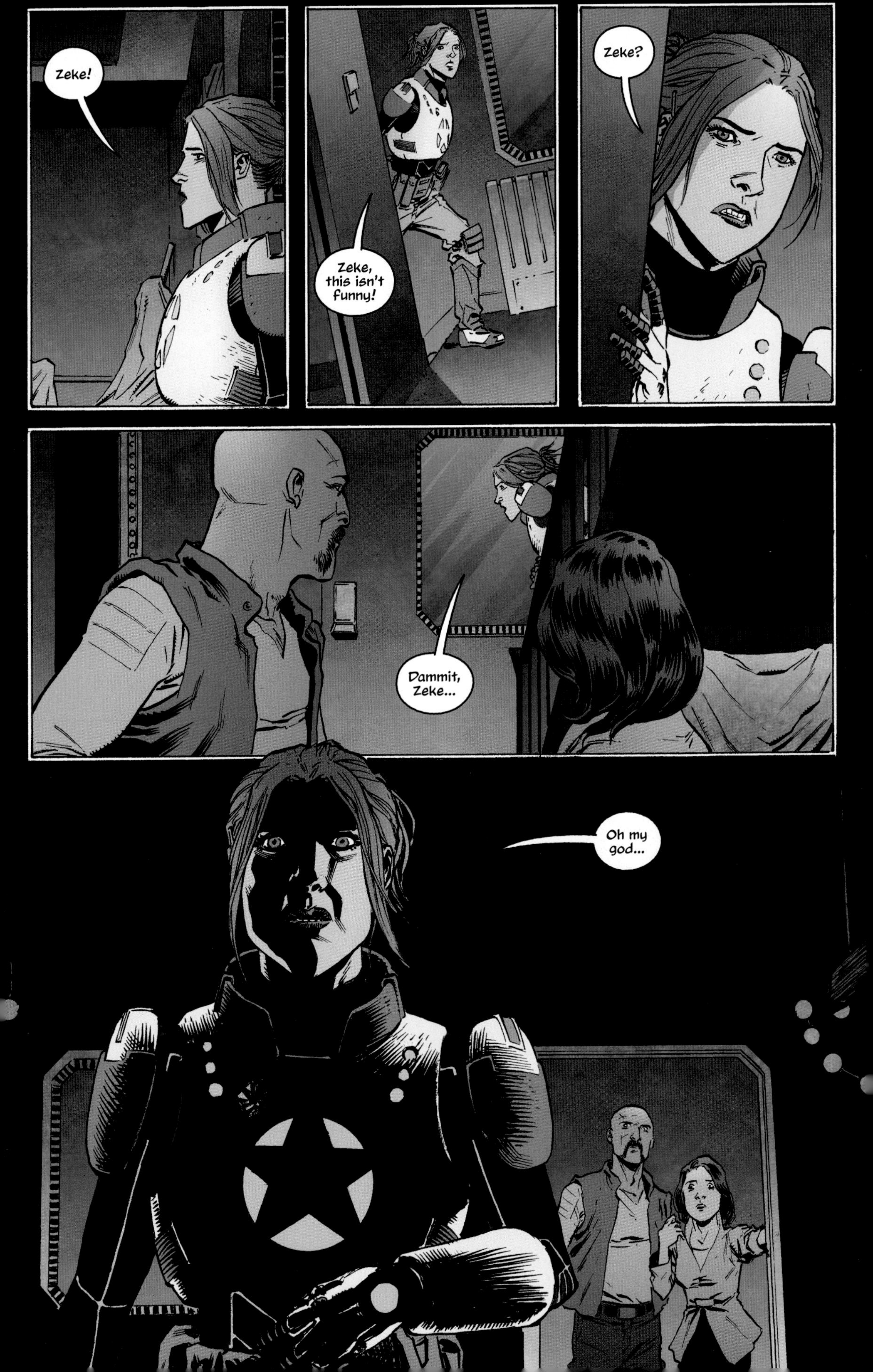
Zeke!
Zeke, this isn't funny!
Zeke?
Dammit, Zeke...
Oh my god...

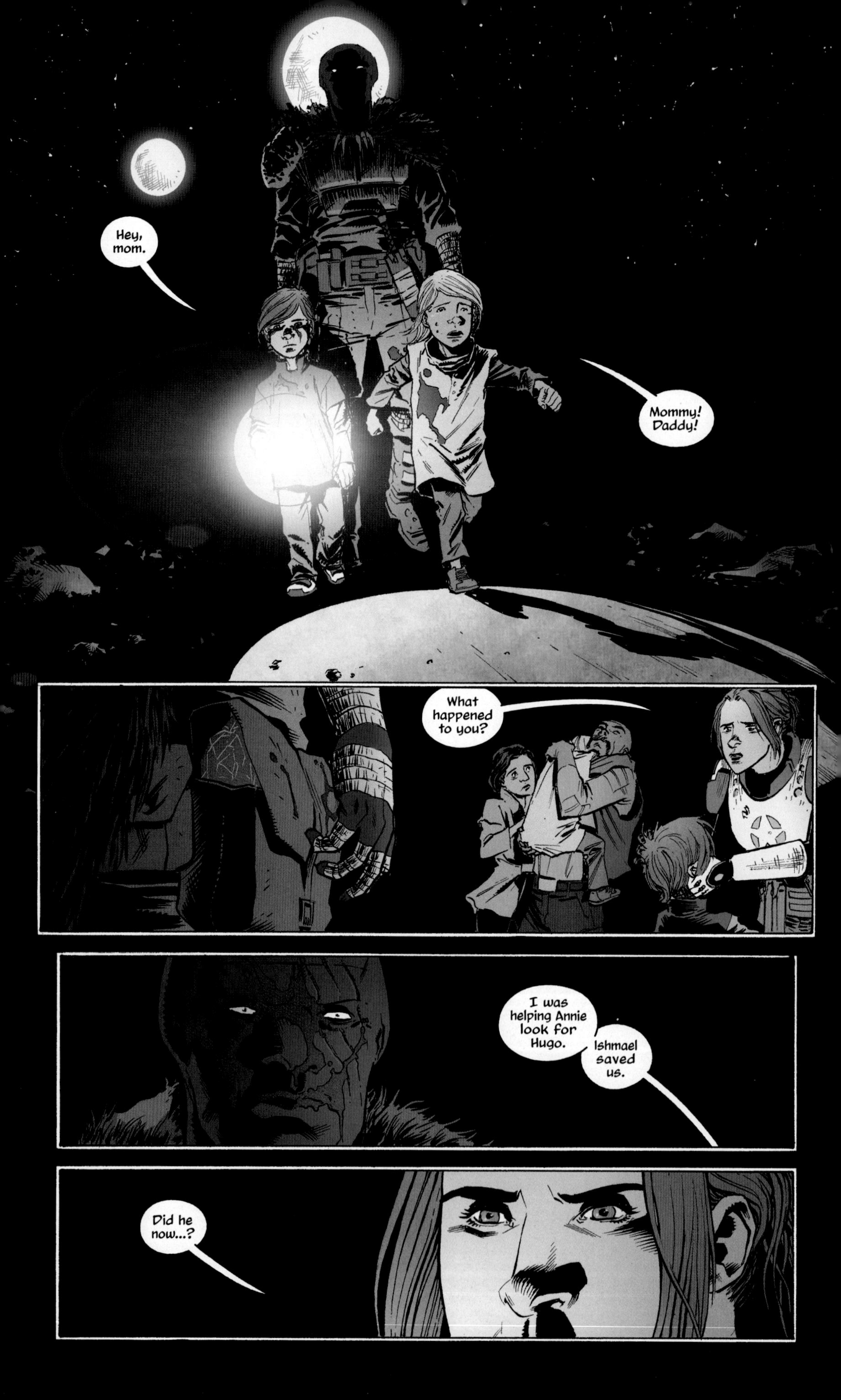
Hey,
mom.
Mommy!
Daddy!
What
happened
to you?
I was
helping Annie
look for
Hugo.
Ishmael
saved
us.
Did he
now...?

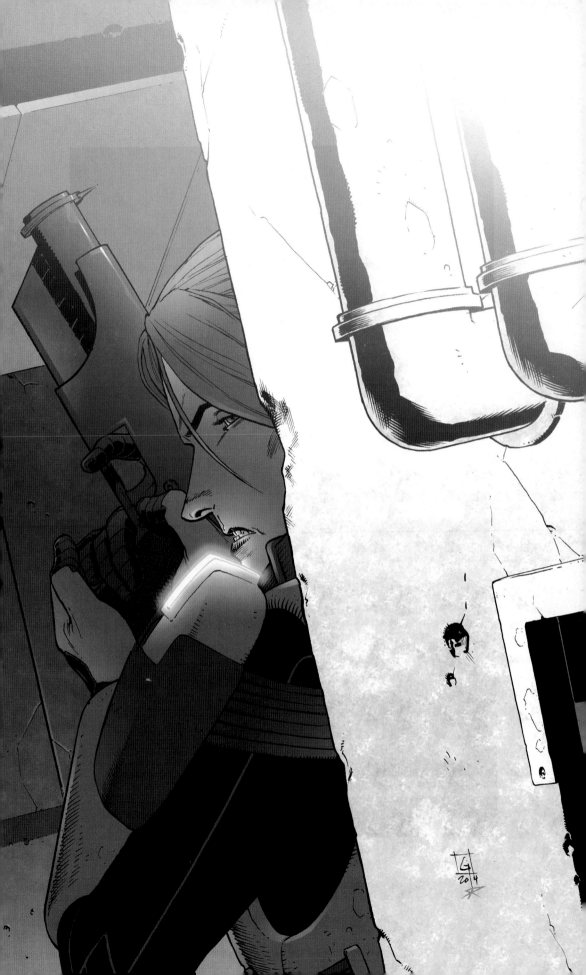

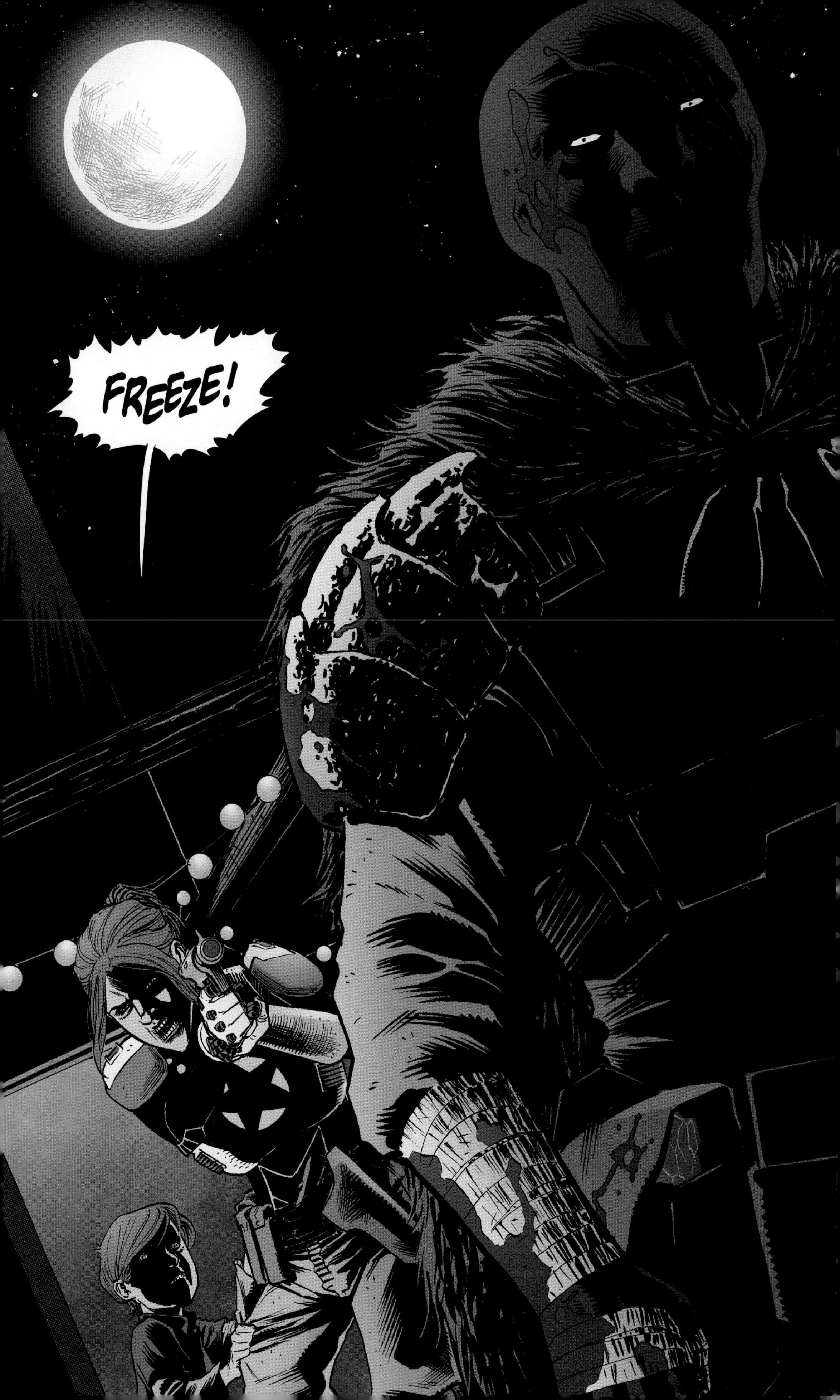
FREEZE!

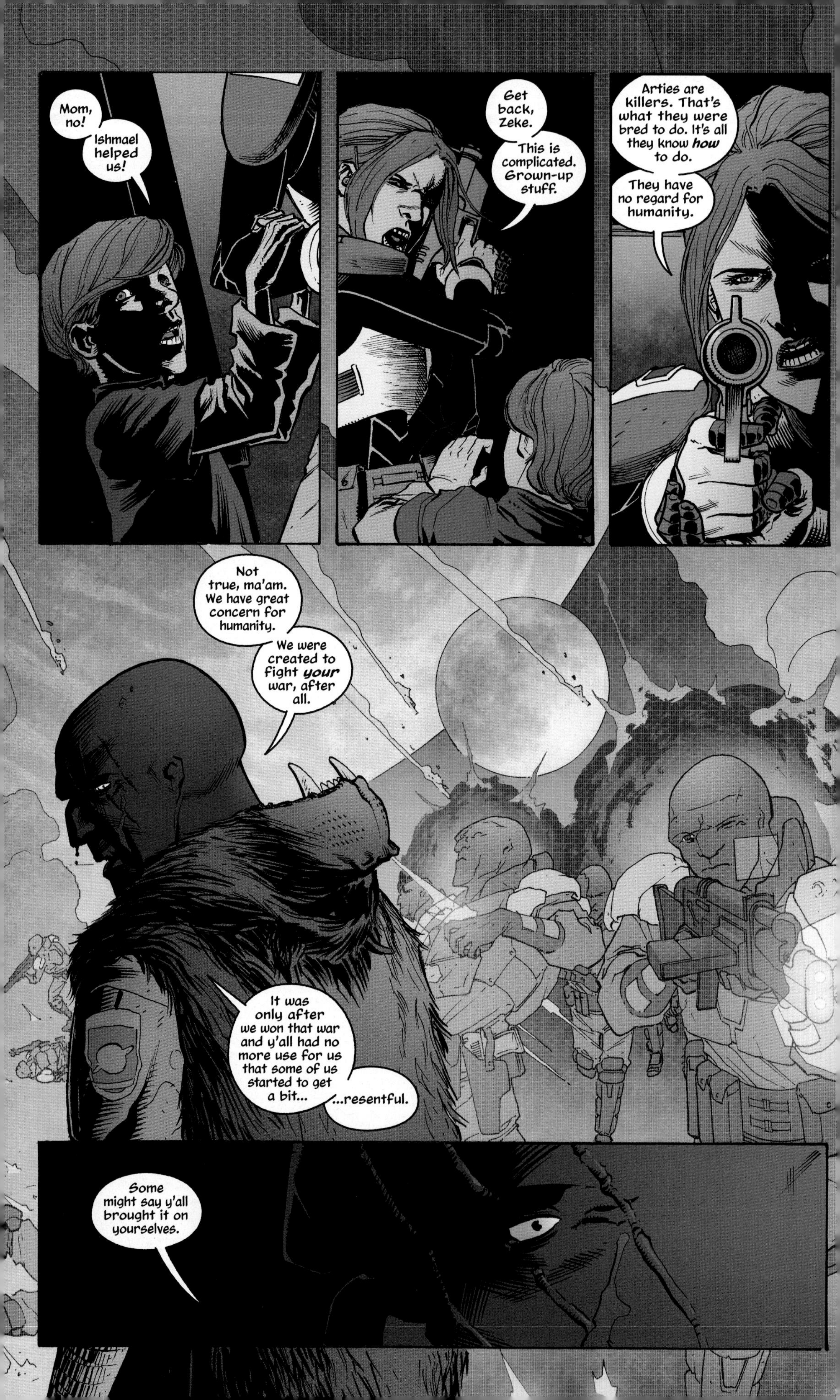
Mom, no!
Ishmael helped us!
Get back, Zeke.
This is complicated. Grown-up stuff.
Arties are killers. That's what they were bred to do. It's all they know *how* to do.
They have no regard for humanity.
Not true, ma'am. We have great concern for humanity.
We were created to fight *your* war, after all.
It was only after we won that war and y'all had no more use for us that some of us started to get a bit...
...resentful.
Some might say y'all brought it on yourselves.

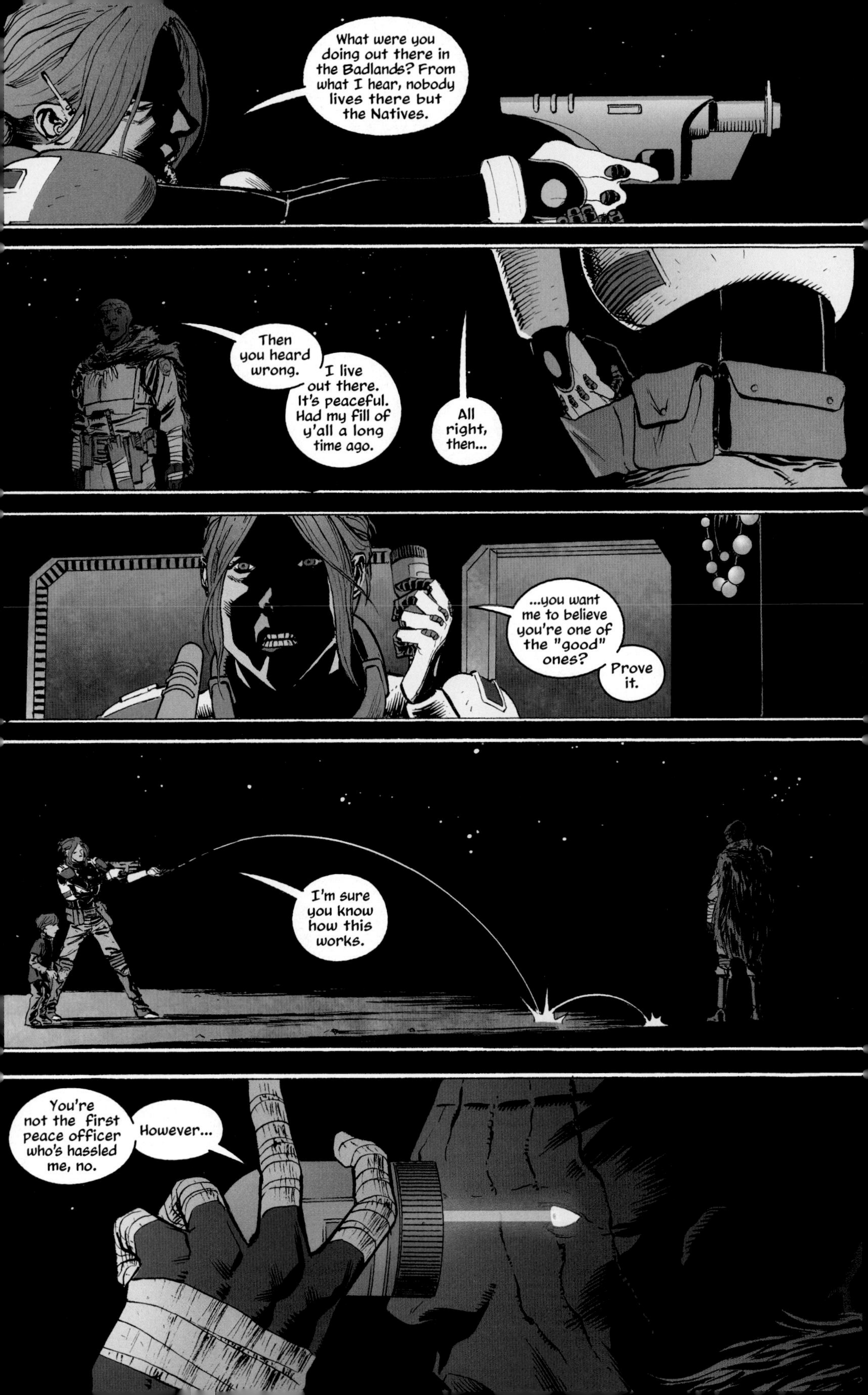
What were you doing out there in the Badlands? From what I hear, nobody lives there but the Natives.
Then you heard wrong.
I live out there. It's peaceful. Had my fill of y'all a long time ago.
All right, then...
...you want me to believe you're one of the "good" ones?
Prove it.
I'm sure you know how this works.
You're not the first peace officer who's hassled me, no.
However...

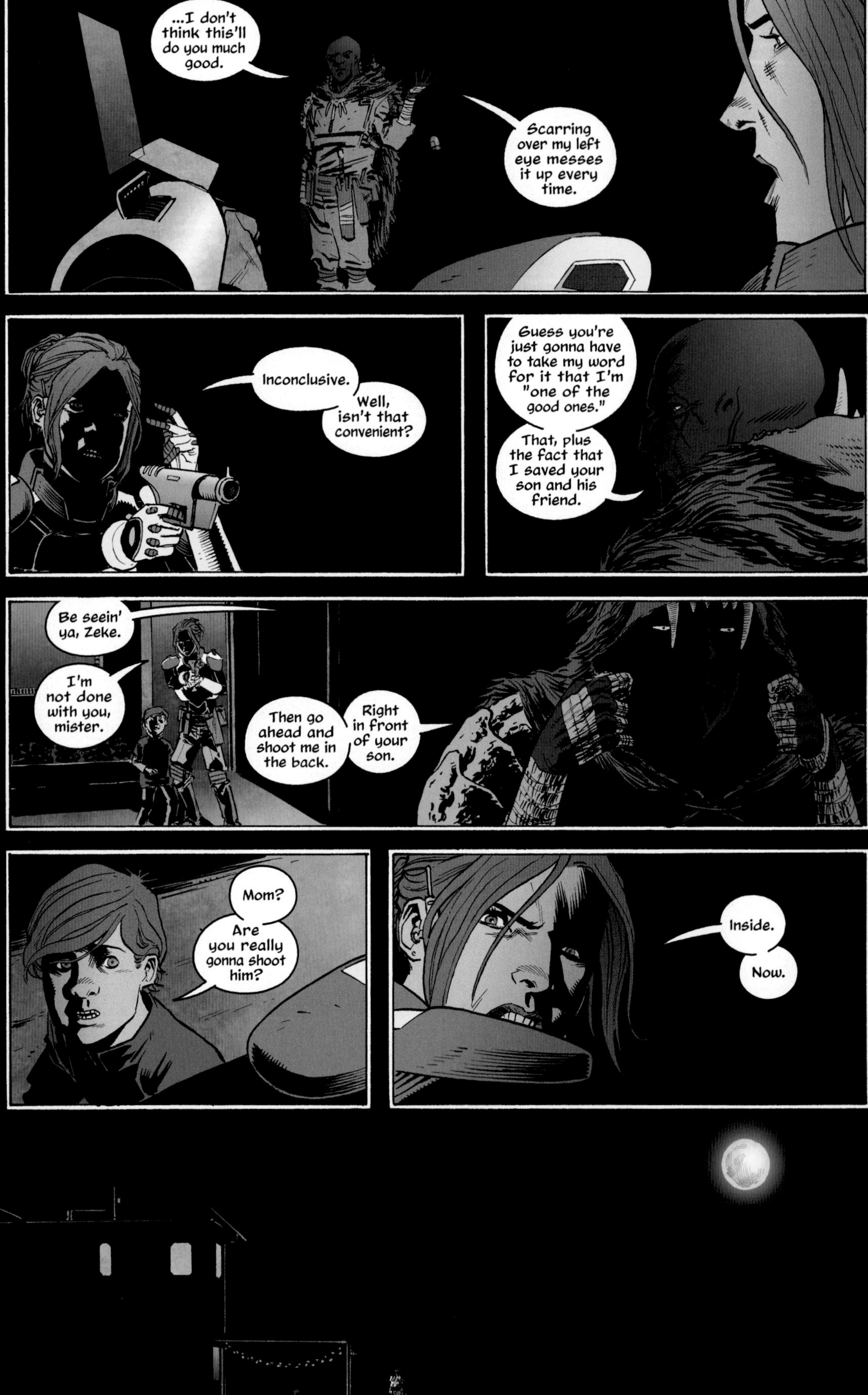
...I don't think this'll do you much good.
Scarring over my left eye messes it up every time.
Inconclusive.
Well, isn't that convenient?
Guess you're just gonna have to take my word for it that I'm "one of the good ones."
That, plus the fact that I saved your son and his friend.
Be seein' ya, Zeke.
I'm not done with you, mister.
Then go ahead and shoot me in the back.
Right in front of your son.
Mom?
Are you really gonna shoot him?
Inside.
Now.

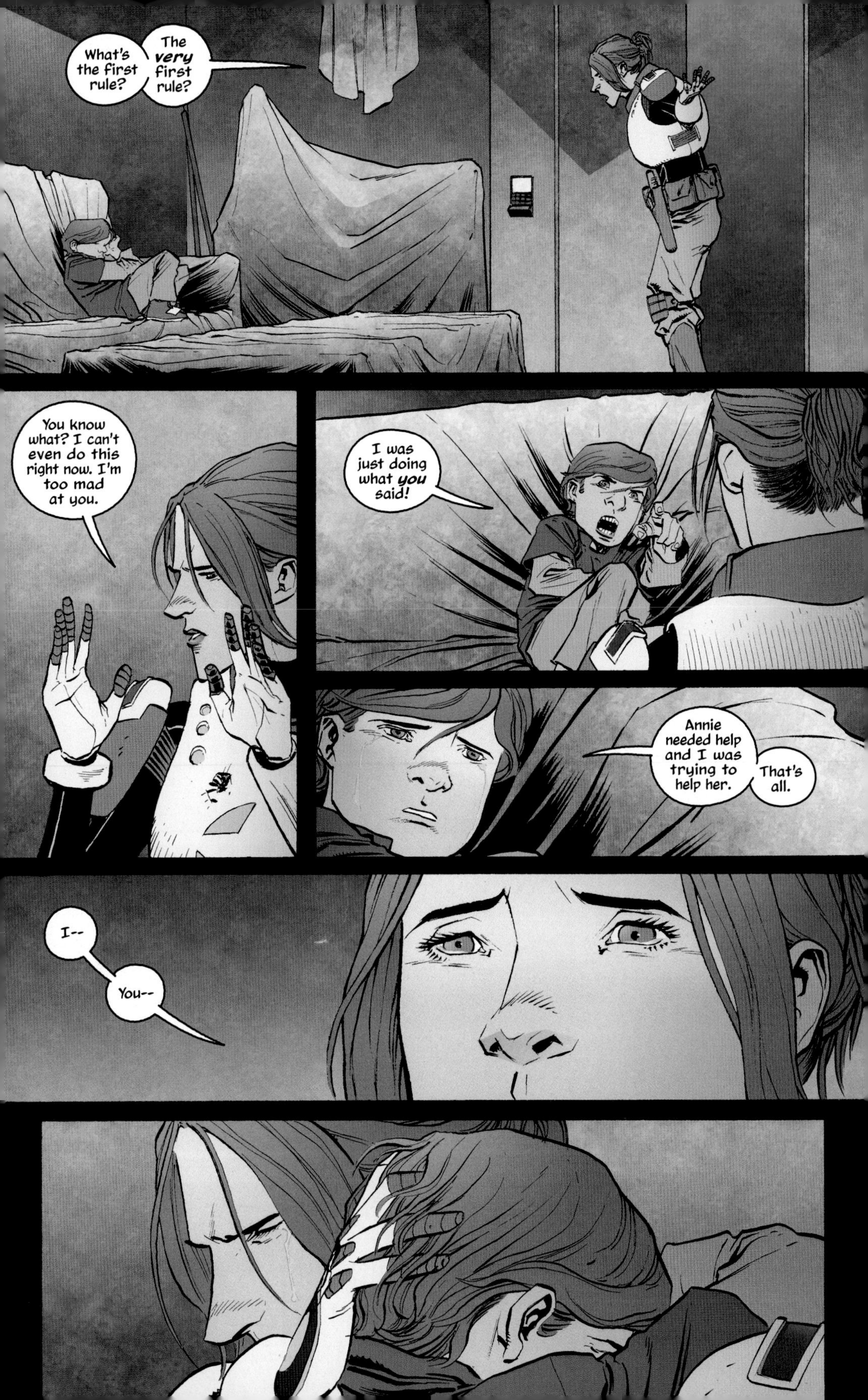
What's the first rule?
The *very* first rule?
You know what? I can't even do this right now. I'm too mad at you.
I was just doing what *you* said!
Annie needed help and I was trying to help her.
That's all.
I--
You--

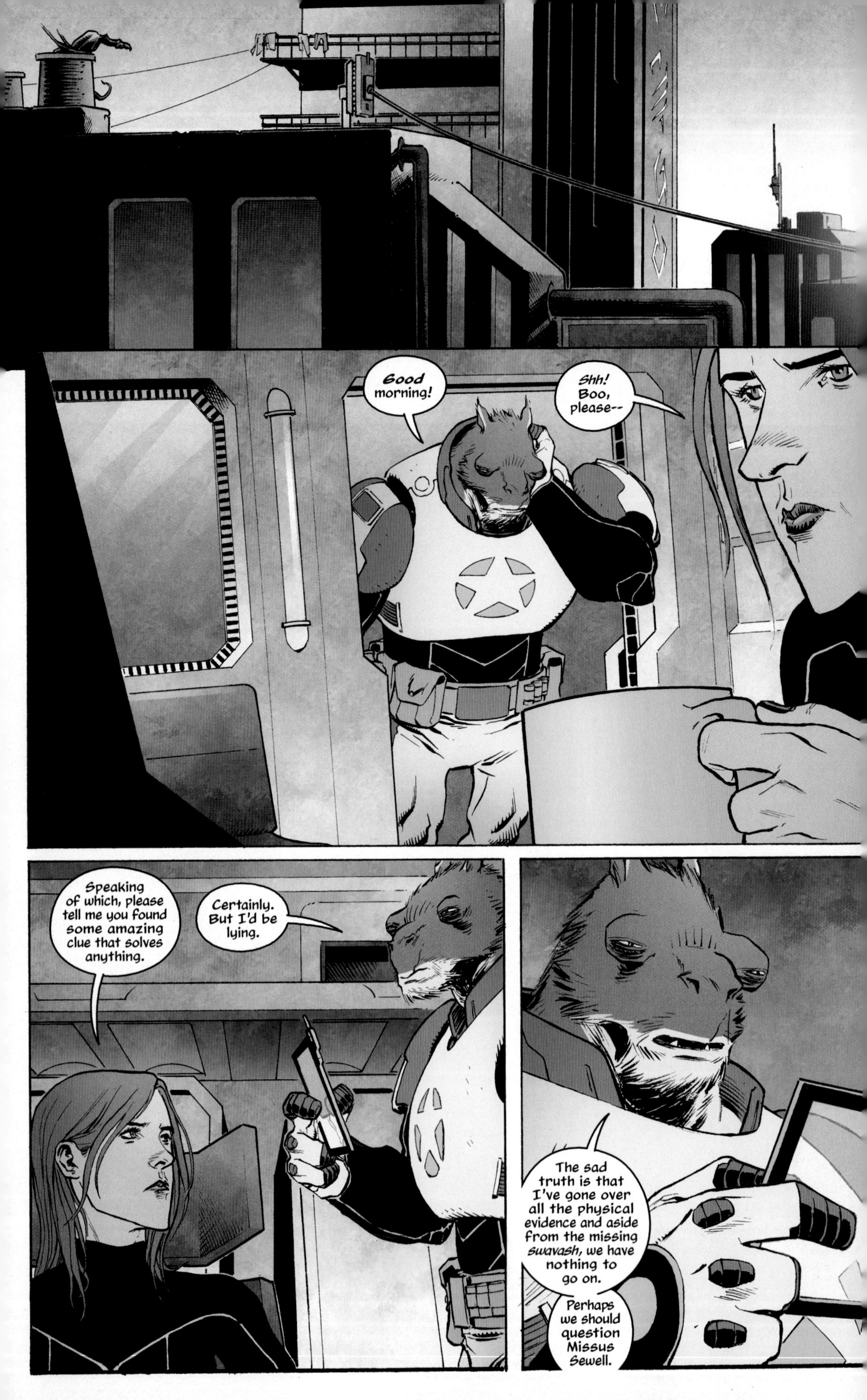
Good morning!
Shh! Boo, please--
Speaking of which, please tell me you found some amazing clue that solves anything.
Certainly. But I'd be lying.
The sad truth is that I've gone over all the physical evidence and aside from the missing *swavash,* we have nothing to go on.
Perhaps we should question Missus Sewell.

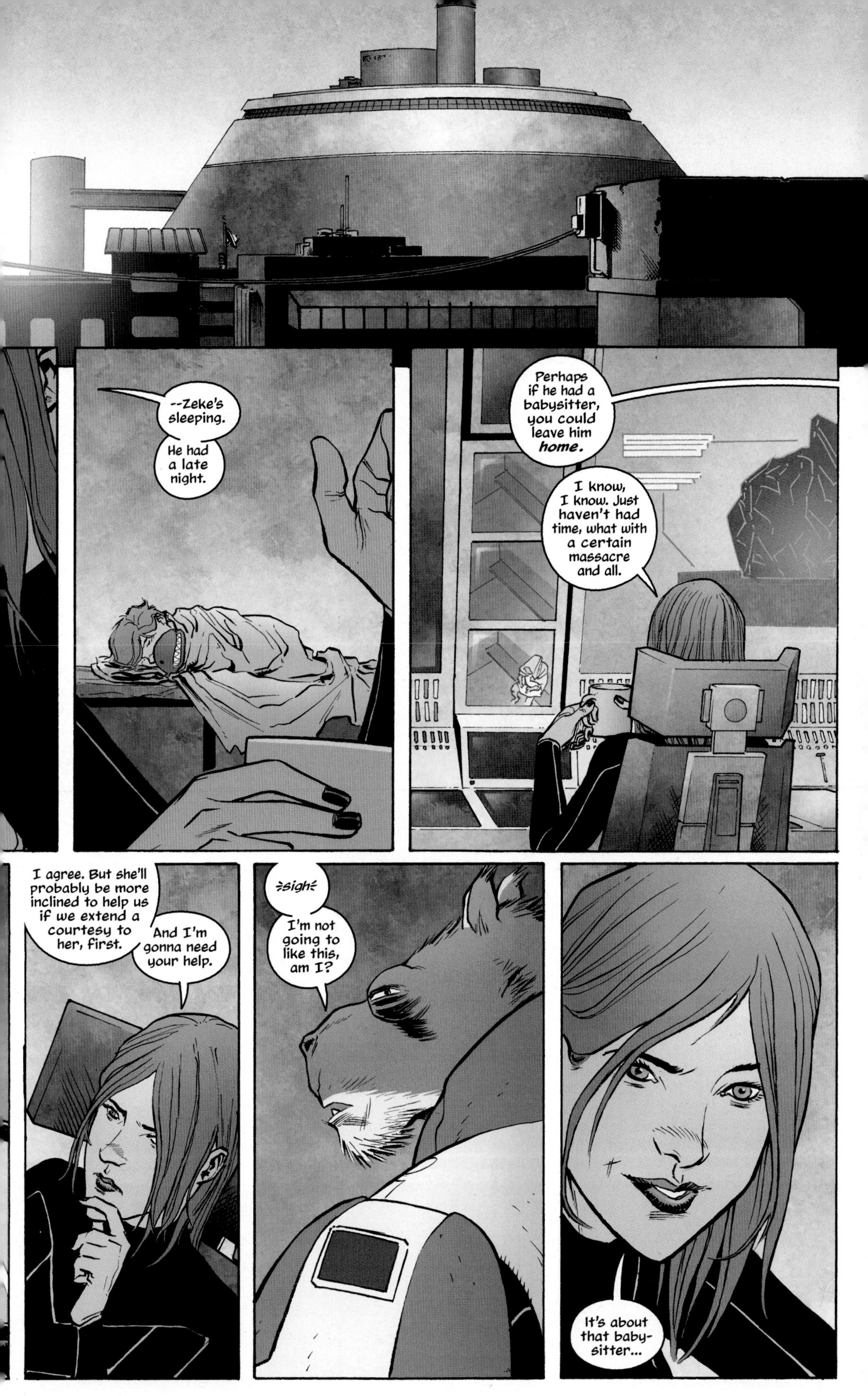
--Zeke's sleeping.
He had a late night.
Perhaps if he had a babysitter, you could leave him *home*.
I know, I know. Just haven't had time, what with a certain massacre and all.
I agree. But she'll probably be more inclined to help us if we extend a courtesy to her, first.
And I'm gonna need your help.
sigh
I'm not going to like this, am I?
It's about that baby-sitter...

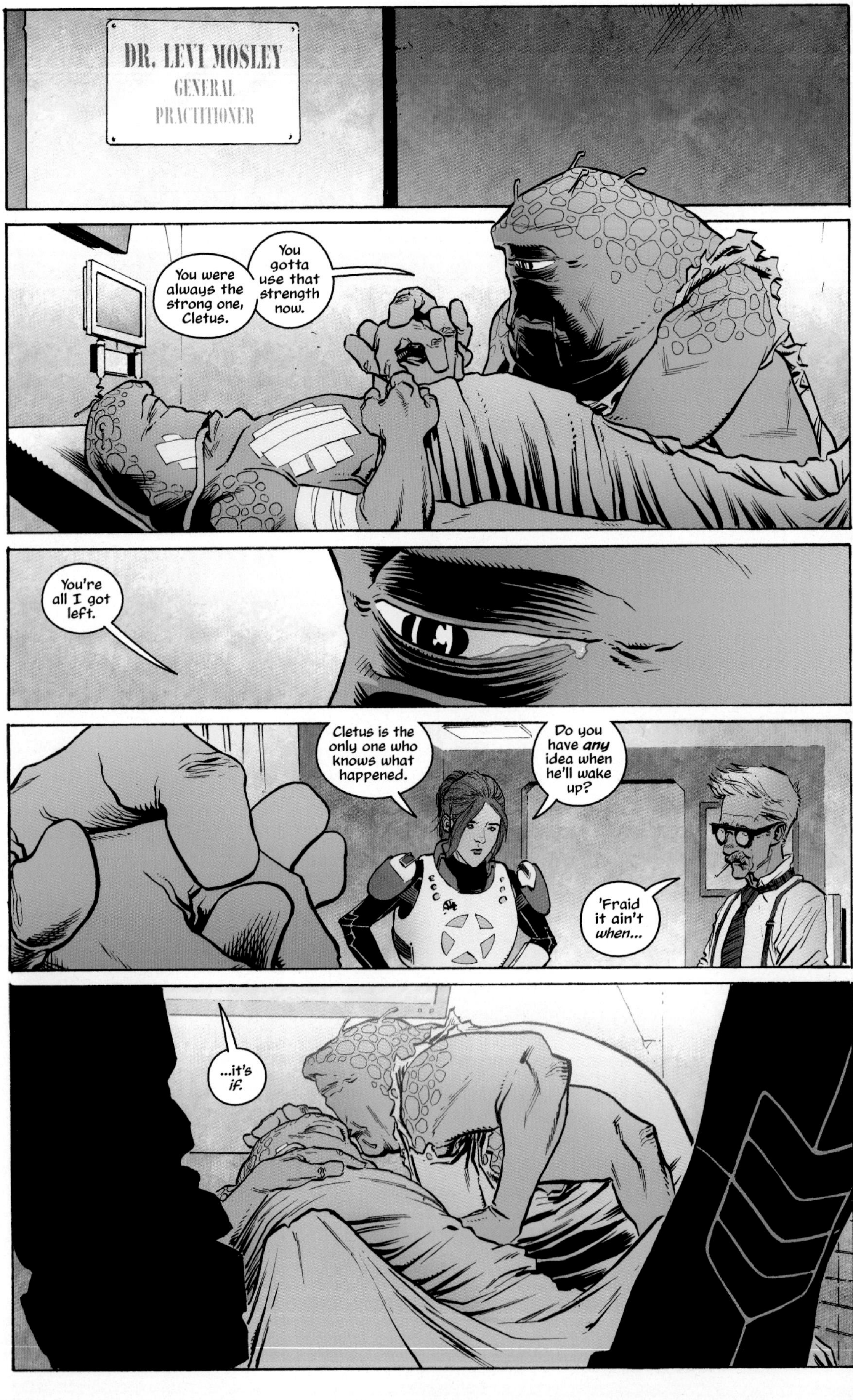

DR. LEVI MOSLEY
GENERAL
PRACTITIONER
You were always the strong one, Cletus.
You gotta use that strength now.
You're all I got left.
Cletus is the only one who knows what happened.
Do you have *any* idea when he'll wake up?
'Fraid it ain't *when*...
...it's *if*.

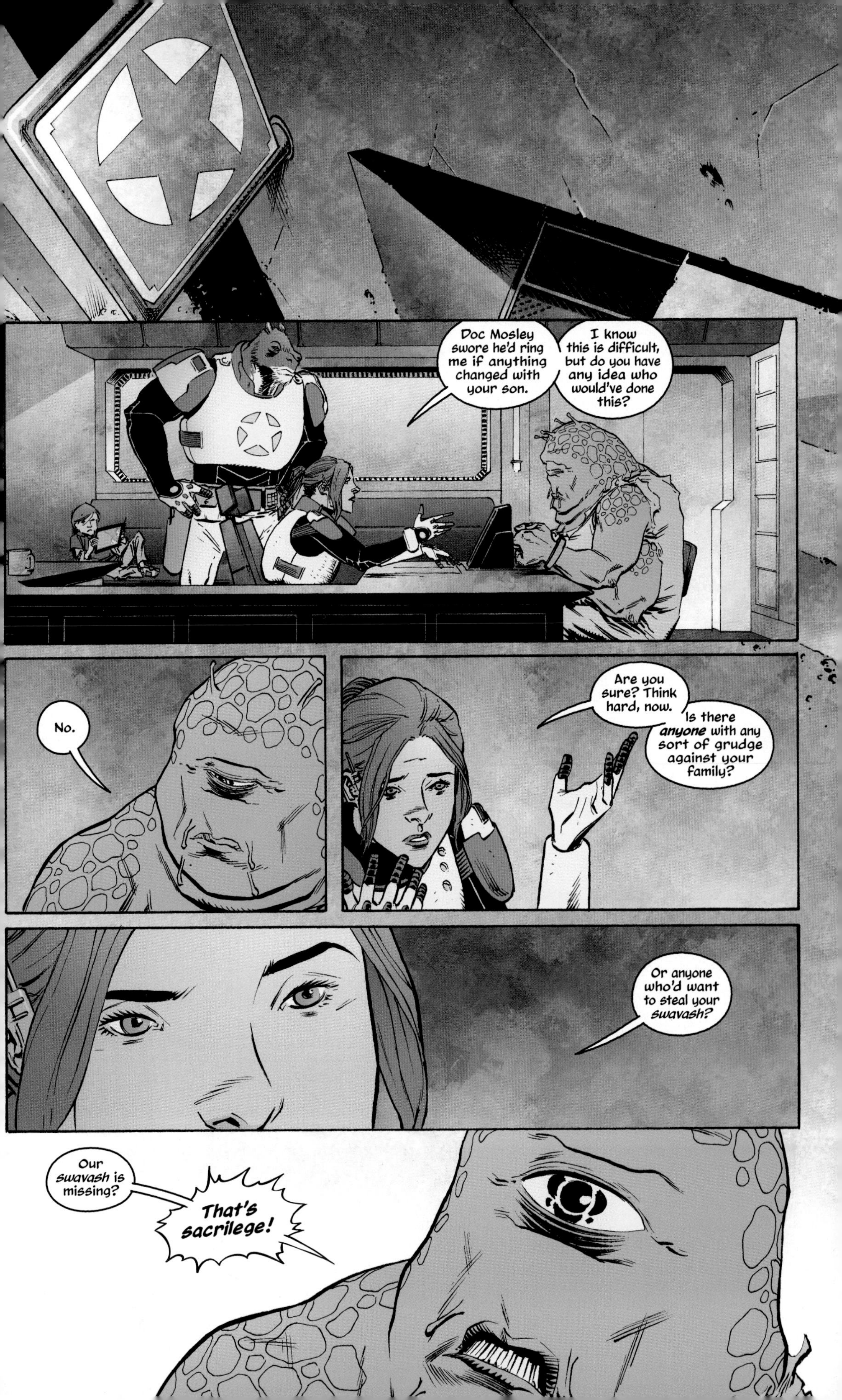

Doc Mosley swore he'd ring me if anything changed with your son.
I know this is difficult, but do you have any idea who would've done this?
No.
Are you sure? Think hard, now.
Is there *anyone* with any sort of grudge against your family?
Or anyone who'd want to steal your *swavash*?
Our *swavash* is missing?
That's sacrilege!

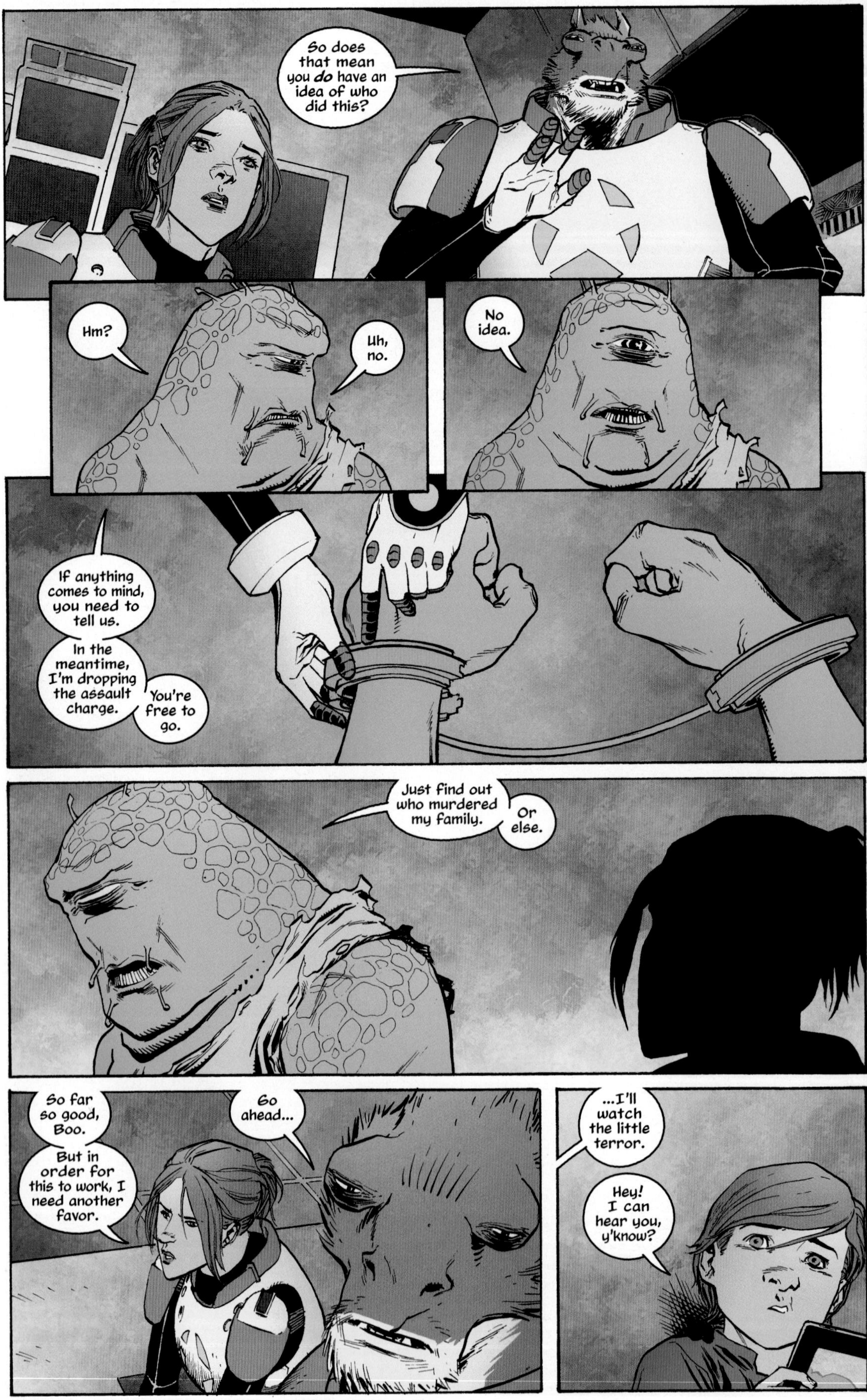

So does that mean you *do* have an idea of who did this?
Hm?
Uh, no.
No idea.
If anything comes to mind, you need to tell us.
In the meantime, I'm dropping the assault charge.
You're free to go.
Just find out who murdered my family.
Or else.
So far so good, Boo.
But in order for this to work, I need another favor.
Go ahead...
...I'll watch the little terror.
Hey! I can hear you, y'know?

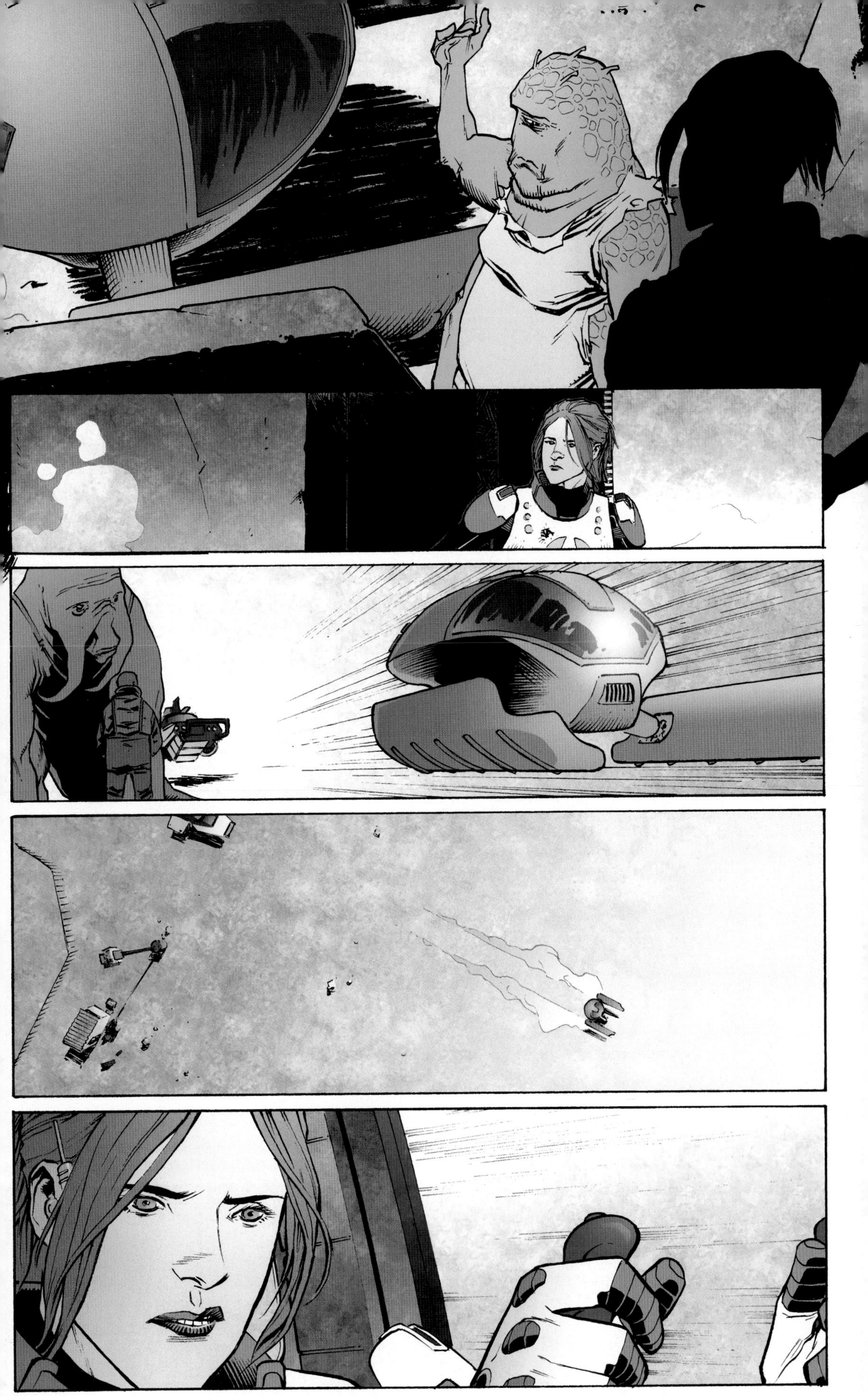

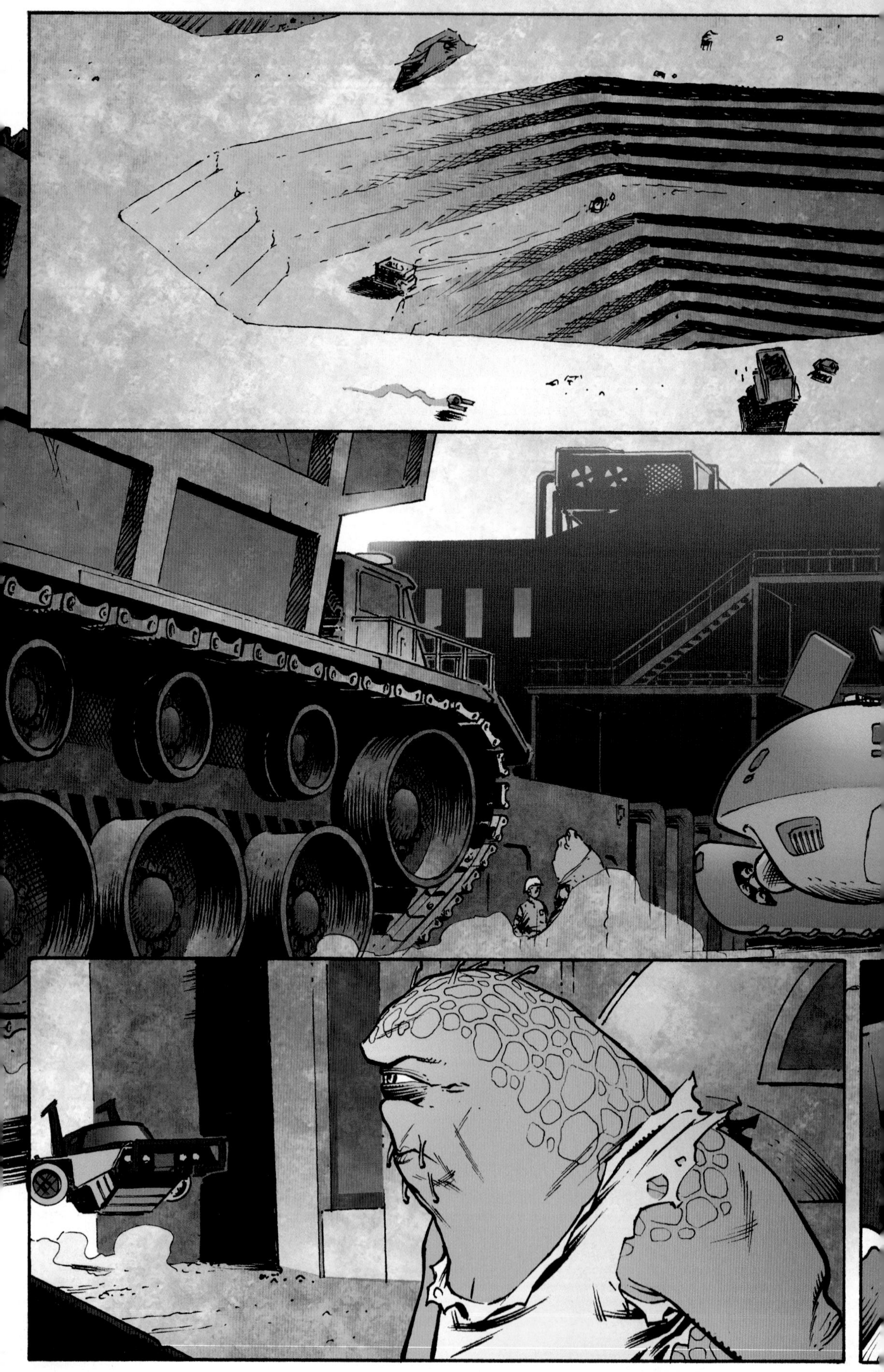

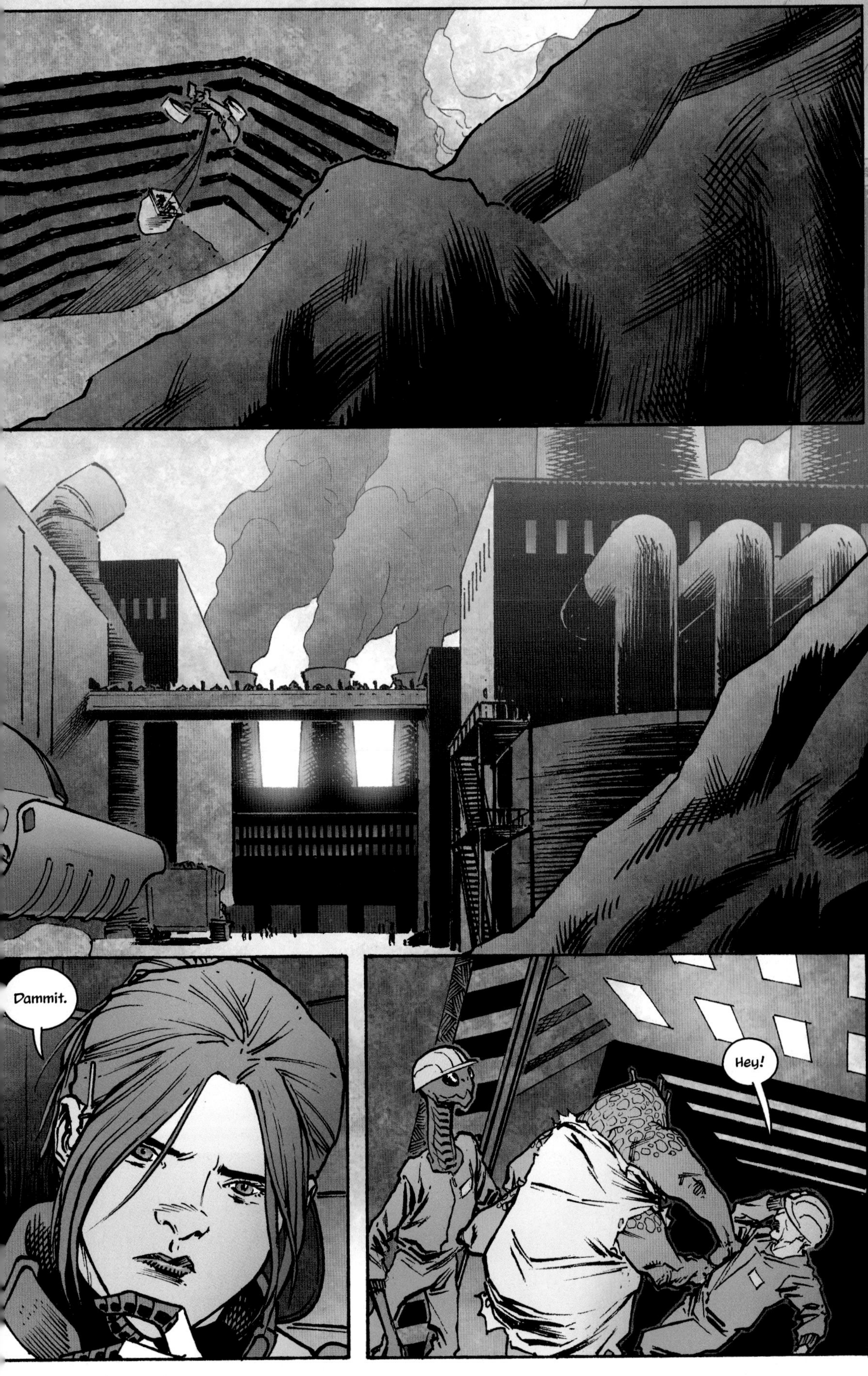
Dammit.
Hey!

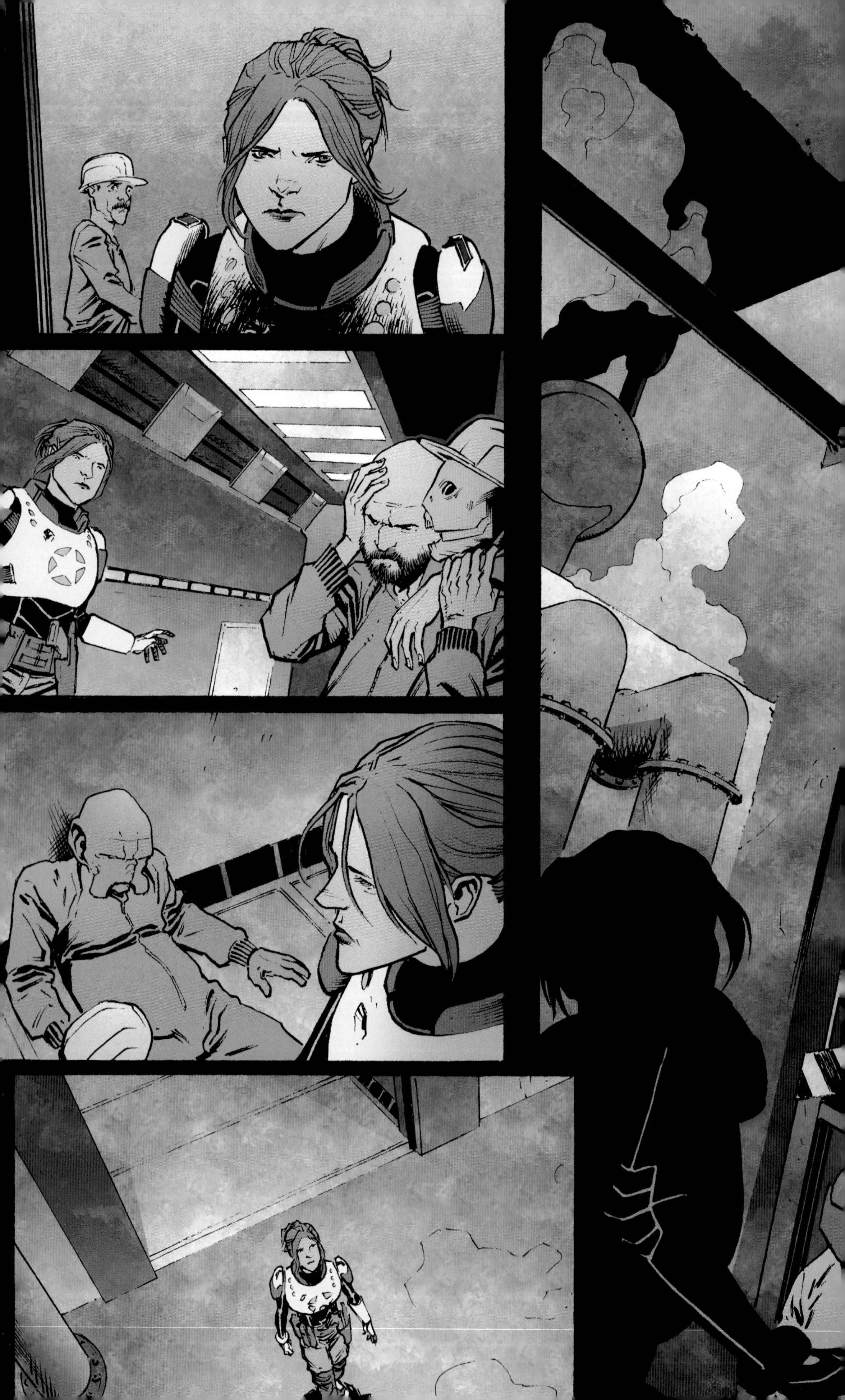

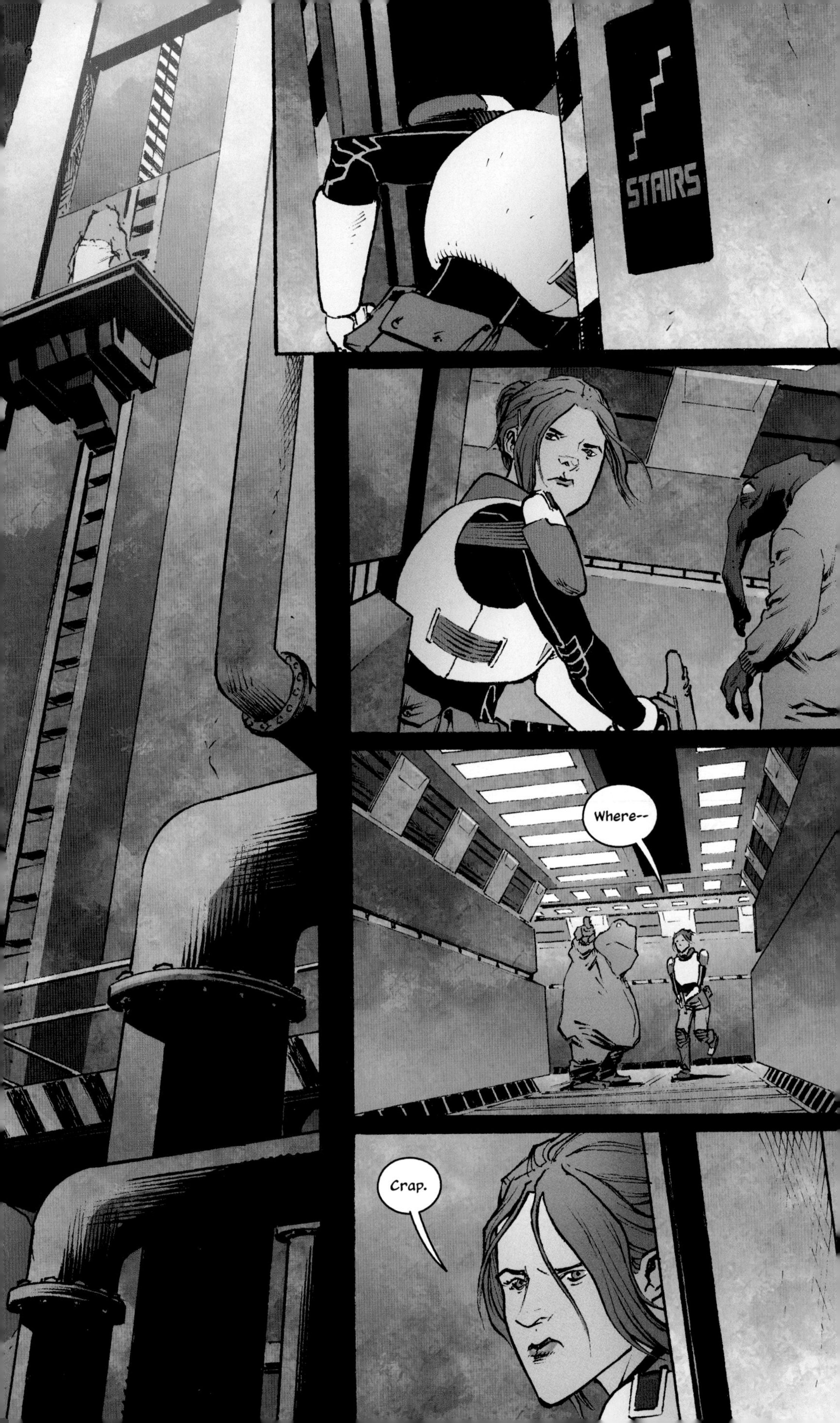
STAIRS
Where--
Crap.

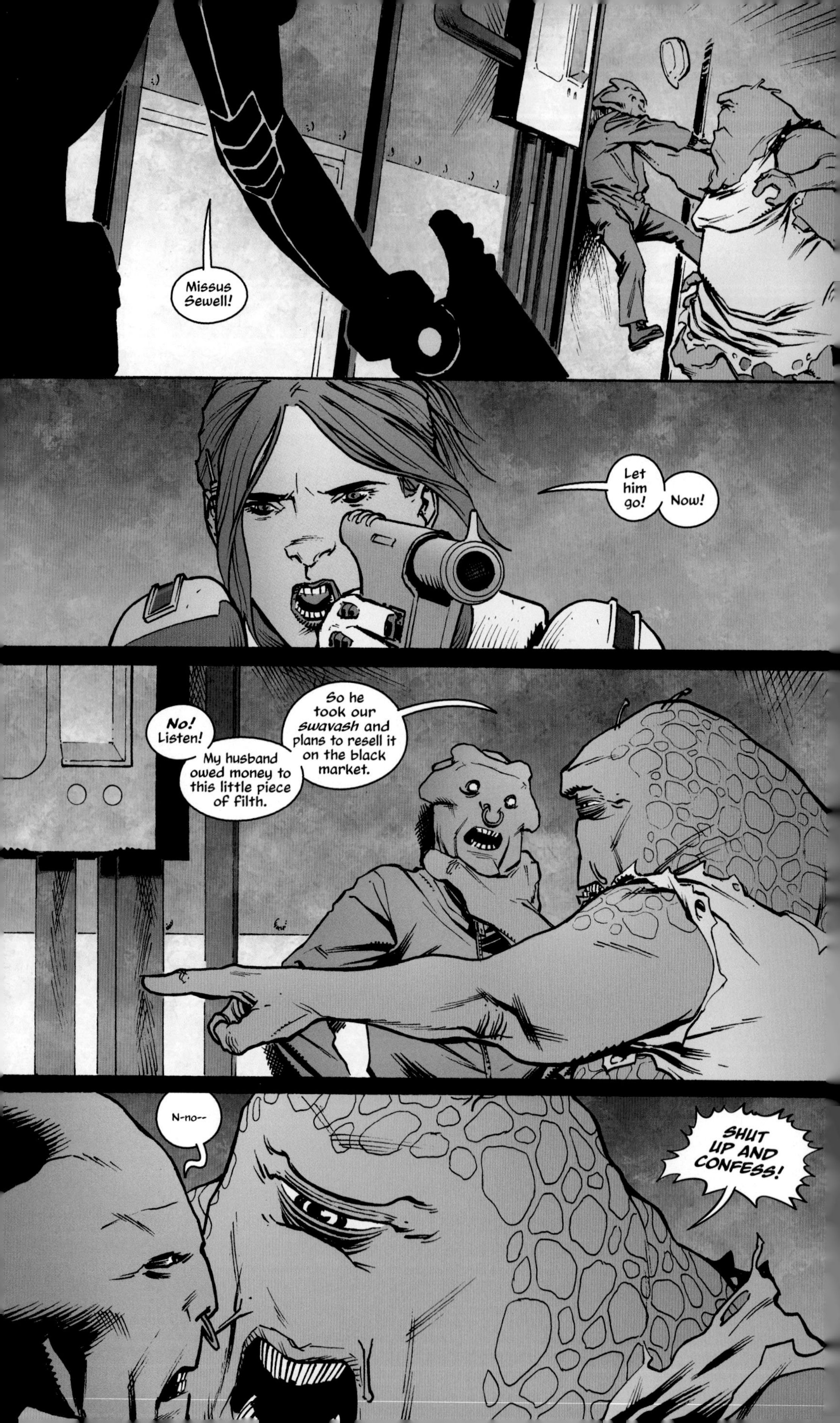
Missus Sewell!
Let him go!
Now!
No! Listen!
My husband owed money to this little piece of filth.
So he took our *swavash* and plans to resell it on the black market.
N-no--
SHUT UP AND CONFESS!

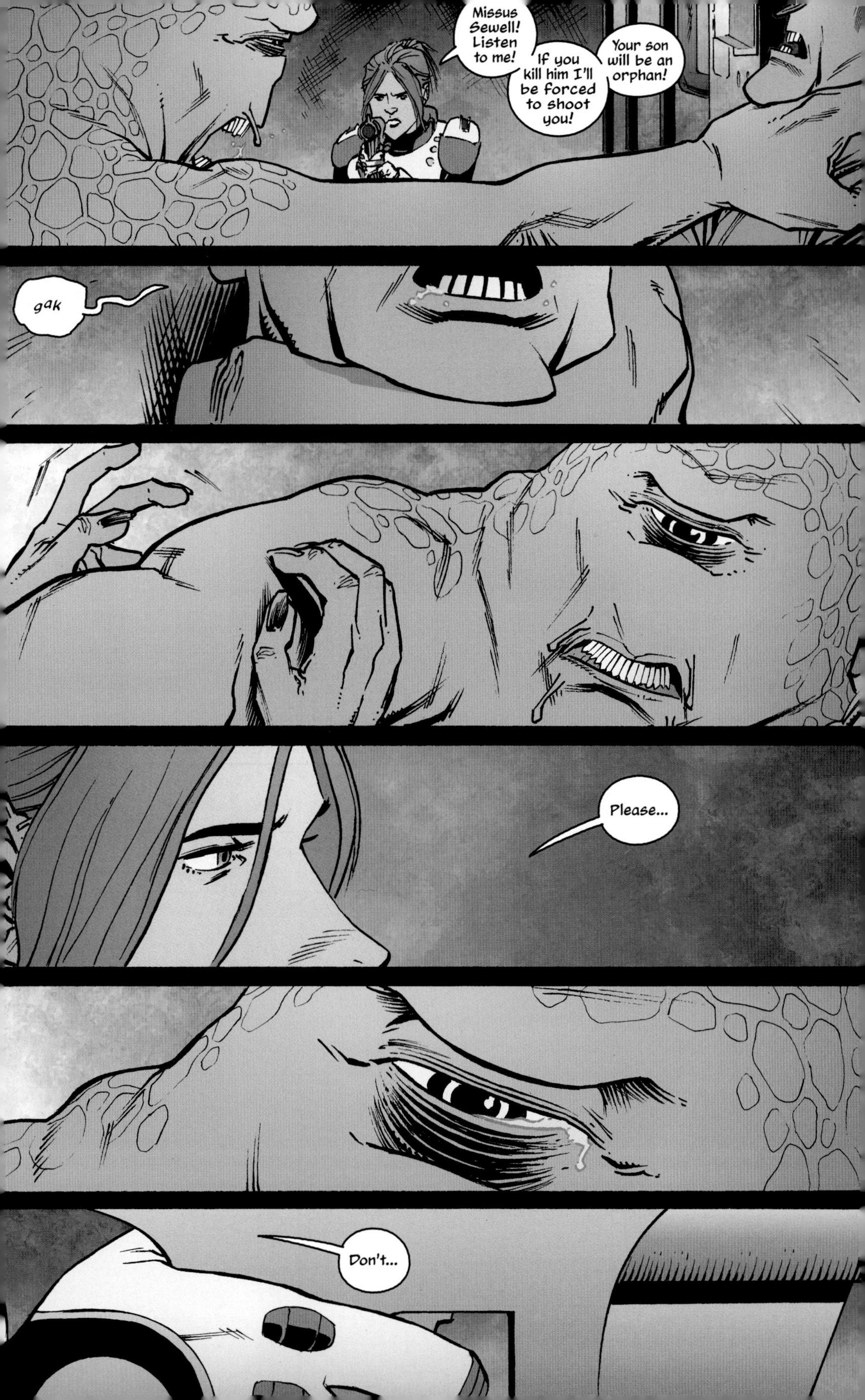
Missus Sewell! Listen to me!
If you kill him I'll be forced to shoot you!
Your son will be an orphan!
gak
Please...
Don't...

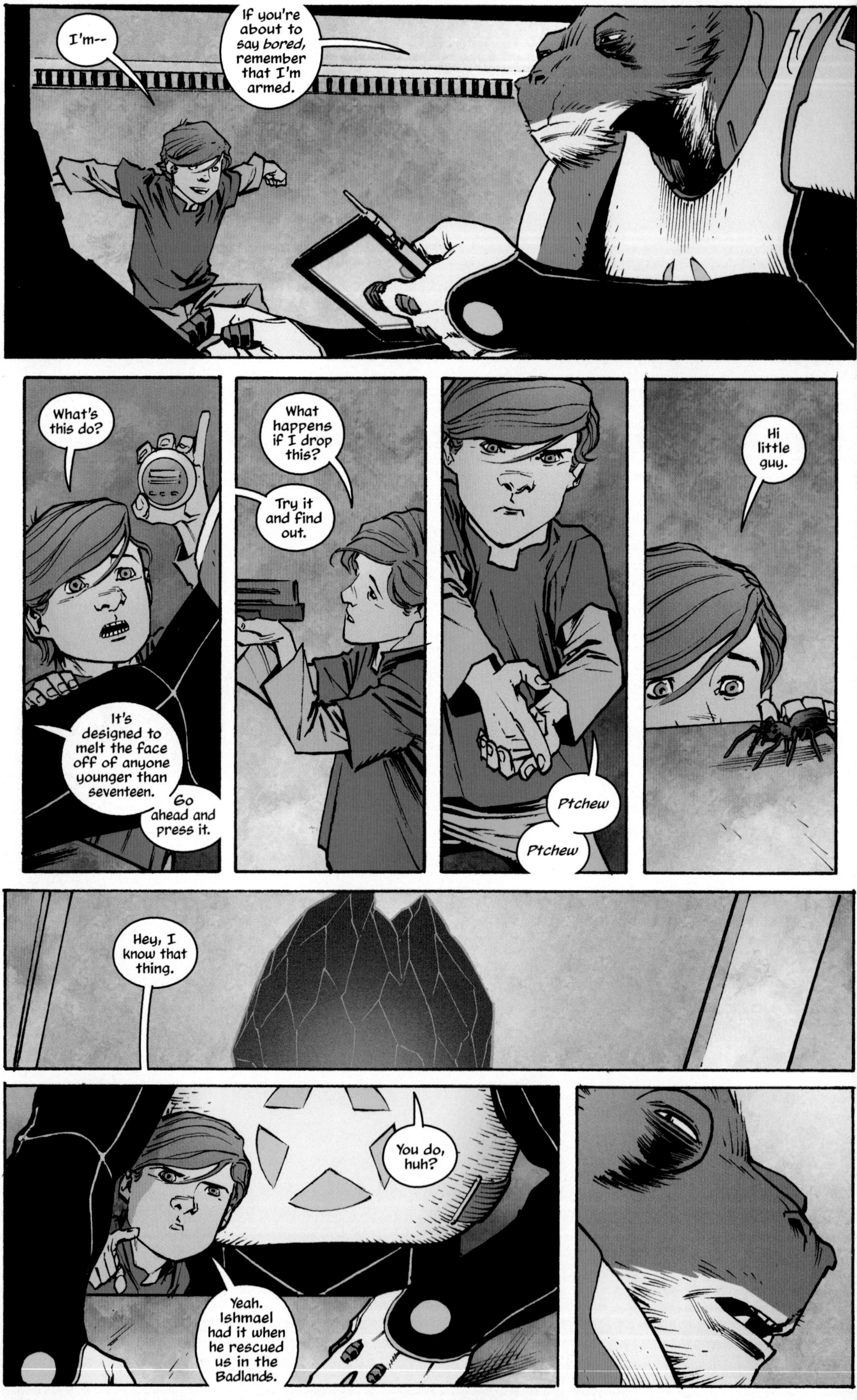
I'm--
If you're about to say *bored*, remember that I'm armed.
What's this do?
It's designed to melt the face off of anyone younger than seventeen.
Go ahead and press it.
What happens if I drop this?
Try it and find out.
Ptchew
Ptchew
Hi little guy.
Hey, I know that thing.
You do, huh?
Yeah. Ishmael had it when he rescued us in the Badlands.

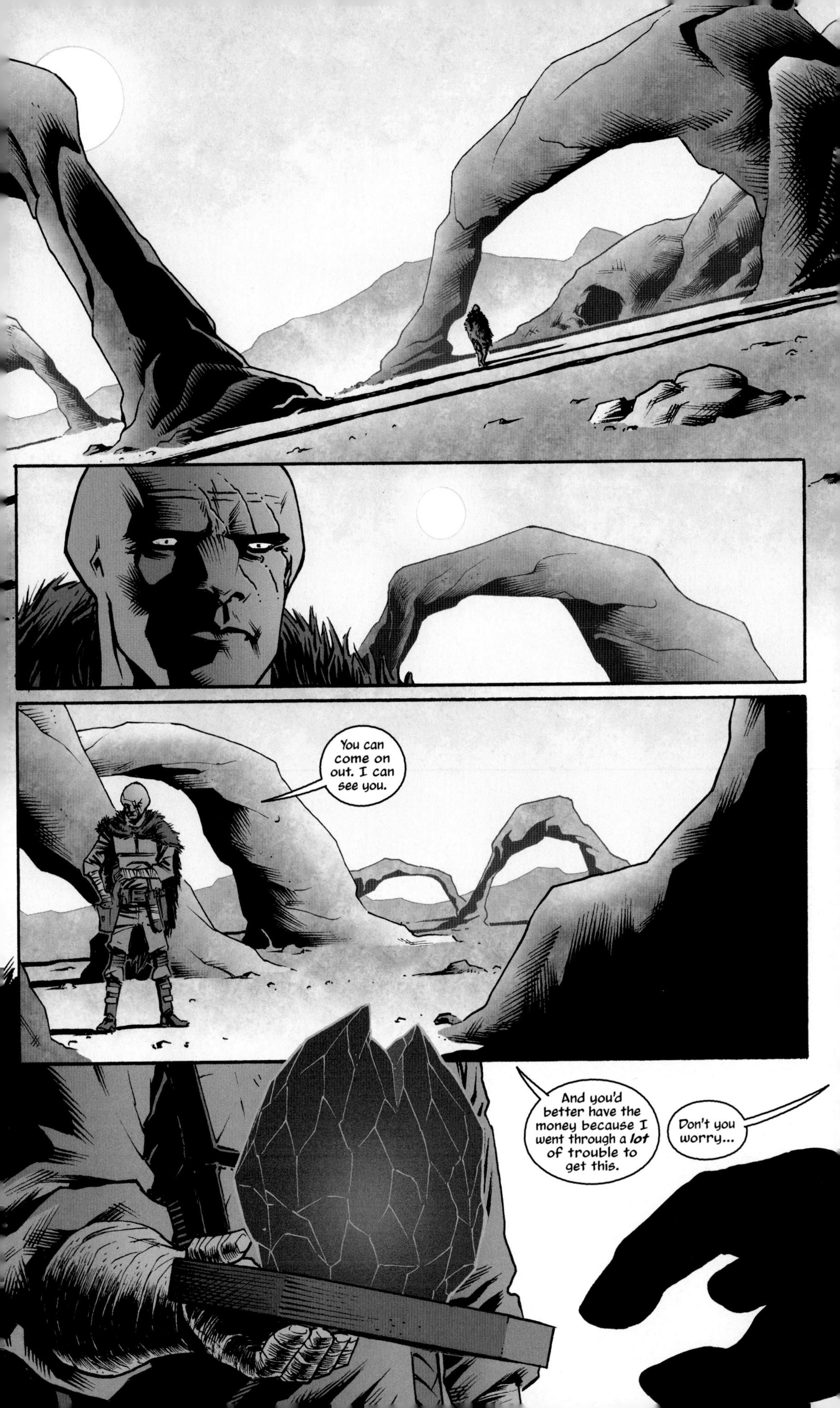
You can come on out. I can see you.
And you'd better have the money because I went through a *lot* of trouble to get this.
Don't you worry...

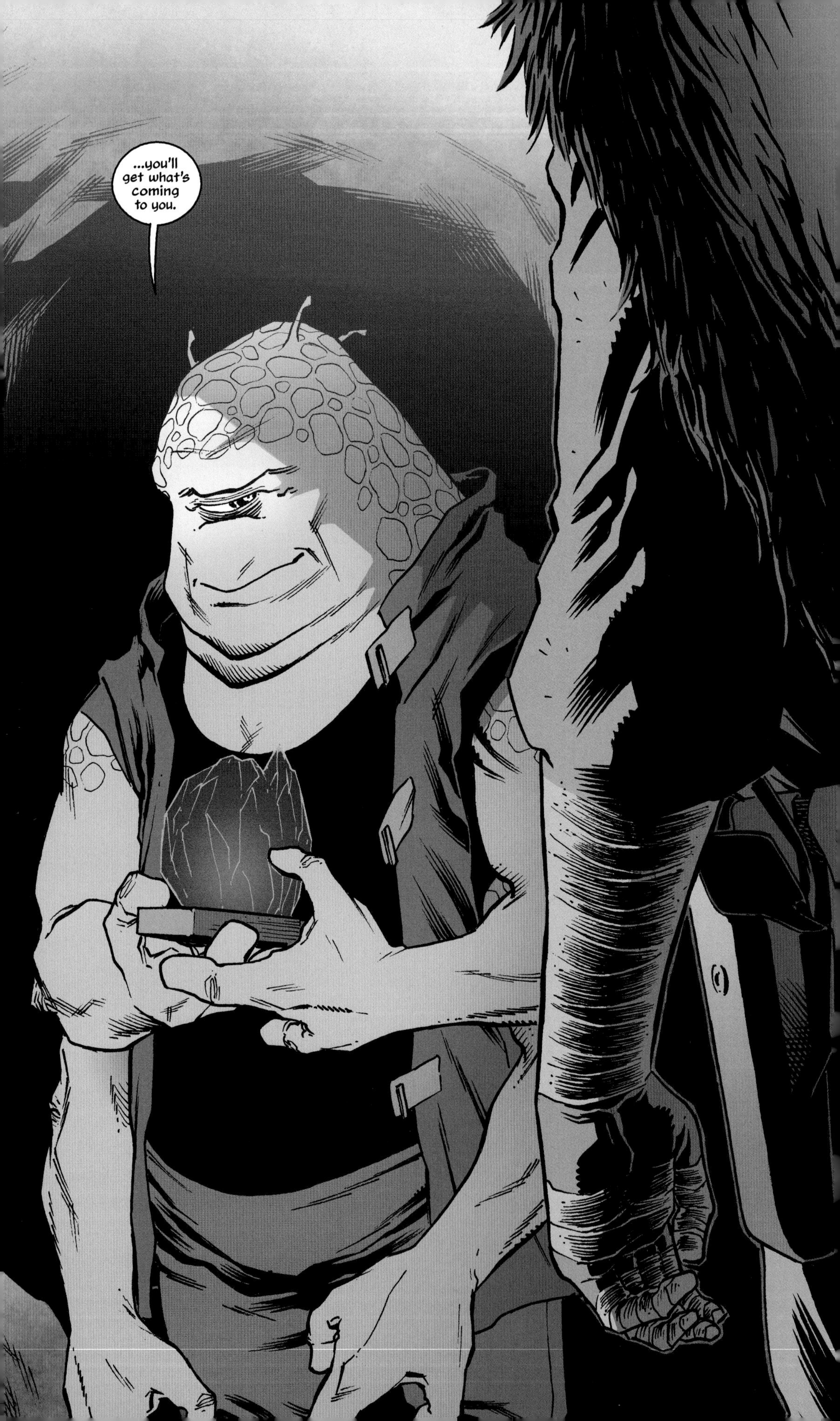
...you'll get what's coming to you.

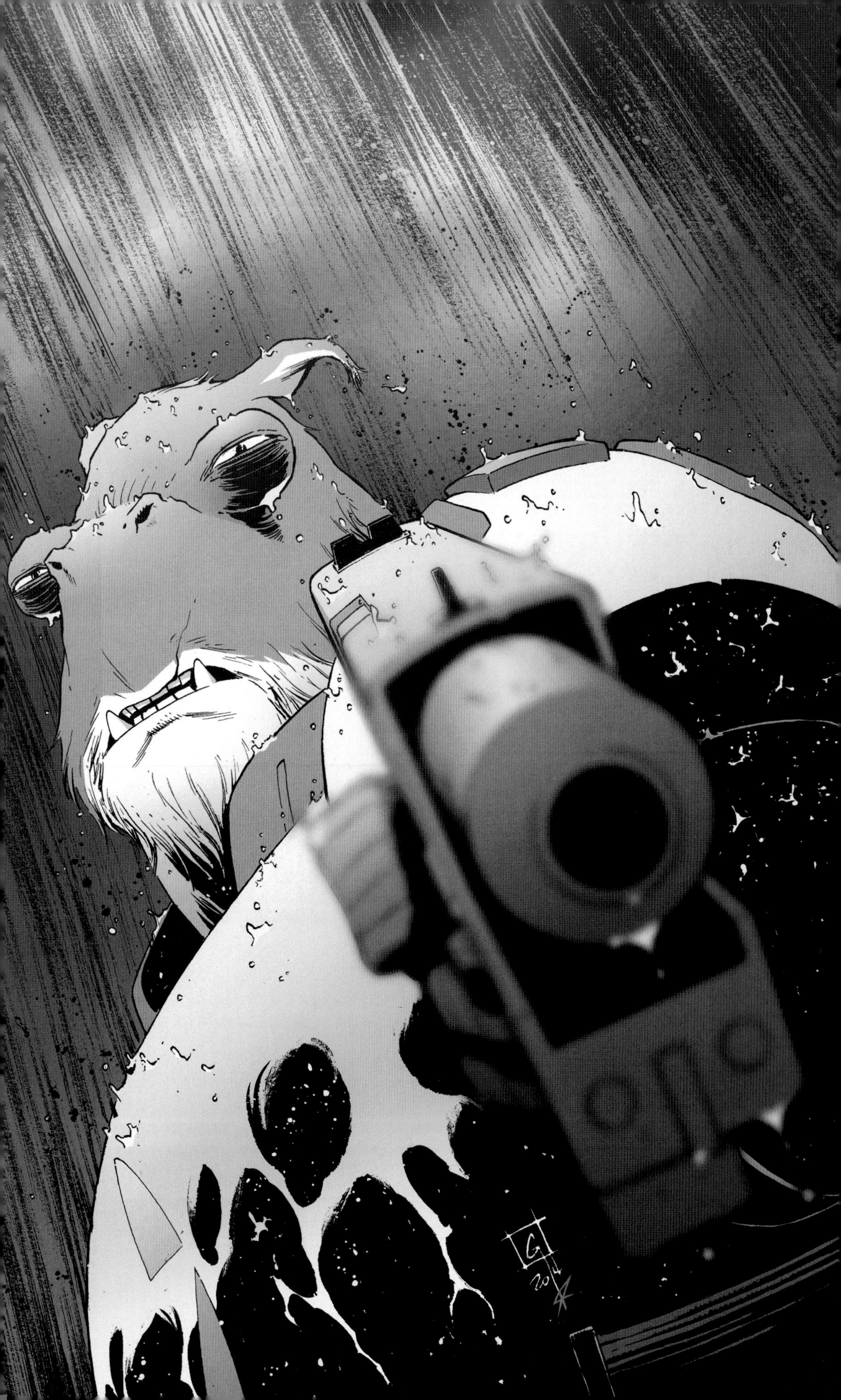

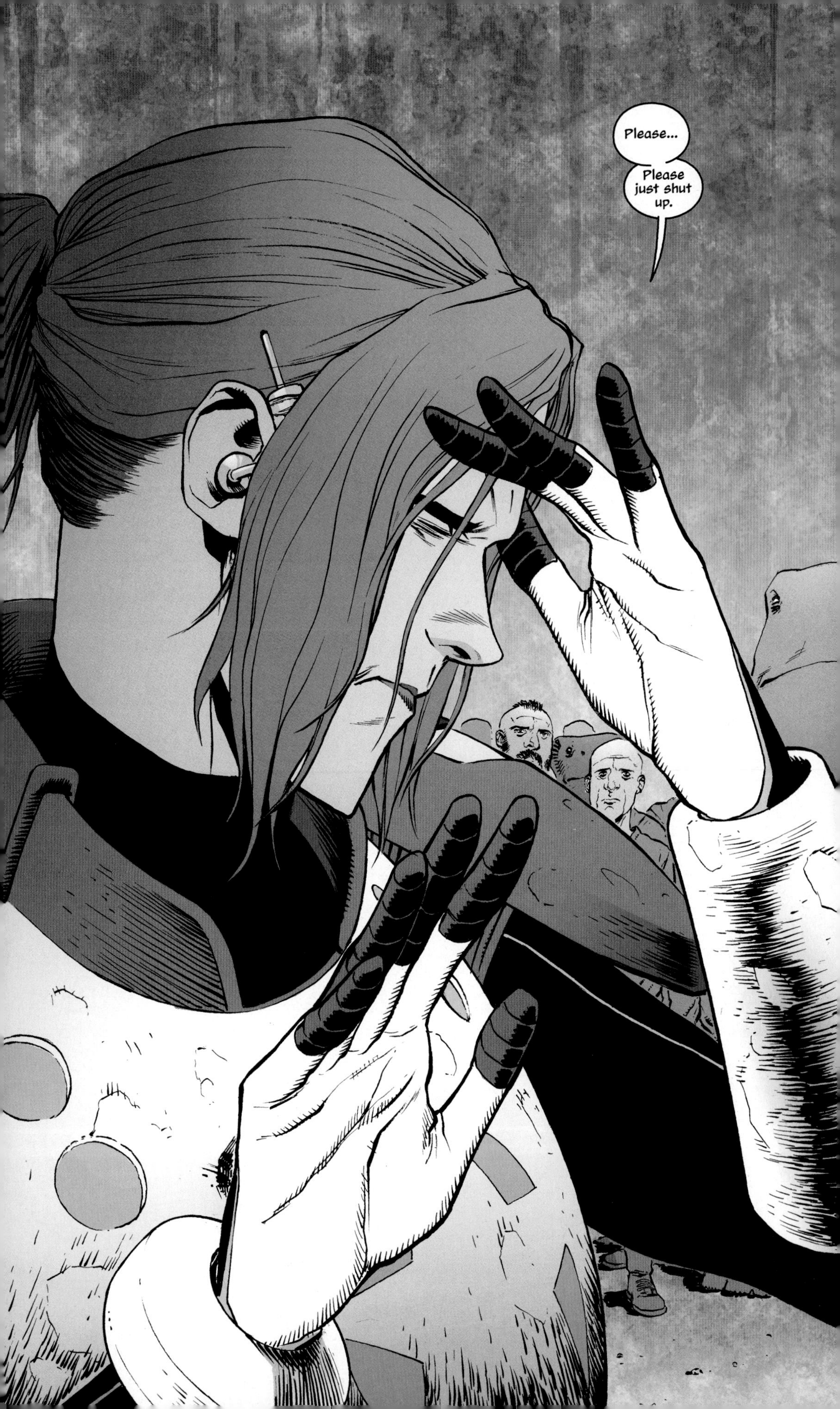
Please...
Please just shut up.

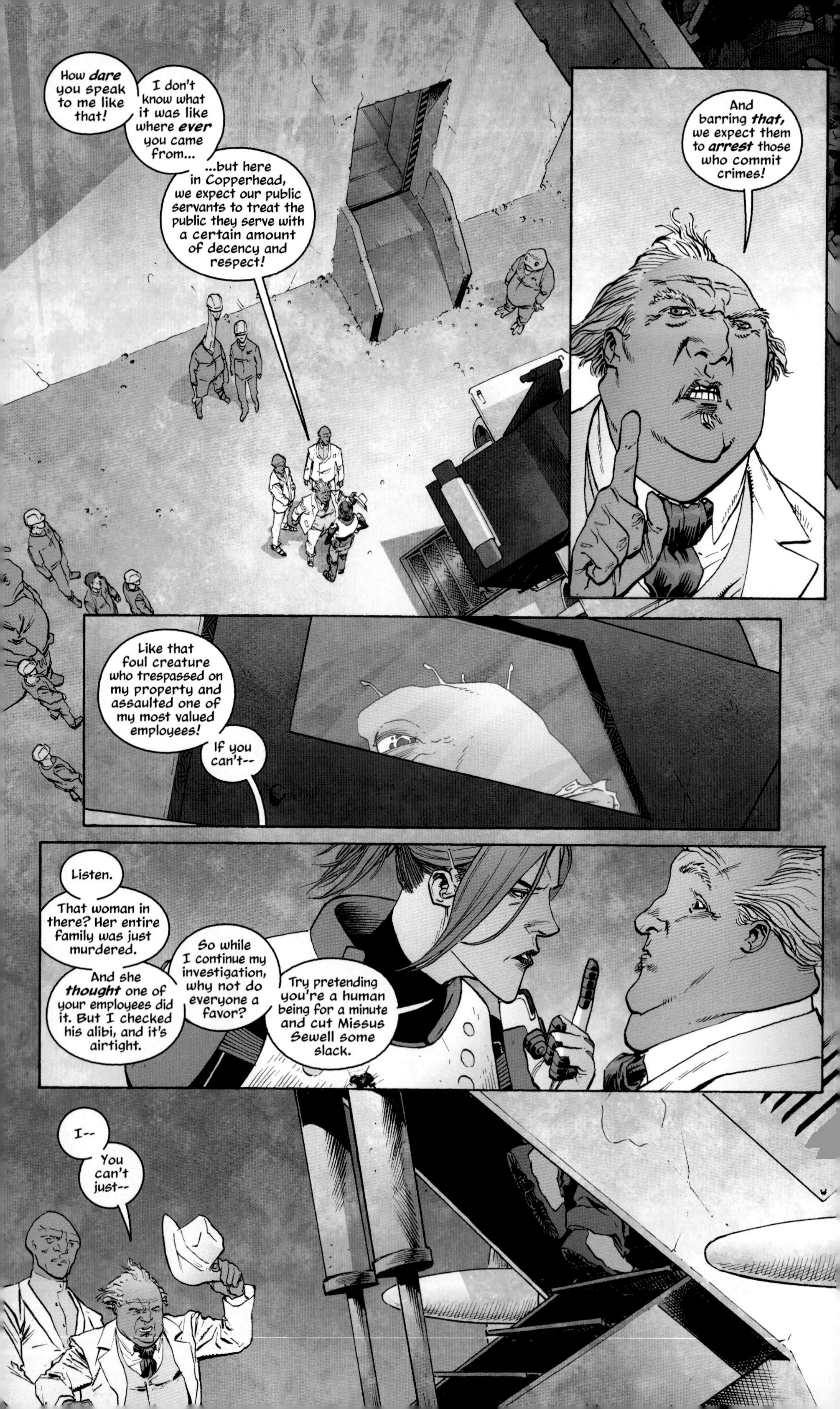
How **dare** you speak to me like that!
I don't know what it was like where **ever** you came from...
...but here in Copperhead, we expect our public servants to treat the public they serve with a certain amount of decency and respect!
And barring **that,** we expect them to **arrest** those who commit crimes!
Like that foul creature who trespassed on my property and assaulted one of my most valued employees!
If you can't--
Listen.
That woman in there? Her entire family was just murdered.
And she **thought** one of your employees did it. But I checked his alibi, and it's airtight.
So while I continue my investigation, why not do everyone a favor?
Try pretending you're a human being for a minute and cut Missus Sewell some slack.
I--
You can't just--

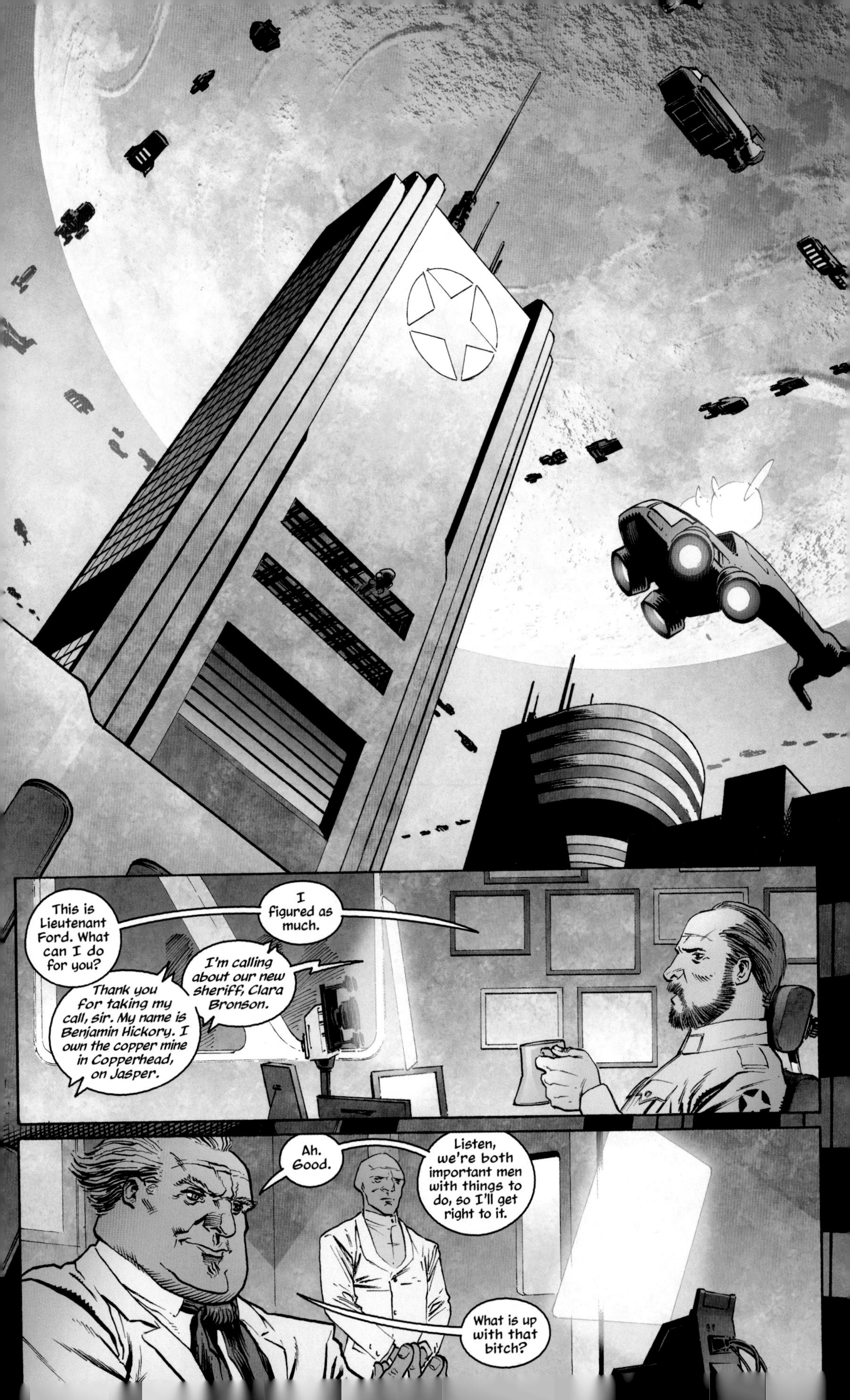
This is Lieutenant Ford. What can I do for you?
Thank you for taking my call, sir. My name is Benjamin Hickory. I own the copper mine in Copperhead, on Jasper.
I'm calling about our new sheriff, Clara Bronson.
I figured as much.
Ah. Good.
Listen, we're both important men with things to do, so I'll get right to it.
What is up with that bitch?

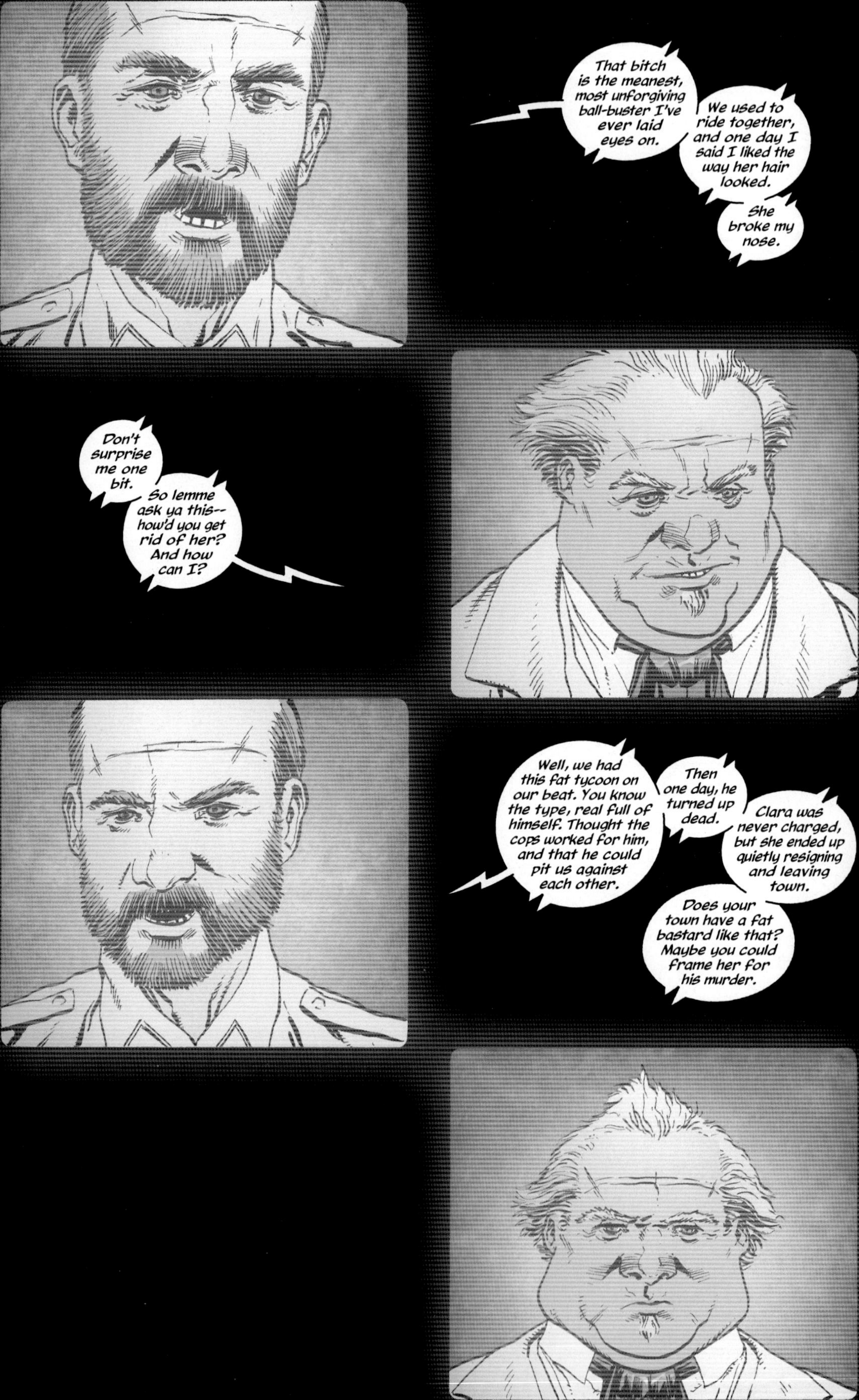
That bitch is the meanest, most unforgiving ball-buster I've ever laid eyes on.
We used to ride together, and one day I said I liked the way her hair looked.
She broke my nose.
Don't surprise me one bit.
So lemme ask ya this--how'd you get rid of her? And how can I?
Well, we had this fat tycoon on our beat. You know the type, real full of himself. Thought the cops worked for him, and that he could pit us against each other.
Then one day, he turned up dead.
Clara was never charged, but she ended up quietly resigning and leaving town.
Does your town have a fat bastard like that? Maybe you could frame her for his murder.

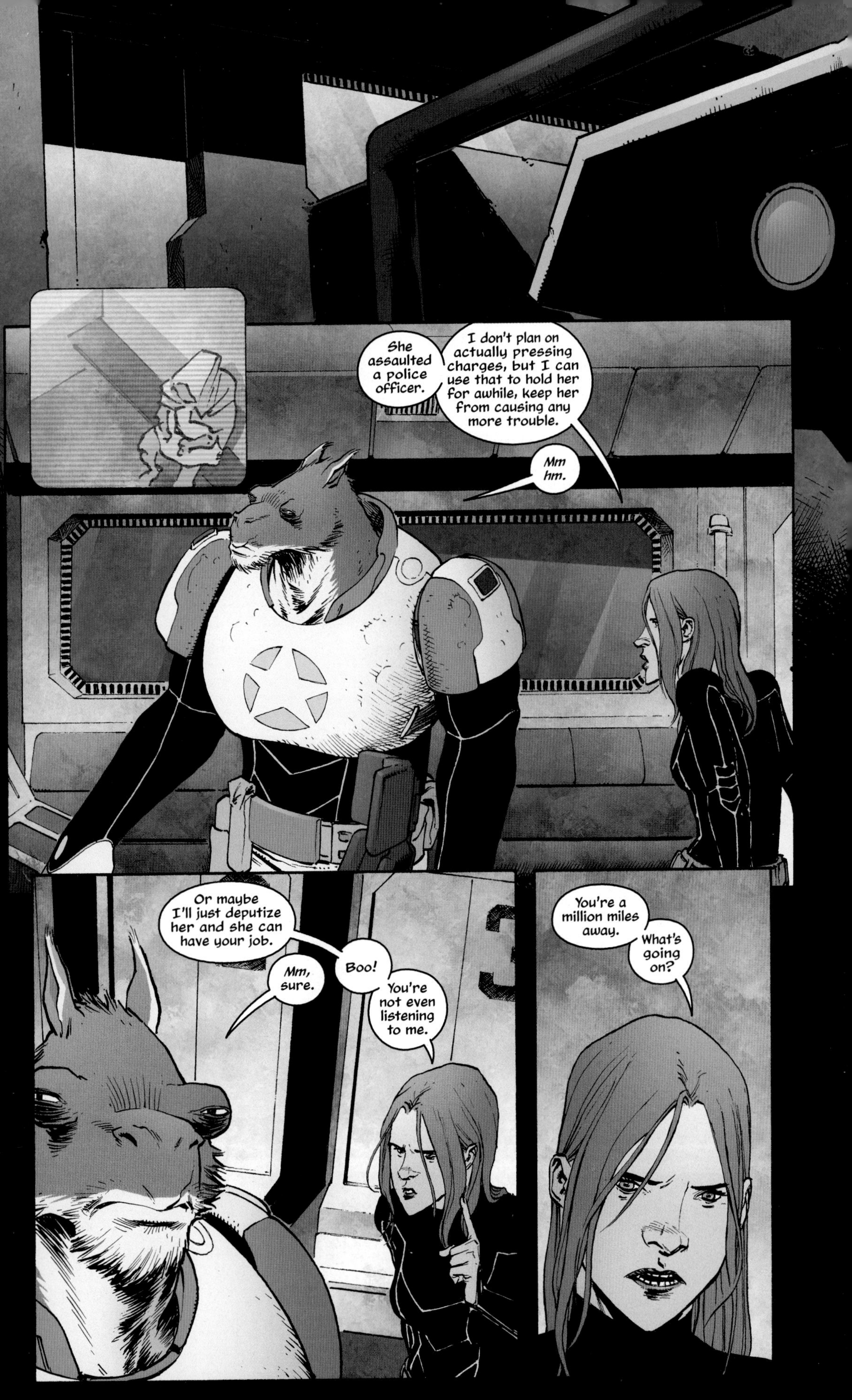

She assaulted a police officer.
I don't plan on actually pressing charges, but I can use that to hold her for awhile, keep her from causing any more trouble.
Mm hm.
Or maybe I'll just deputize her and she can have your job.
Mm, sure.
Boo!
You're not even listening to me.
You're a million miles away.
What's going on?

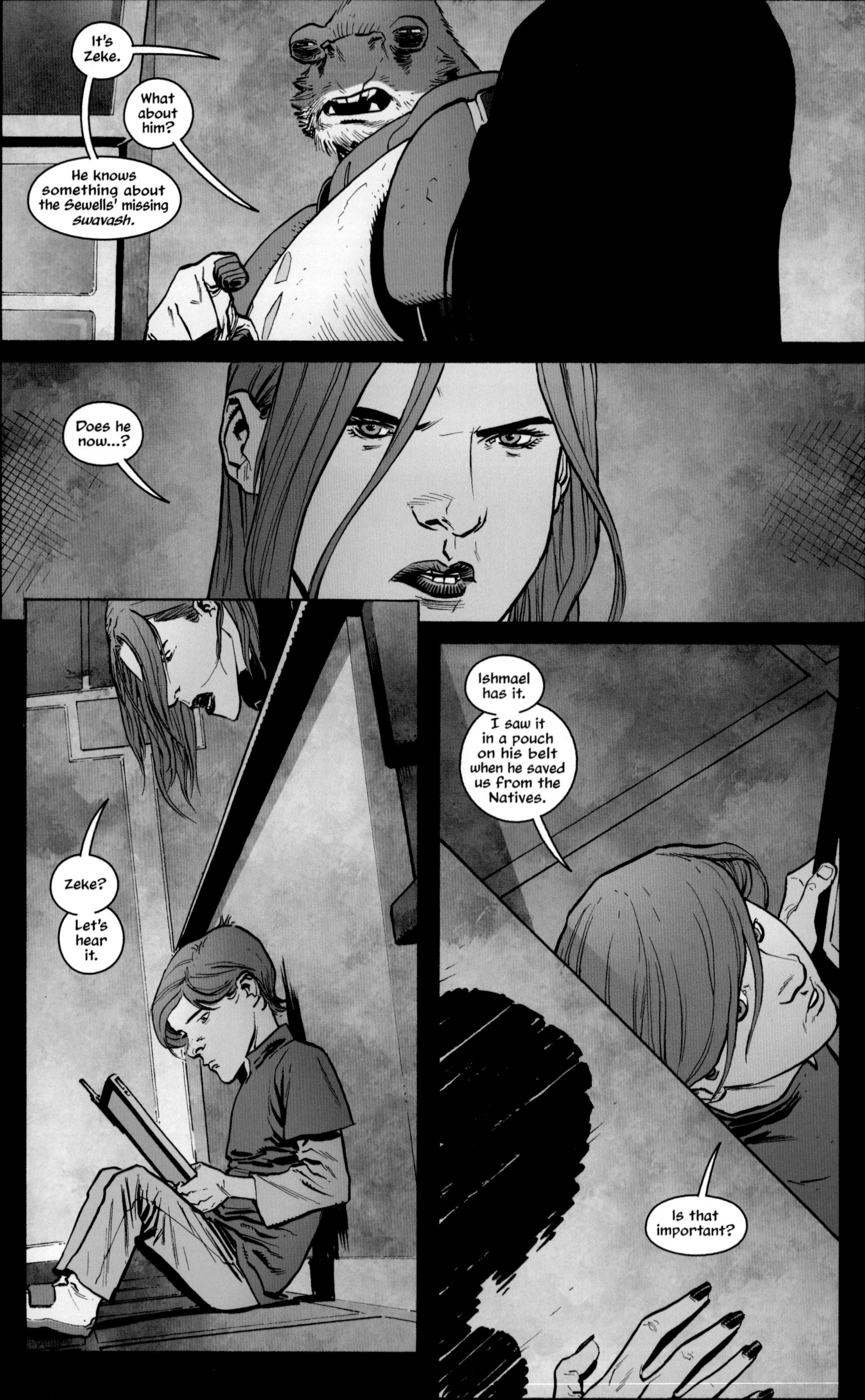
It's Zeke.
What about him?
He knows something about the Sewells' missing *swavash.*
Does he now...?
Zeke?
Let's hear it.
Ishmael has it.
I saw it in a pouch on his belt when he saved us from the Natives.
Is that important?

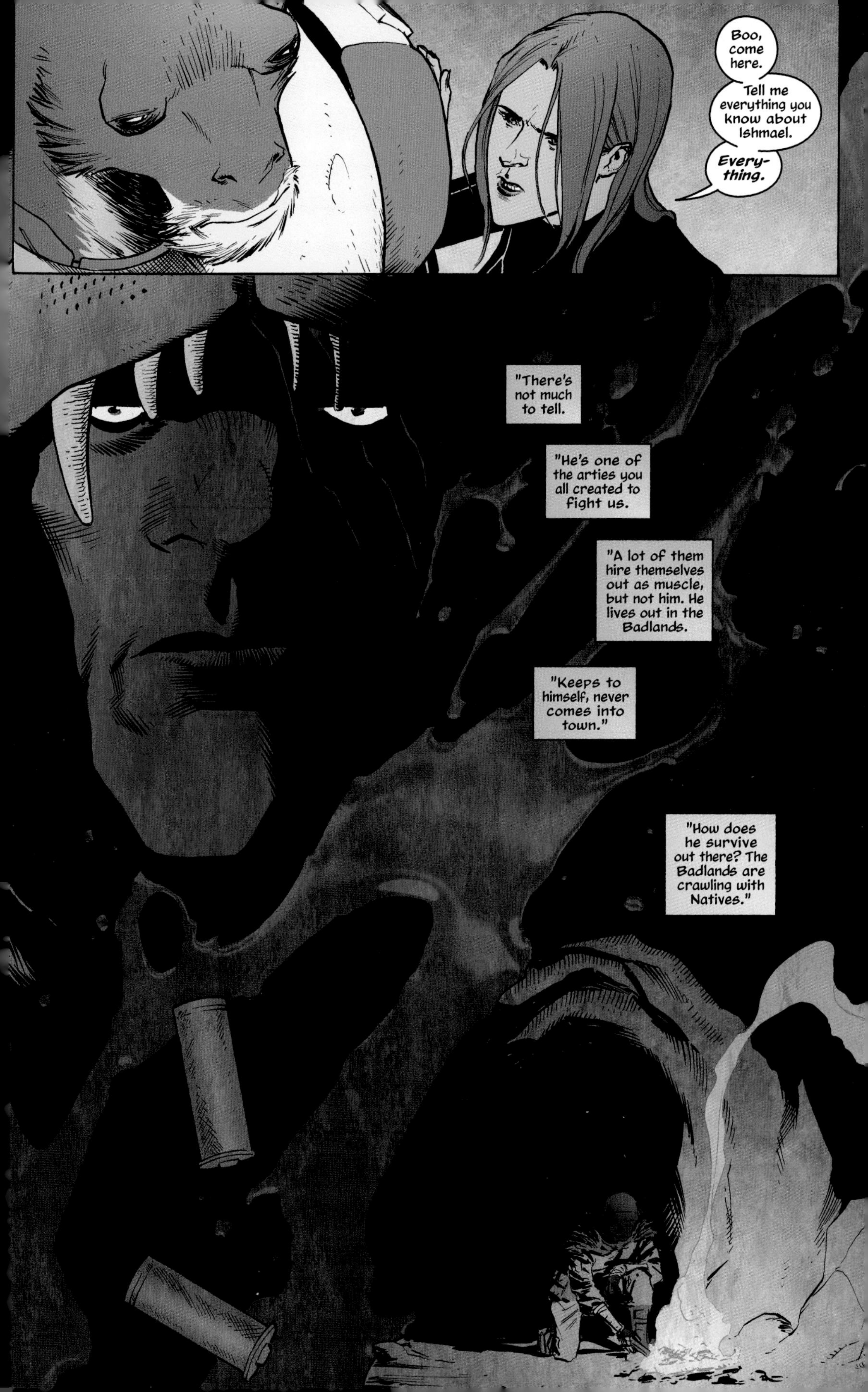
Boo, come here.
Tell me everything you know about Ishmael.
Every-thing.
"There's not much to tell.
"He's one of the arties you all created to fight us.
"A lot of them hire themselves out as muscle, but not him. He lives out in the Badlands.
"Keeps to himself, never comes into town."
"How does he survive out there? The Badlands are crawling with Natives."

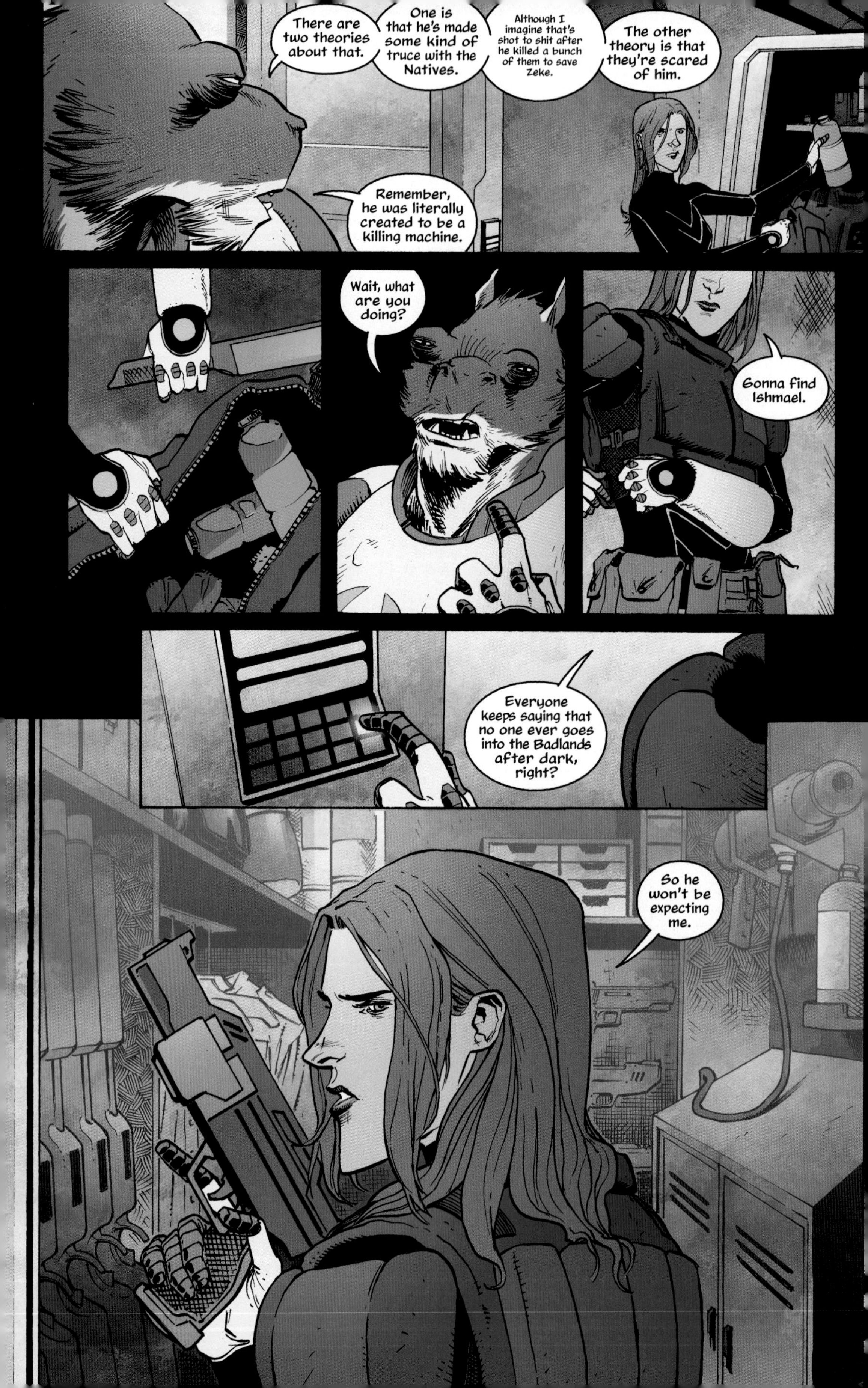
There are two theories about that.
One is that he's made some kind of truce with the Natives.
Although I imagine that's shot to shit after he killed a bunch of them to save Zeke.
The other theory is that they're scared of him.
Remember, he was literally created to be a killing machine.
Wait, what are you doing?
Gonna find Ishmael.
Everyone keeps saying that no one ever goes into the Badlands after dark, right?
So he won't be expecting me.

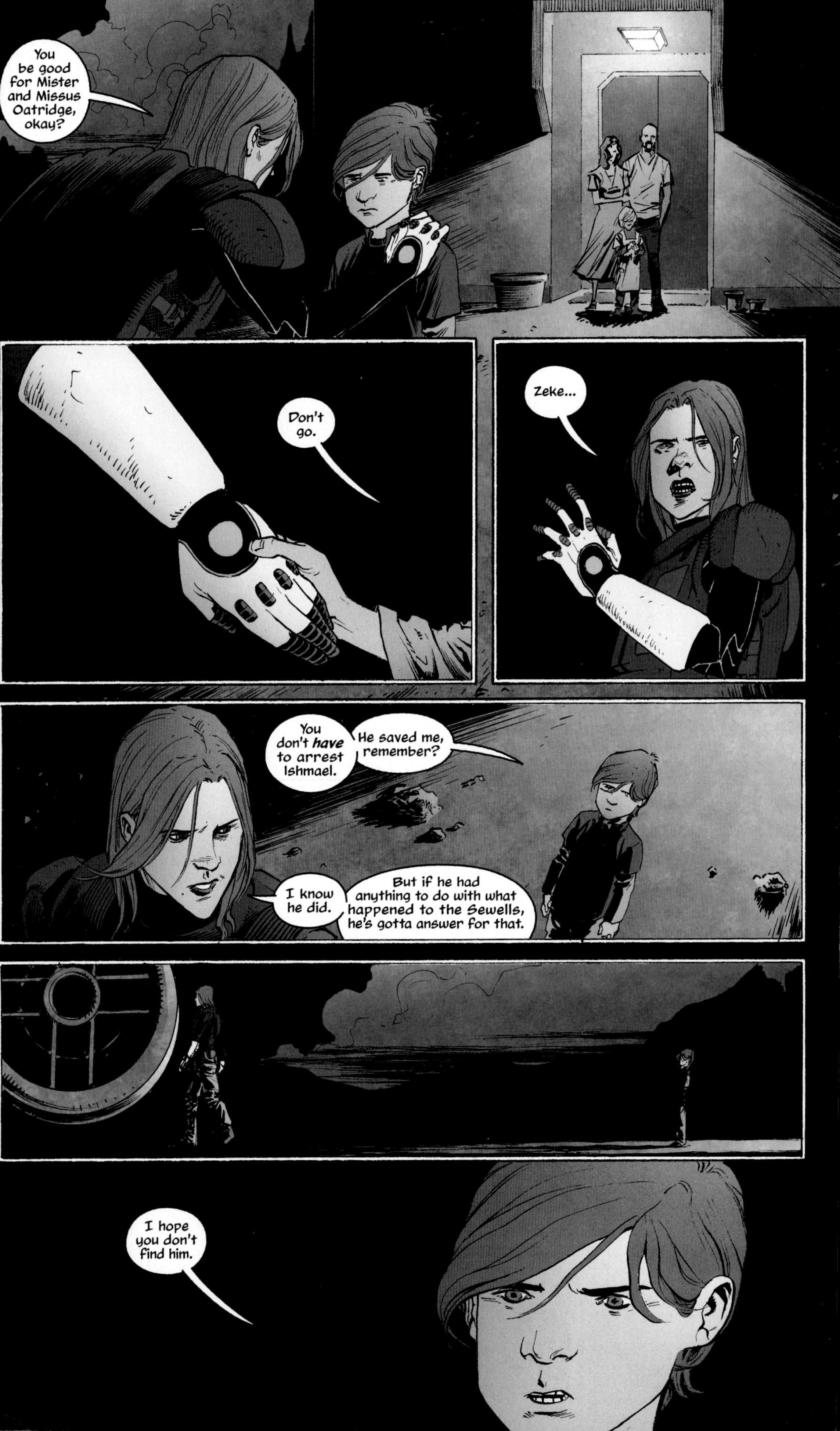
You be good for Mister and Missus Oatridge, okay?
Don't go.
Zeke...
You don't *have* to arrest Ishmael.
He saved me, remember?
I know he did.
But if he had anything to do with what happened to the Sewells, he's gotta answer for that.
I hope you don't find him.

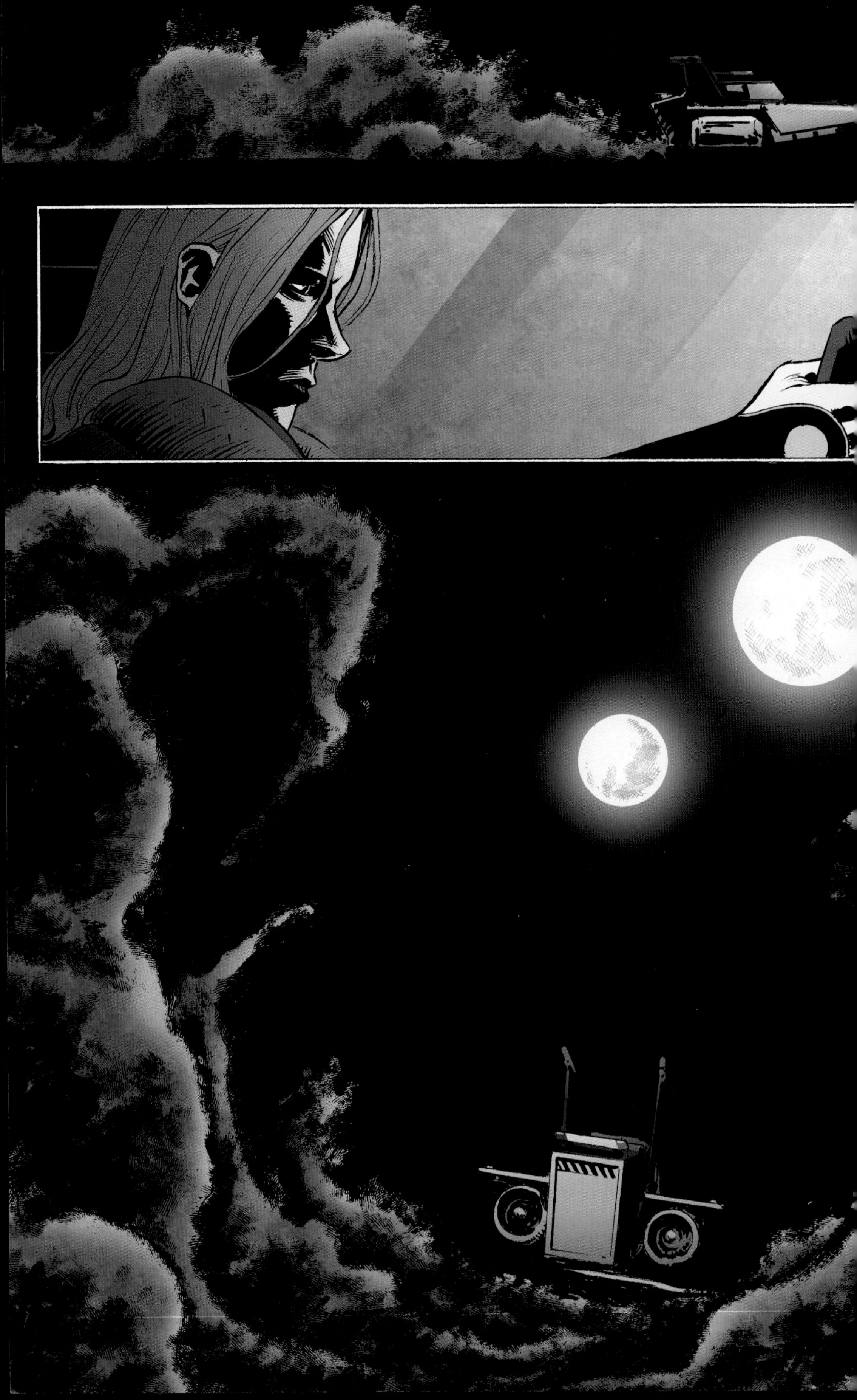

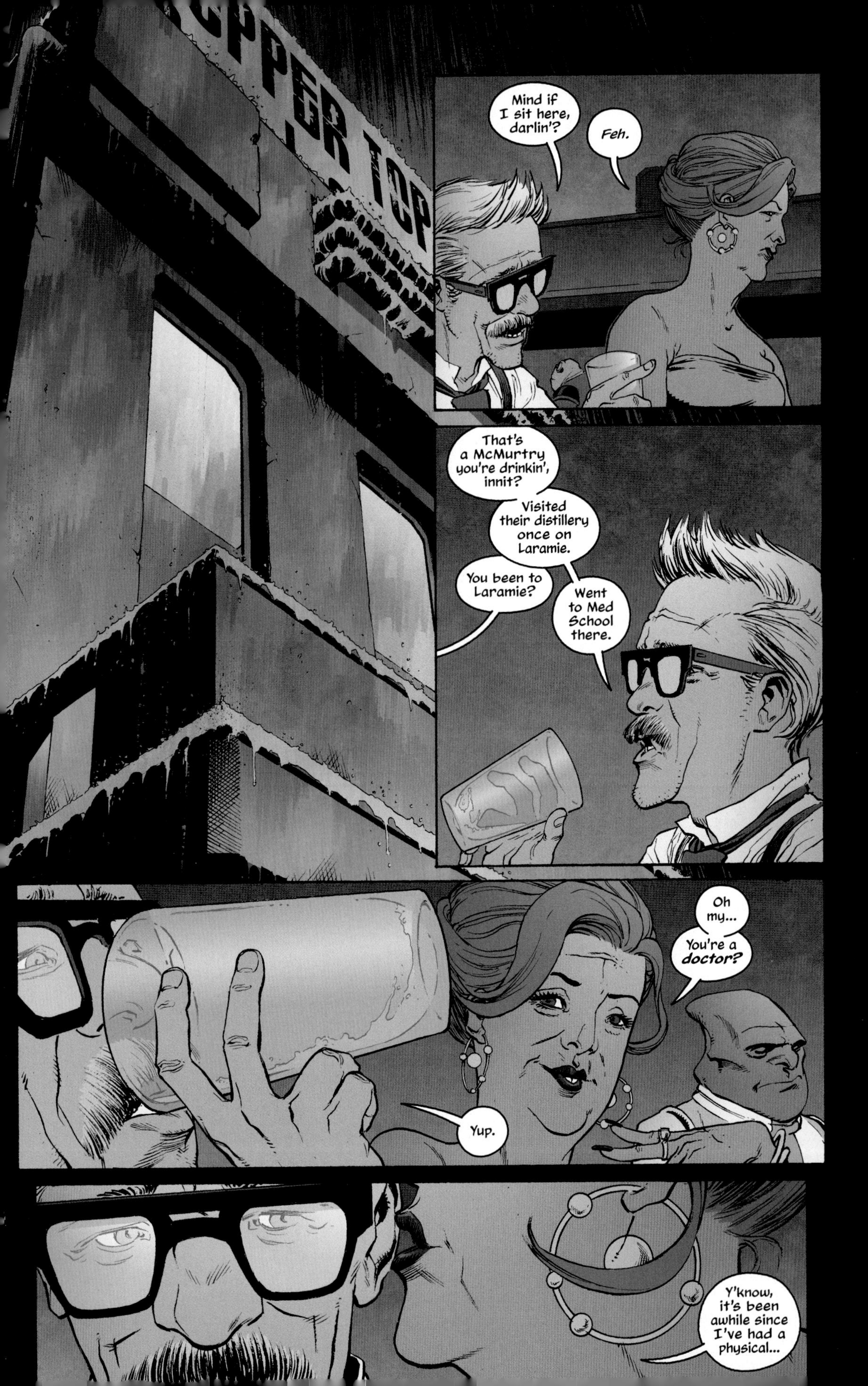

Mind if I sit here, darlin'?
Feh.
That's a McMurtry you're drinkin', innit?
Visited their distillery once on Laramie.
You been to Laramie?
Went to Med School there.
Oh my...
You're a *doctor?*
Yup.
Y'know, it's been awhile since I've had a physical...

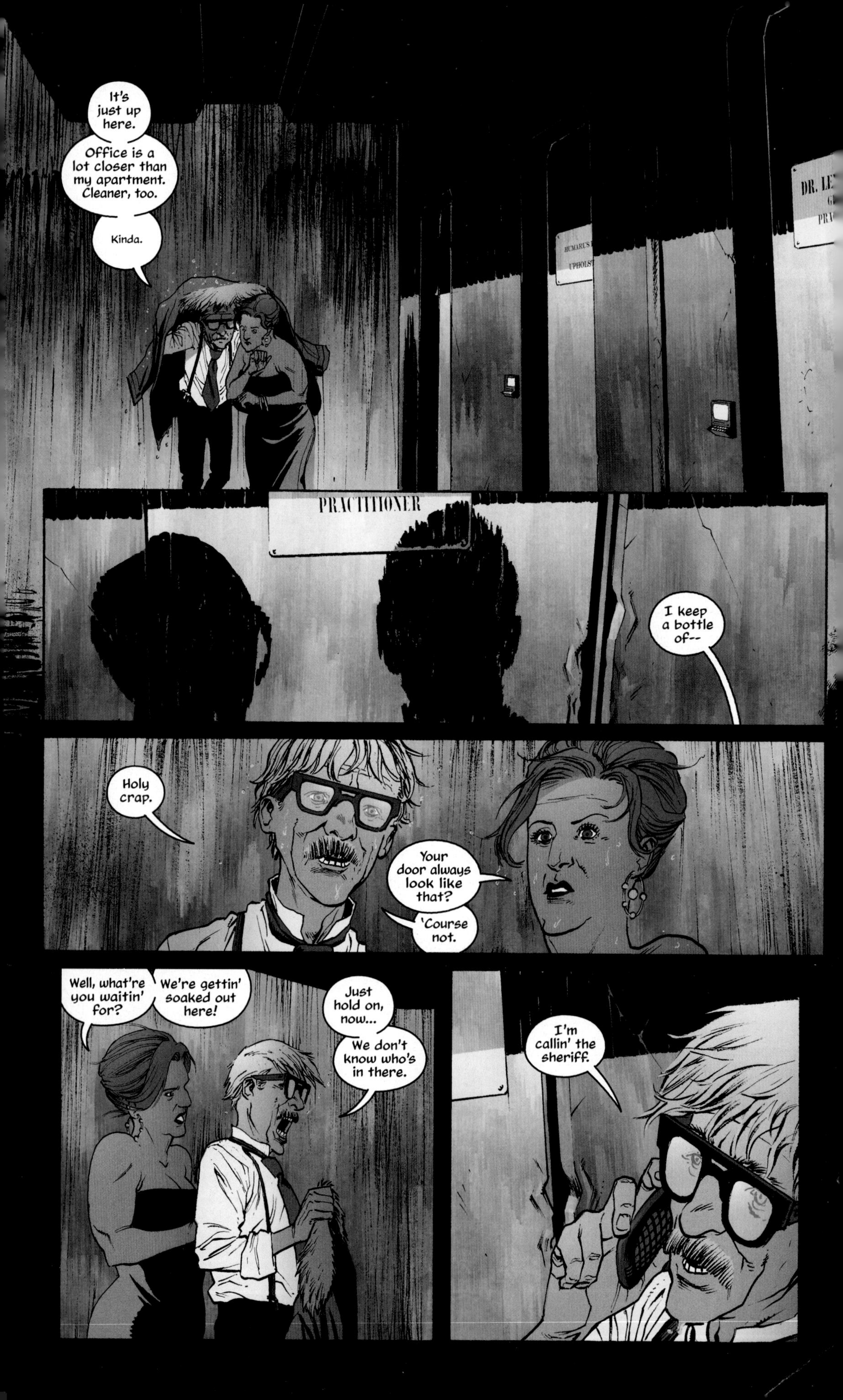
It's just up here.
Office is a lot closer than my apartment. Cleaner, too.
Kinda.
HUMARUS
UPHOLST
DR. LE
PRACTITIONER
I keep a bottle of--
Holy crap.
Your door always look like that?
'Course not.
Well, what're you waitin' for?
We're gettin' soaked out here!
Just hold on, now...
We don't know who's in there.
I'm callin' the sheriff.

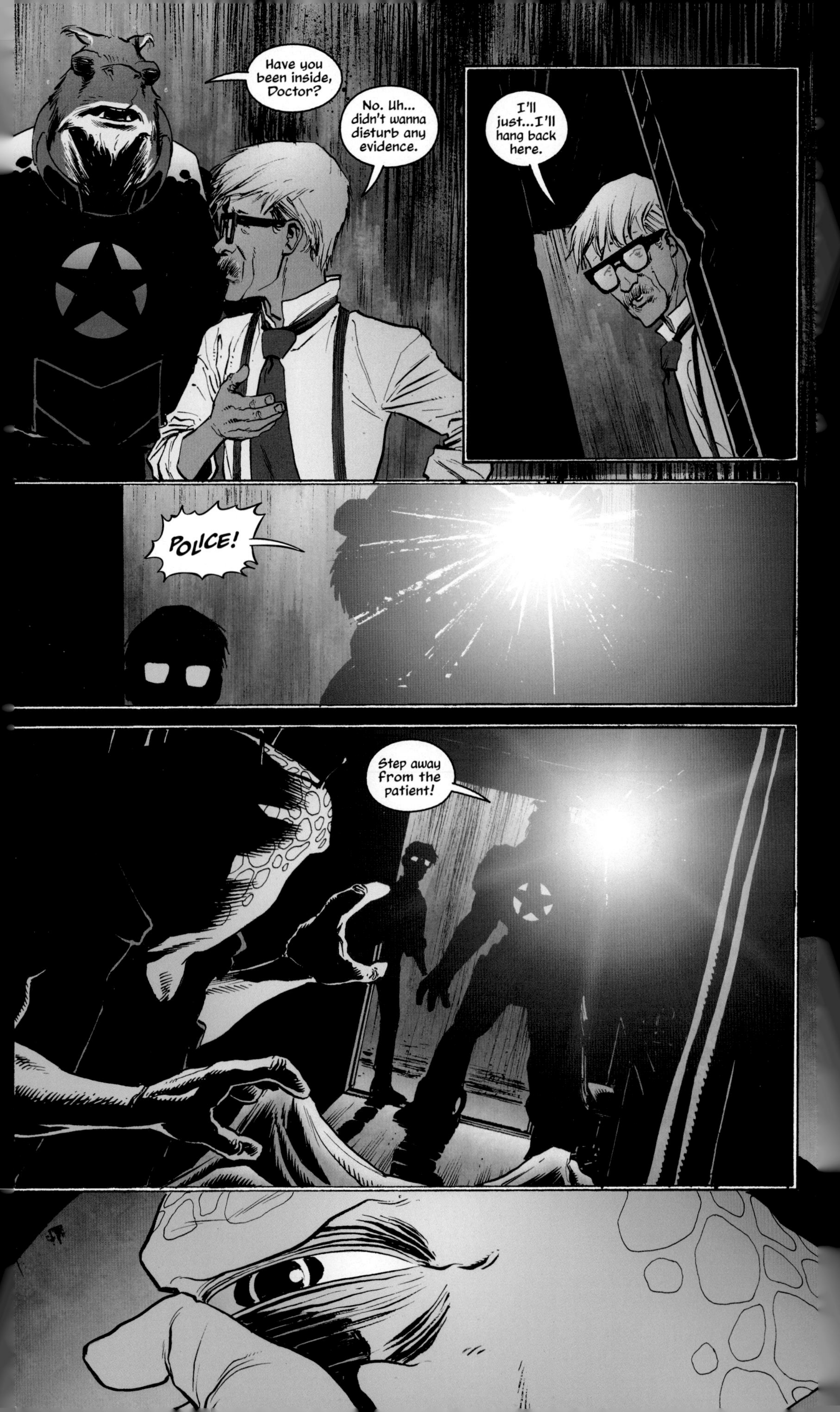
Have you been inside, Doctor?
No. Uh... didn't wanna disturb any evidence.
I'll just...I'll hang back here.
POLICE!
Step away from the patient!

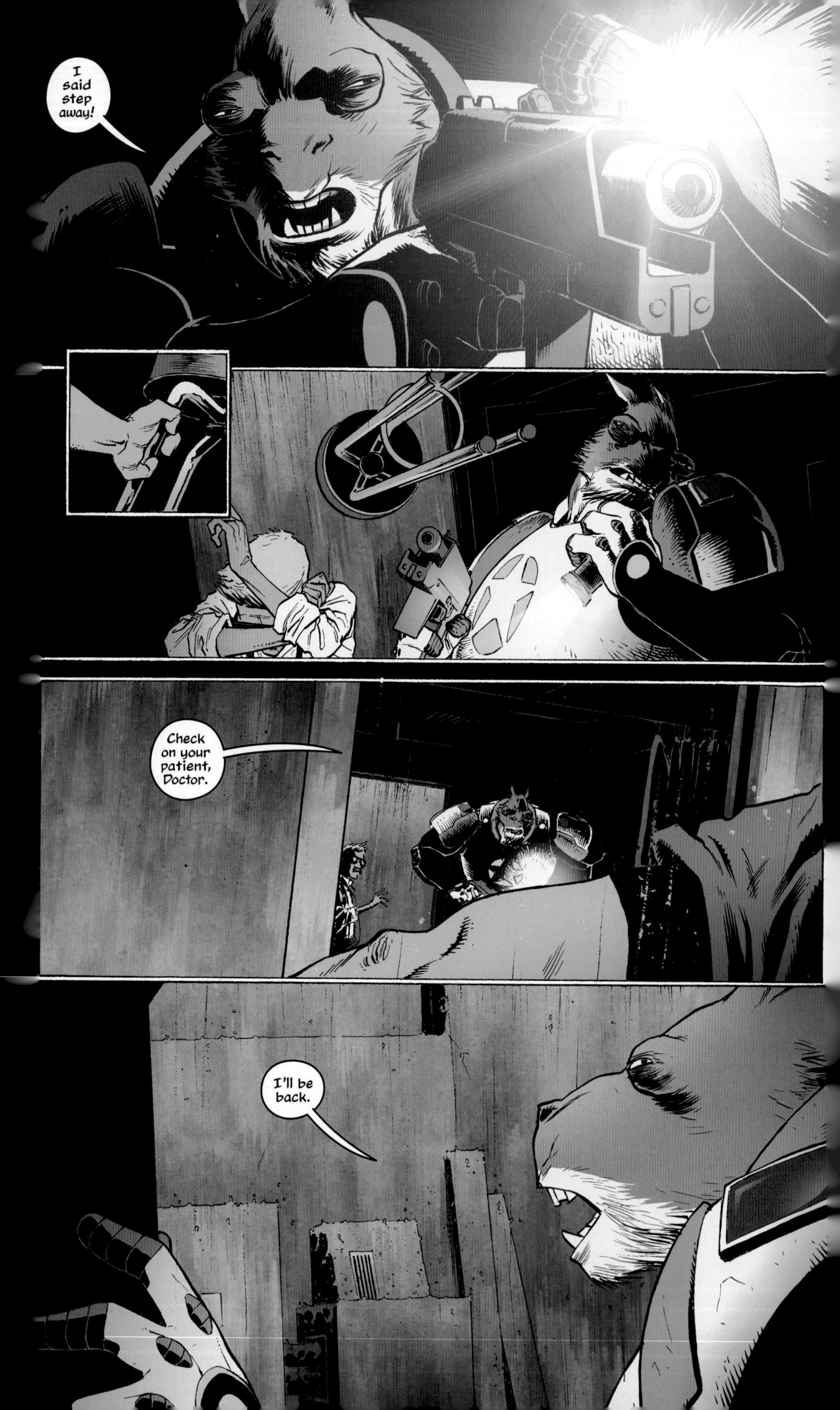
I said step away!
Check on your patient, Doctor.
I'll be back.

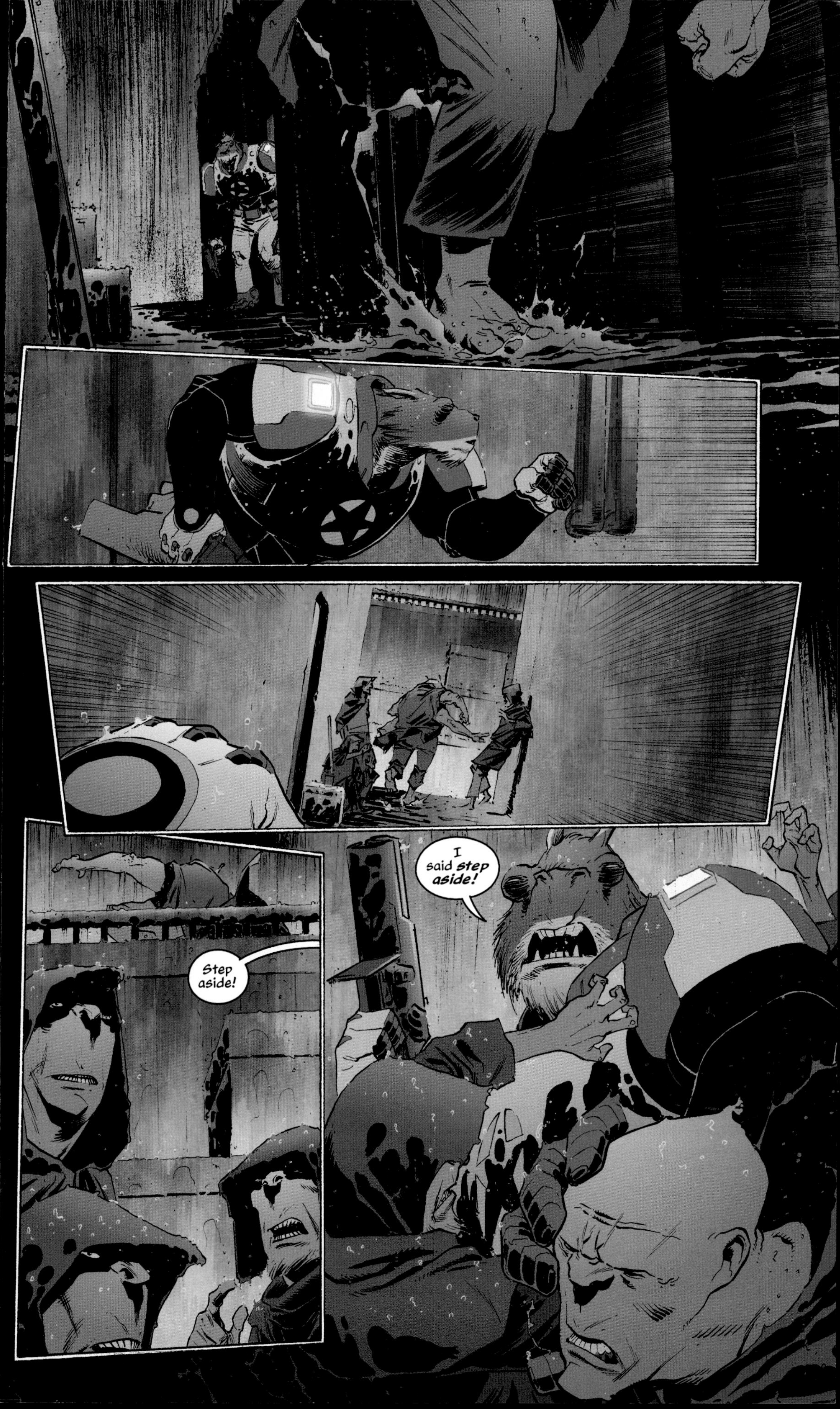
Step aside!
I said step aside!

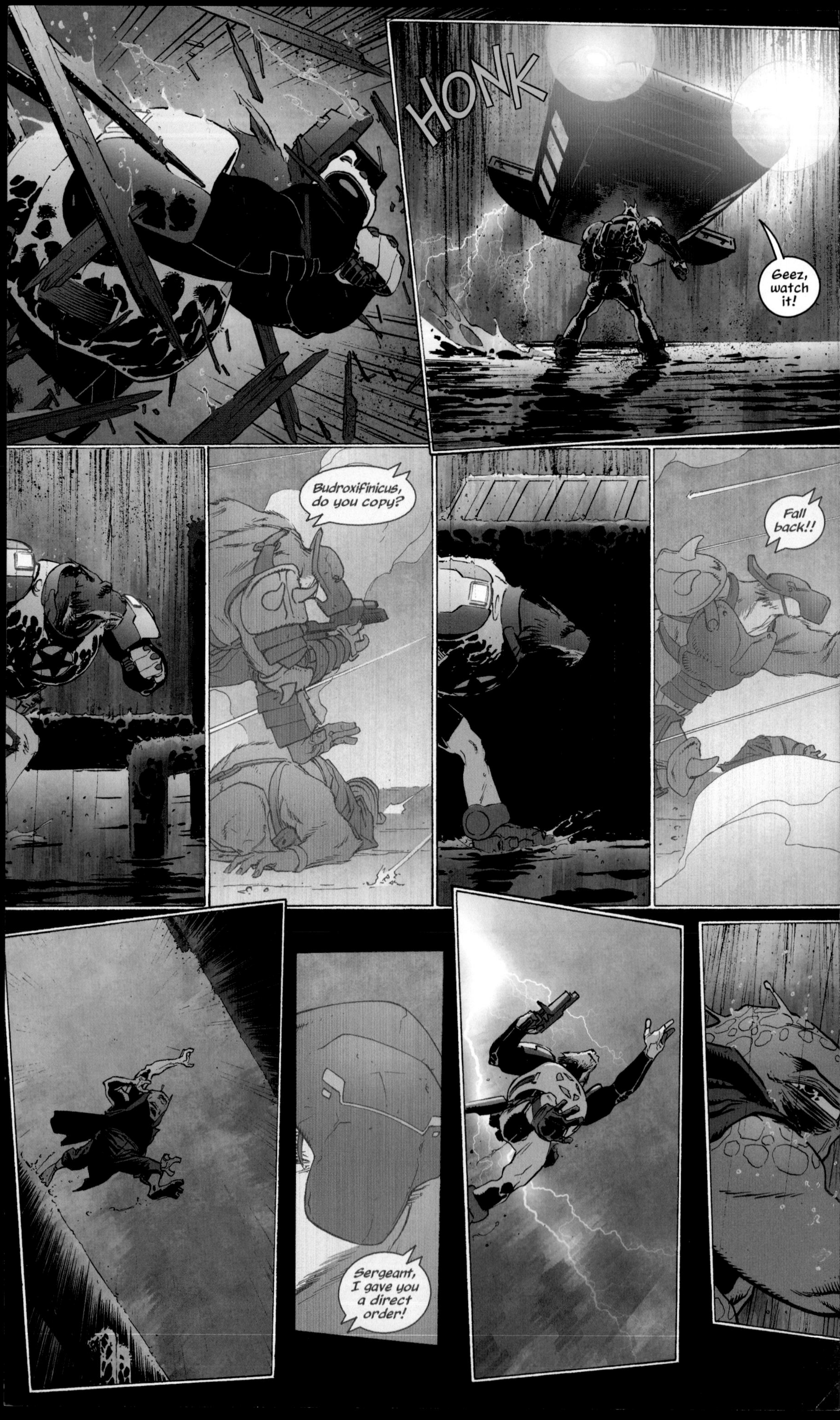
HONK
Geez, watch it!
Budroxifinicus, do you copy?
Fall back!!
Sergeant, I gave you a direct order!

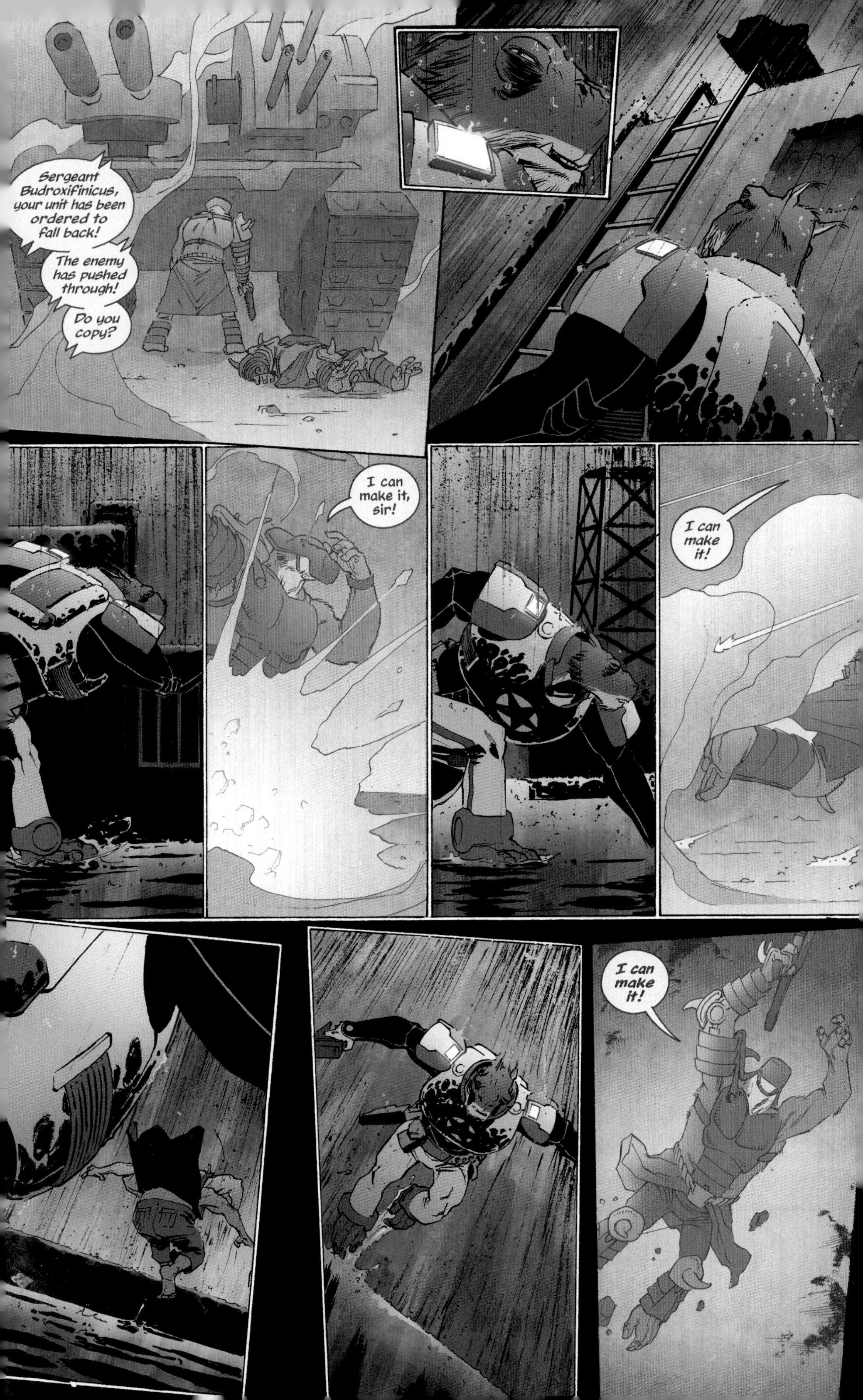
Sergeant Budroxifinicus, your unit has been ordered to fall back!
The enemy has pushed through!
Do you copy?
I can make it, sir!
I can make it!
I can make it!

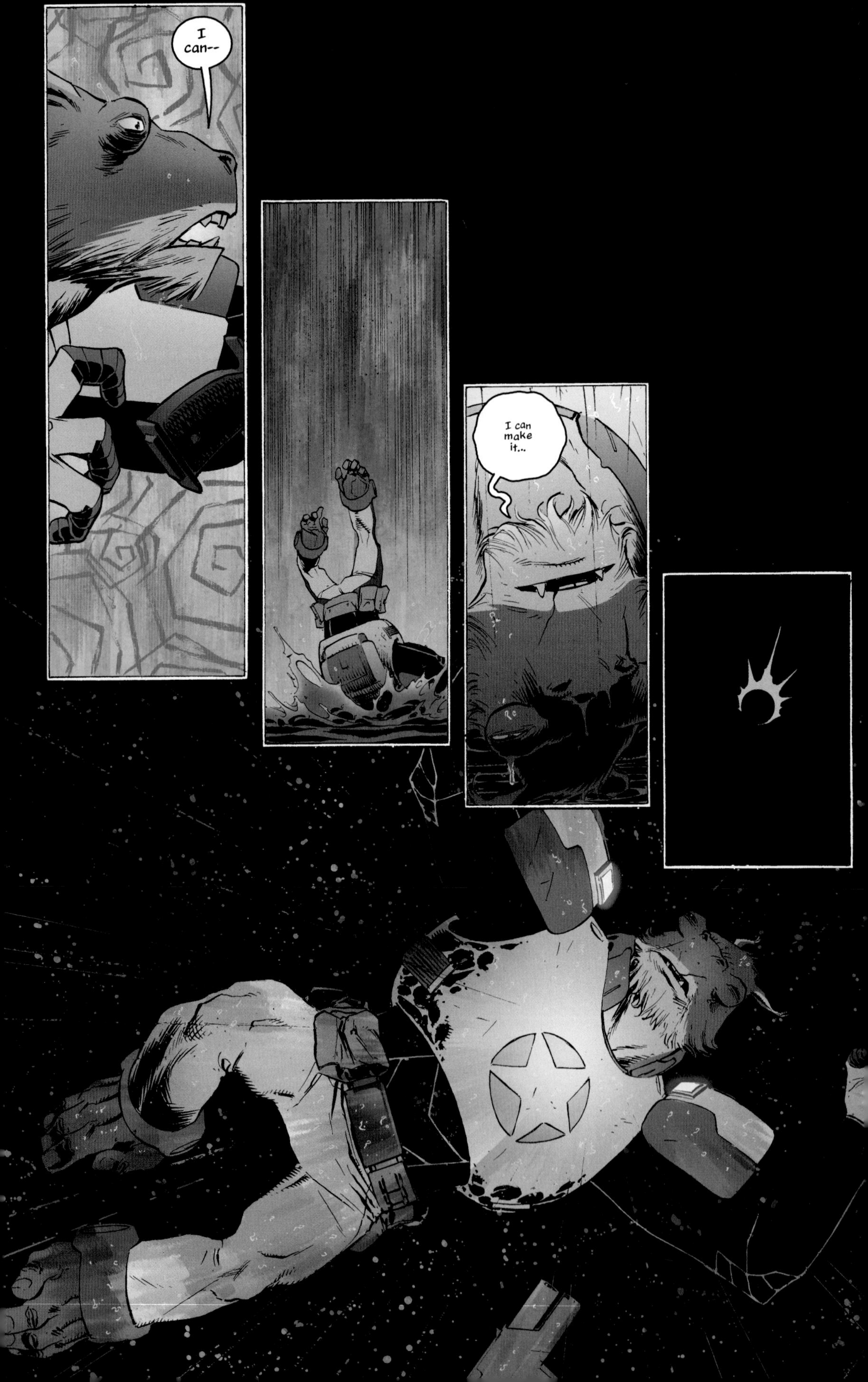
I can--
I can make it...

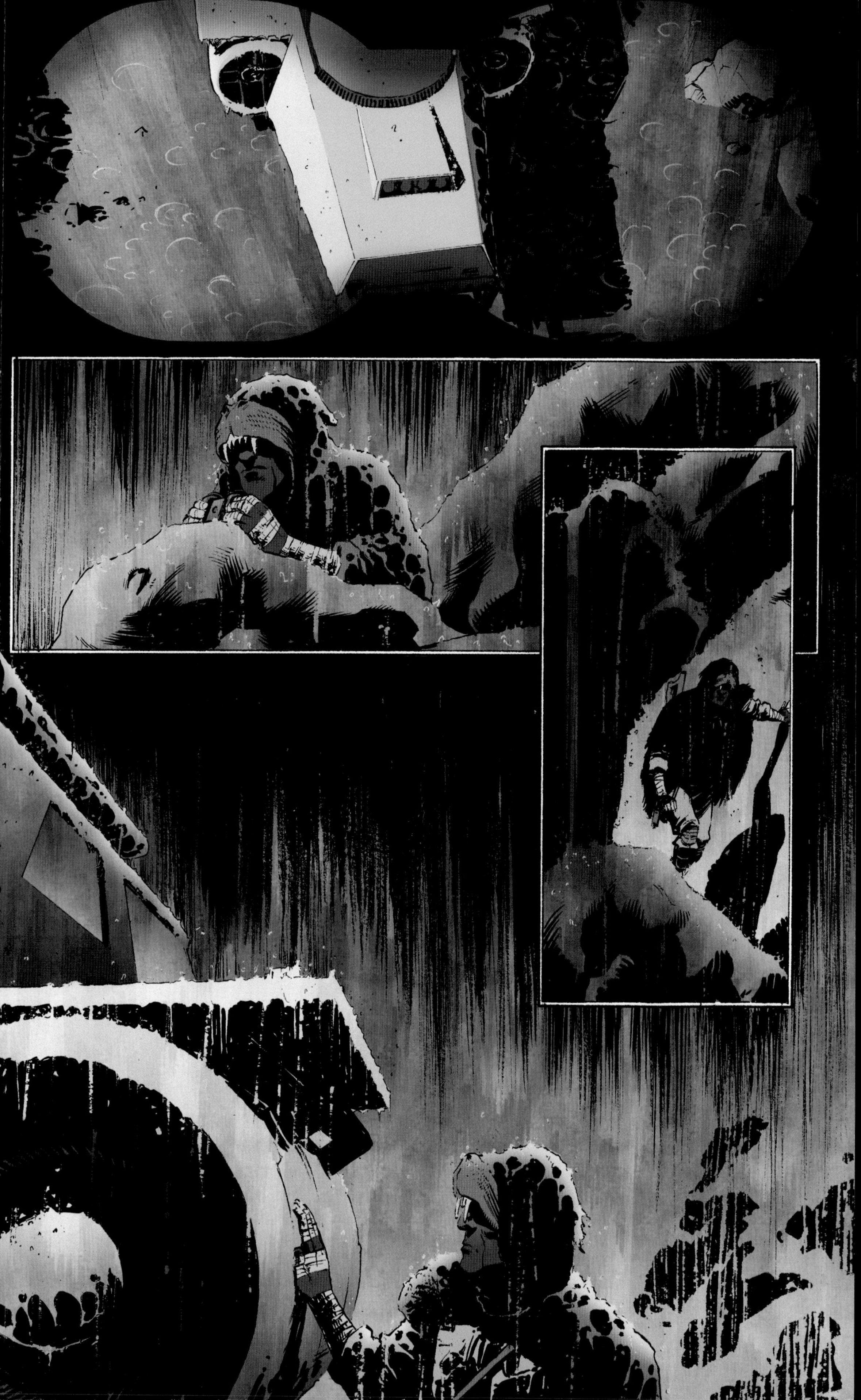

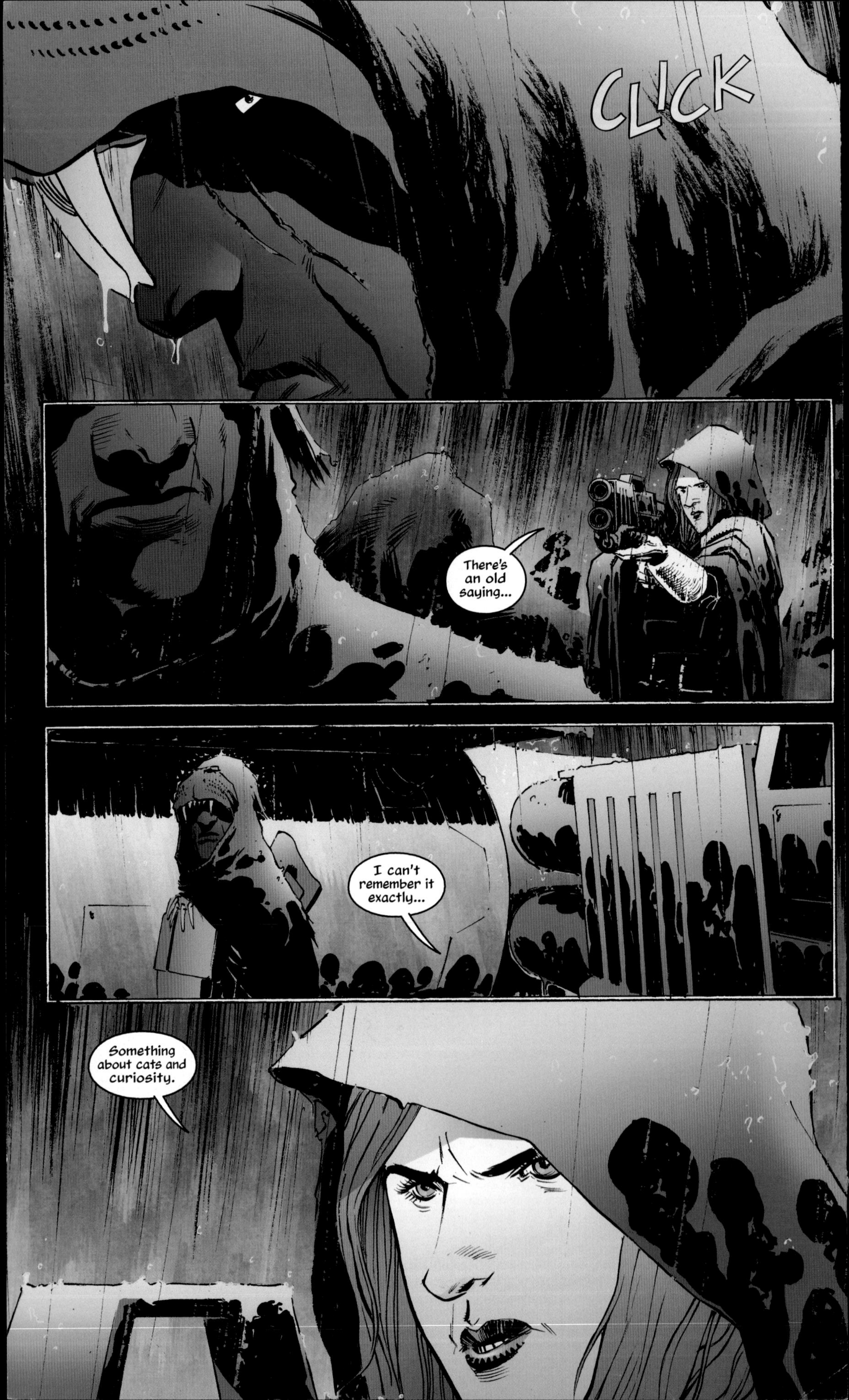
CLICK
There's an old saying...
I can't remember it exactly...
Something about cats and curiosity.

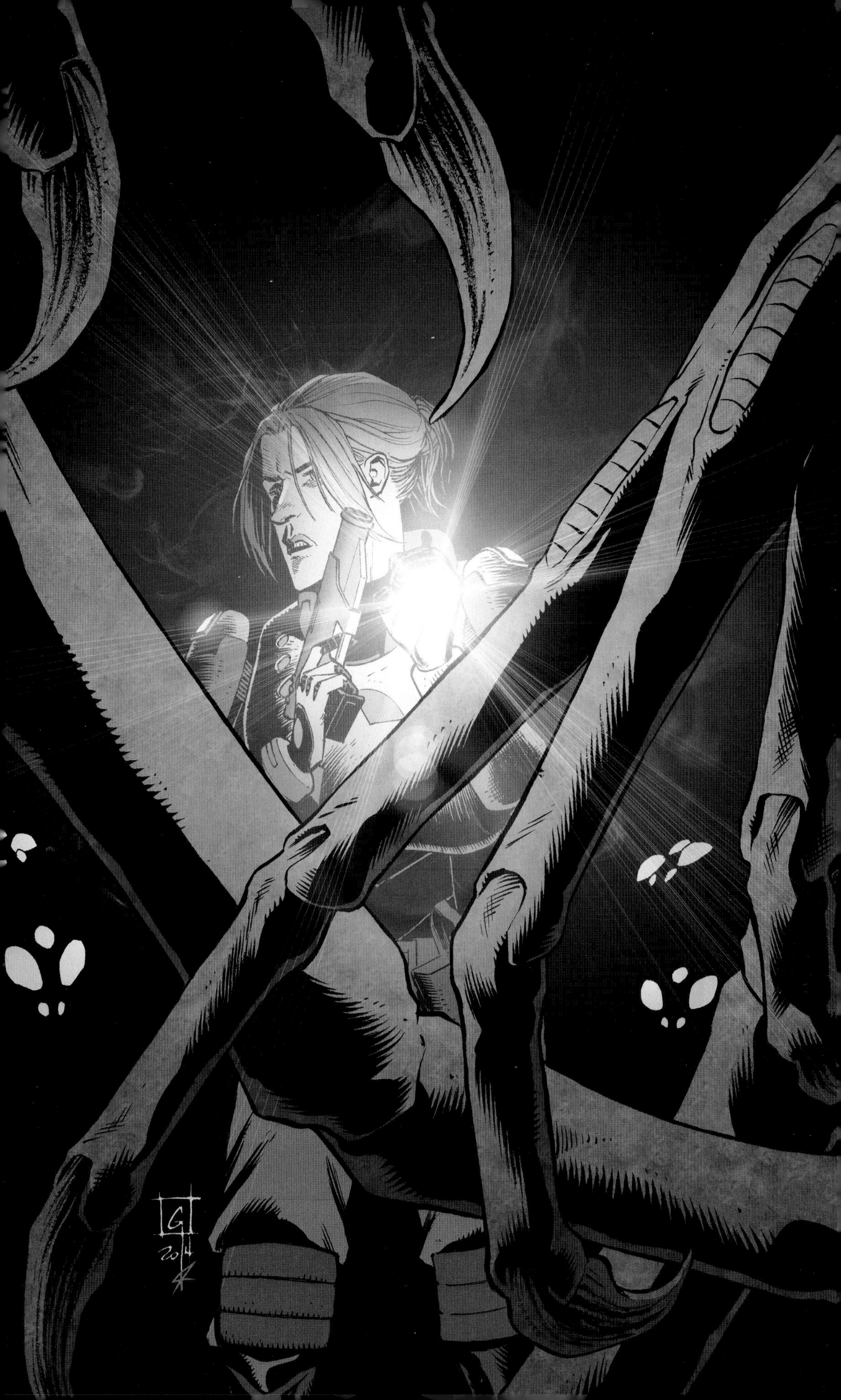

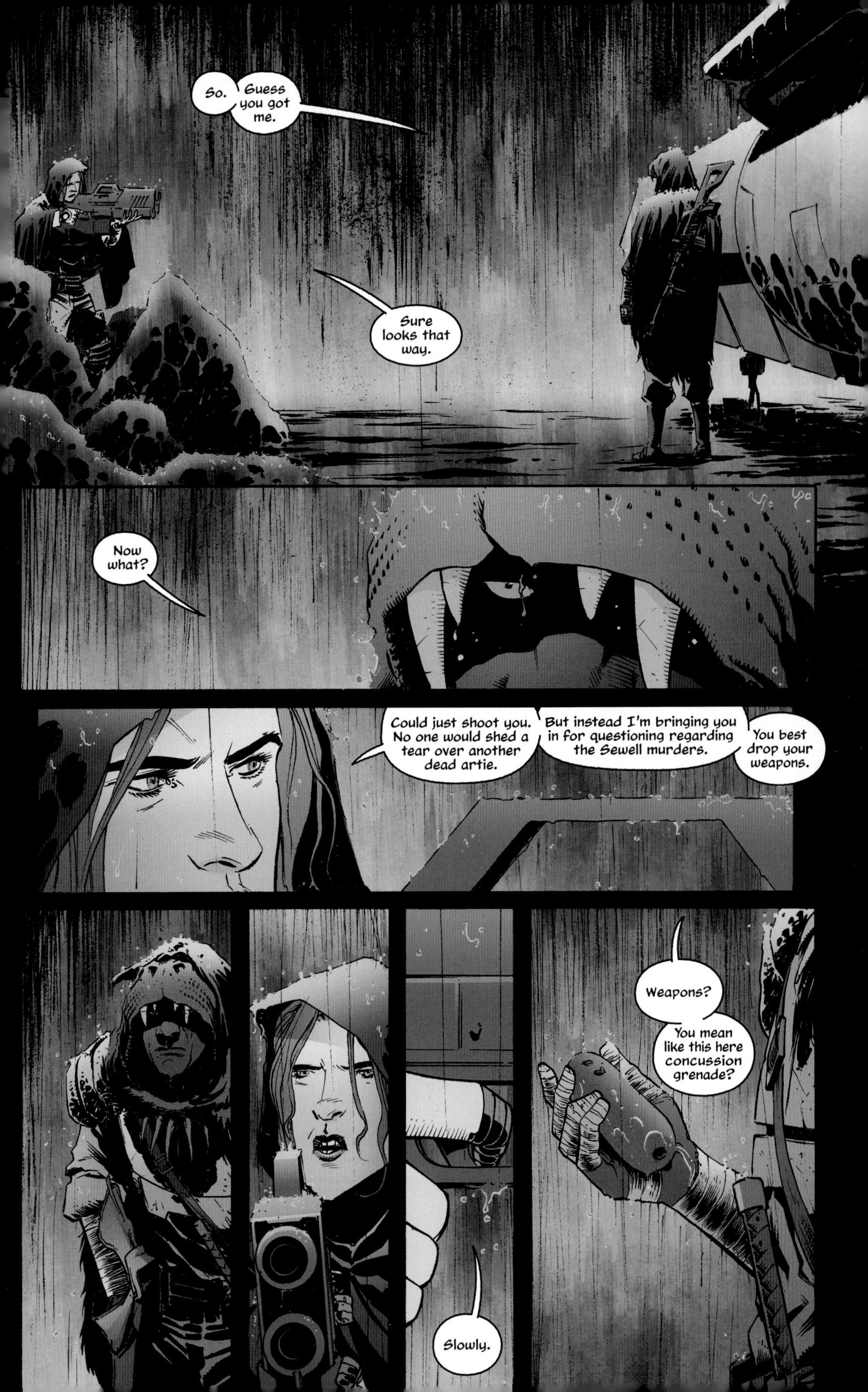

So.
Guess you got me.
Sure looks that way.
Now what?
Could just shoot you. No one would shed a tear over another dead artie.
But instead I'm bringing you in for questioning regarding the Sewell murders.
You best drop your weapons.
Weapons?
You mean like this here concussion grenade?
Slowly.

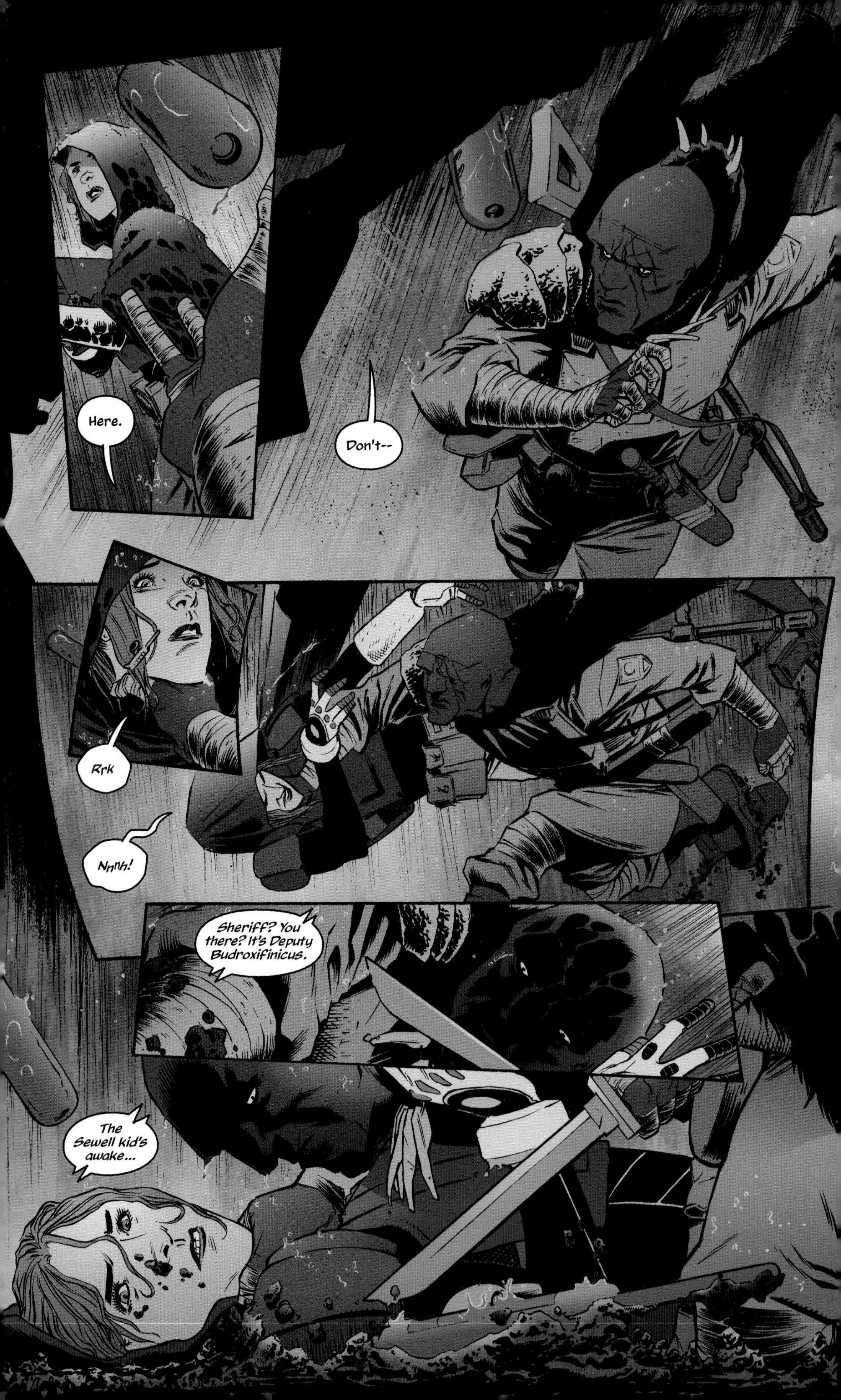
Here.
Don't--
Rrk
Nnnh!
Sheriff? You there? It's Deputy Budroxifinicus.
The Sewell kid's awake...

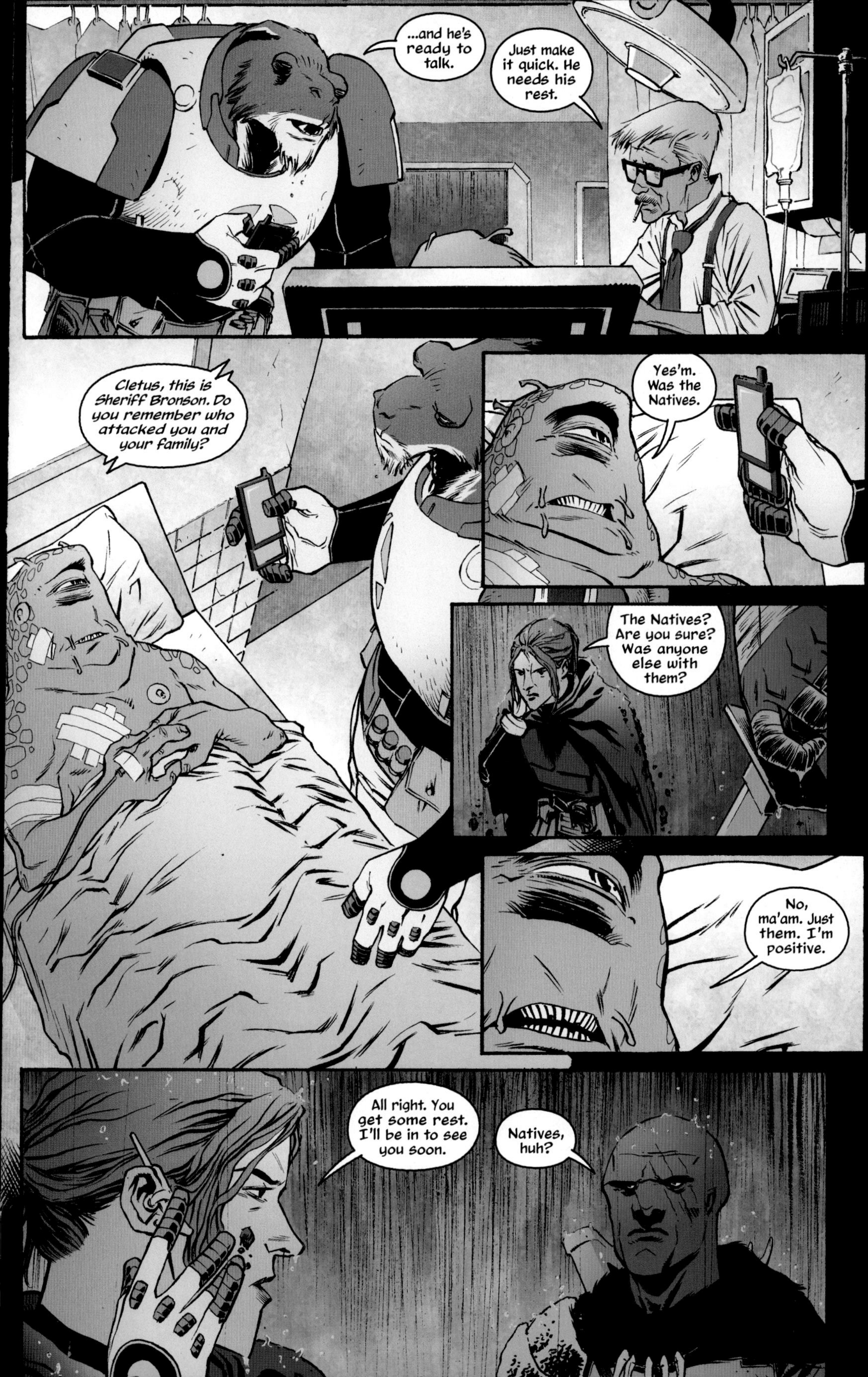
...and he's ready to talk.
Just make it quick. He needs his rest.
Cletus, this is Sheriff Bronson. Do you remember who attacked you and your family?
Yes'm. Was the Natives.
The Natives? Are you sure? Was anyone else with them?
No, ma'am. Just them. I'm positive.
All right. You get some rest. I'll be in to see you soon.
Natives, huh?

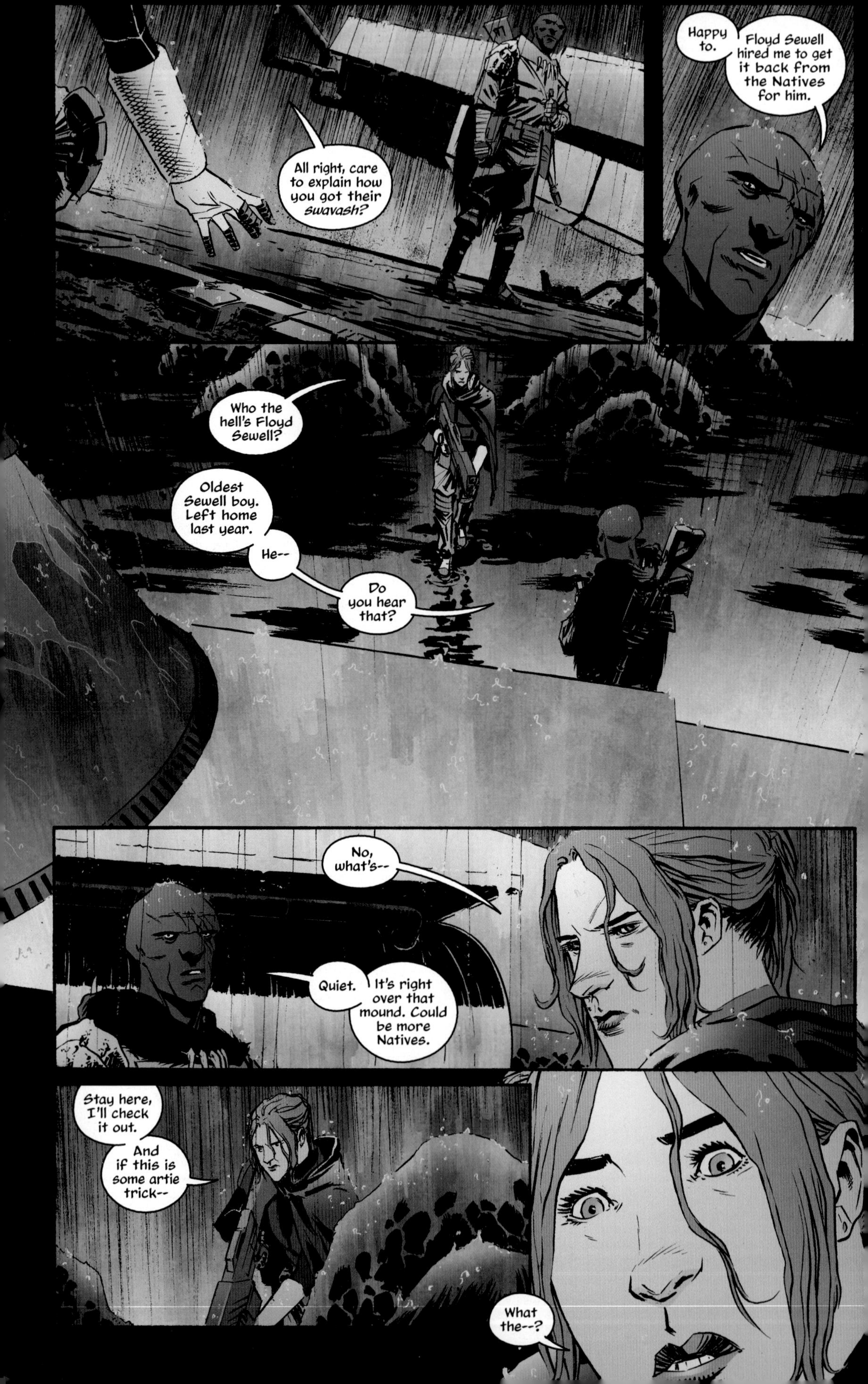
All right, care to explain how you got their *swavash?*
Happy to.
Floyd Sewell hired me to get it back from the Natives for him.
Who the hell's Floyd Sewell?
Oldest Sewell boy. Left home last year.
He--
Do you hear that?
No, what's--
Quiet.
It's right over that mound. Could be more Natives.
Stay here, I'll check it out.
And if this is some artie trick--
What the--?

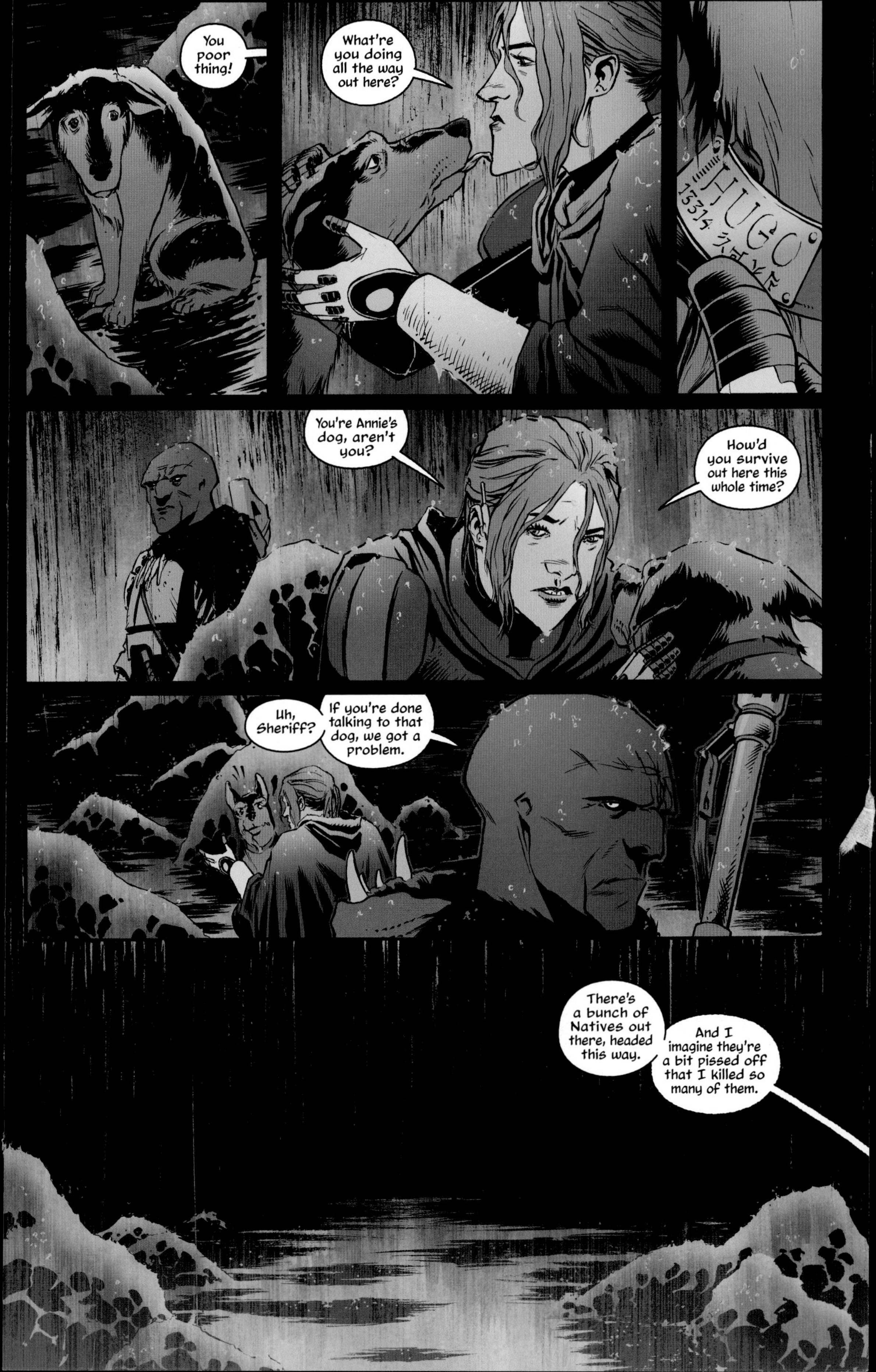
You poor thing!
What're you doing all the way out here?
HUGO
13314
You're Annie's dog, aren't you?
How'd you survive out here this whole time?
Uh, Sheriff?
If you're done talking to that dog, we got a problem.
There's a bunch of Natives out there, headed this way.
And I imagine they're a bit pissed off that I killed so many of them.

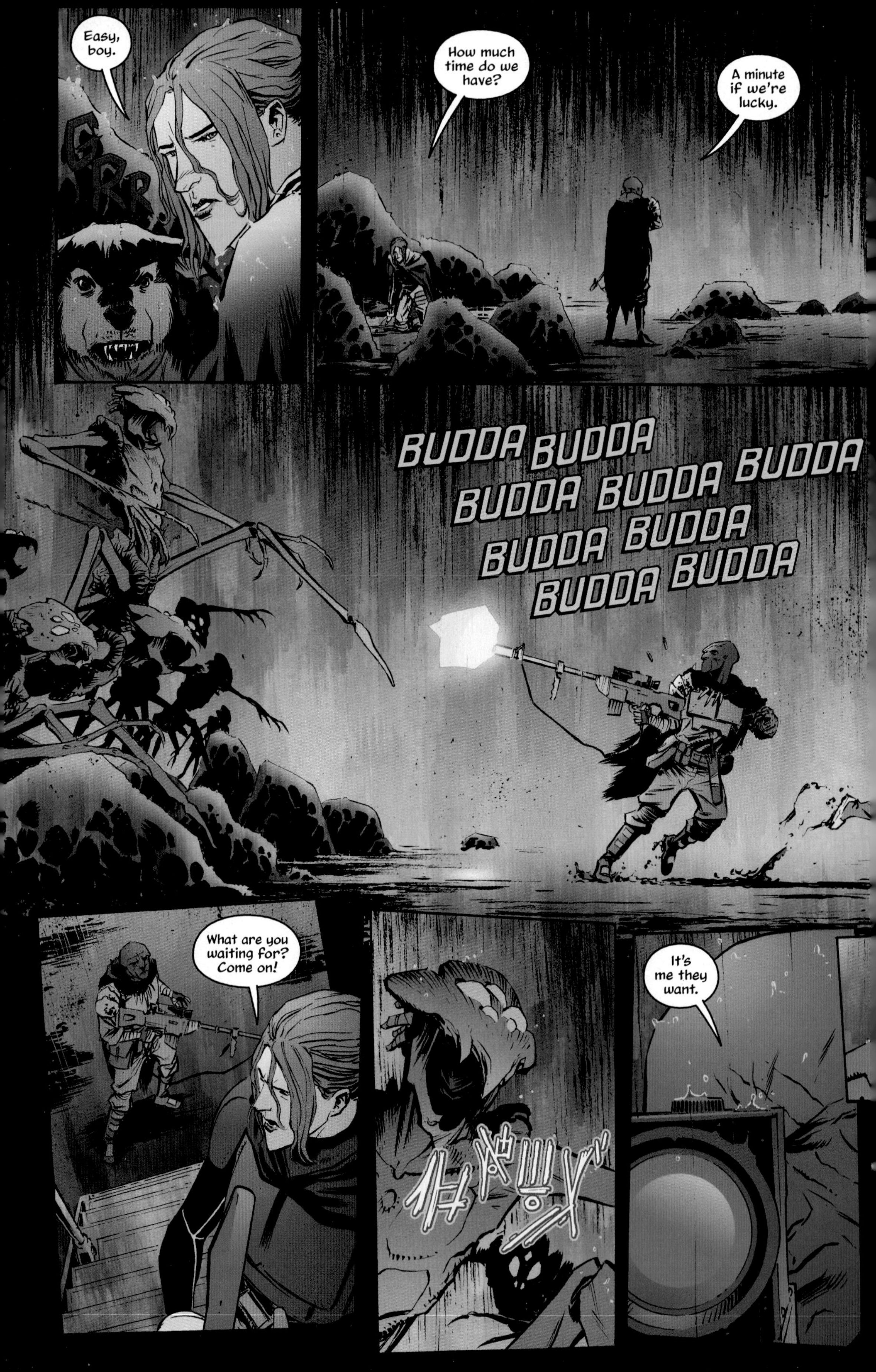
Easy, boy.
GRR
How much time do we have?
A minute if we're lucky.
BUDDA BUDDA
BUDDA BUDDA BUDDA
BUDDA BUDDA
BUDDA BUDDA
What are you waiting for? Come on!
It's me they want.

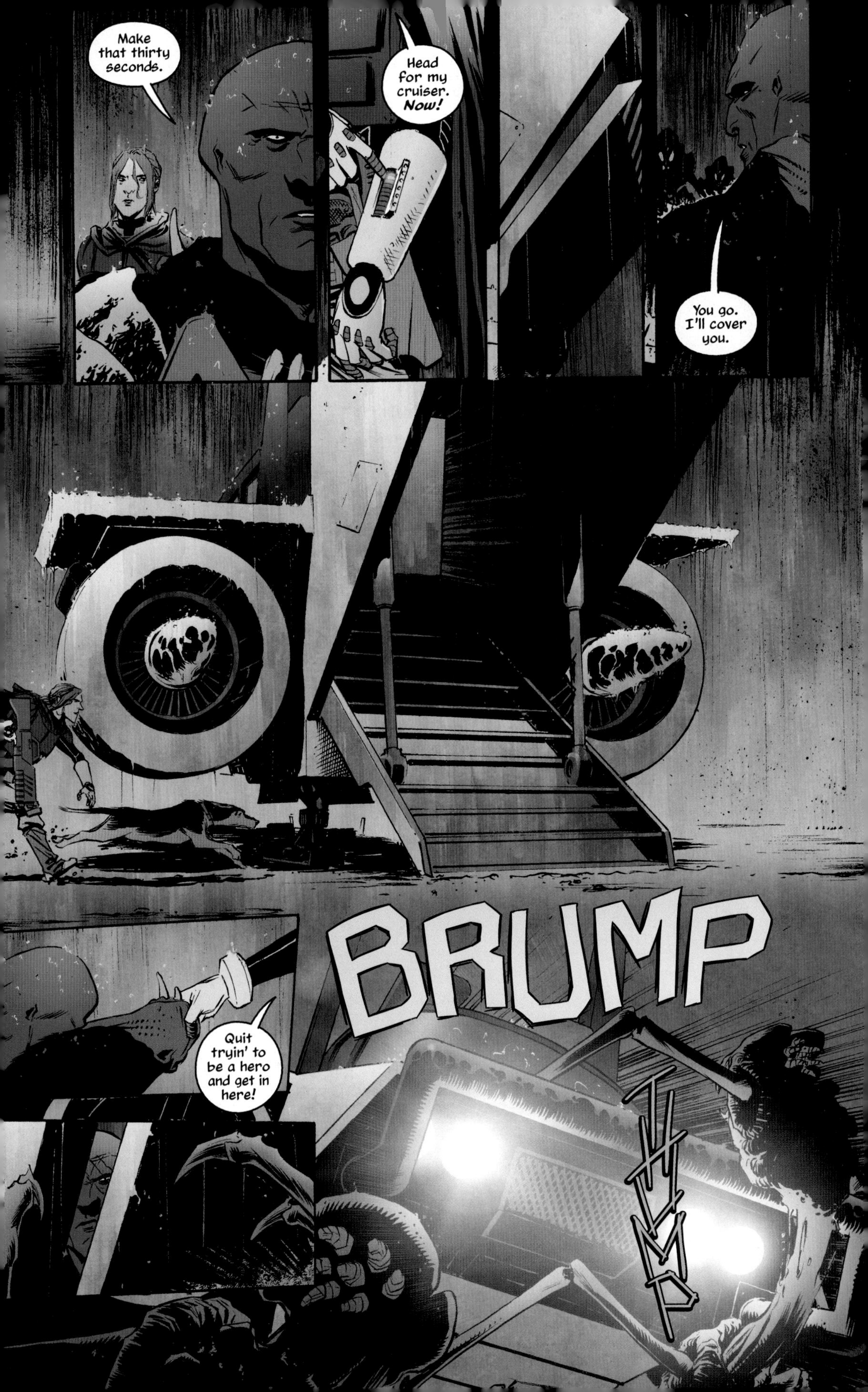
Make that thirty seconds.
Head for my cruiser. *Now!*
You go. I'll cover you.
BRUMP
Quit tryin' to be a hero and get in here!
THUMP

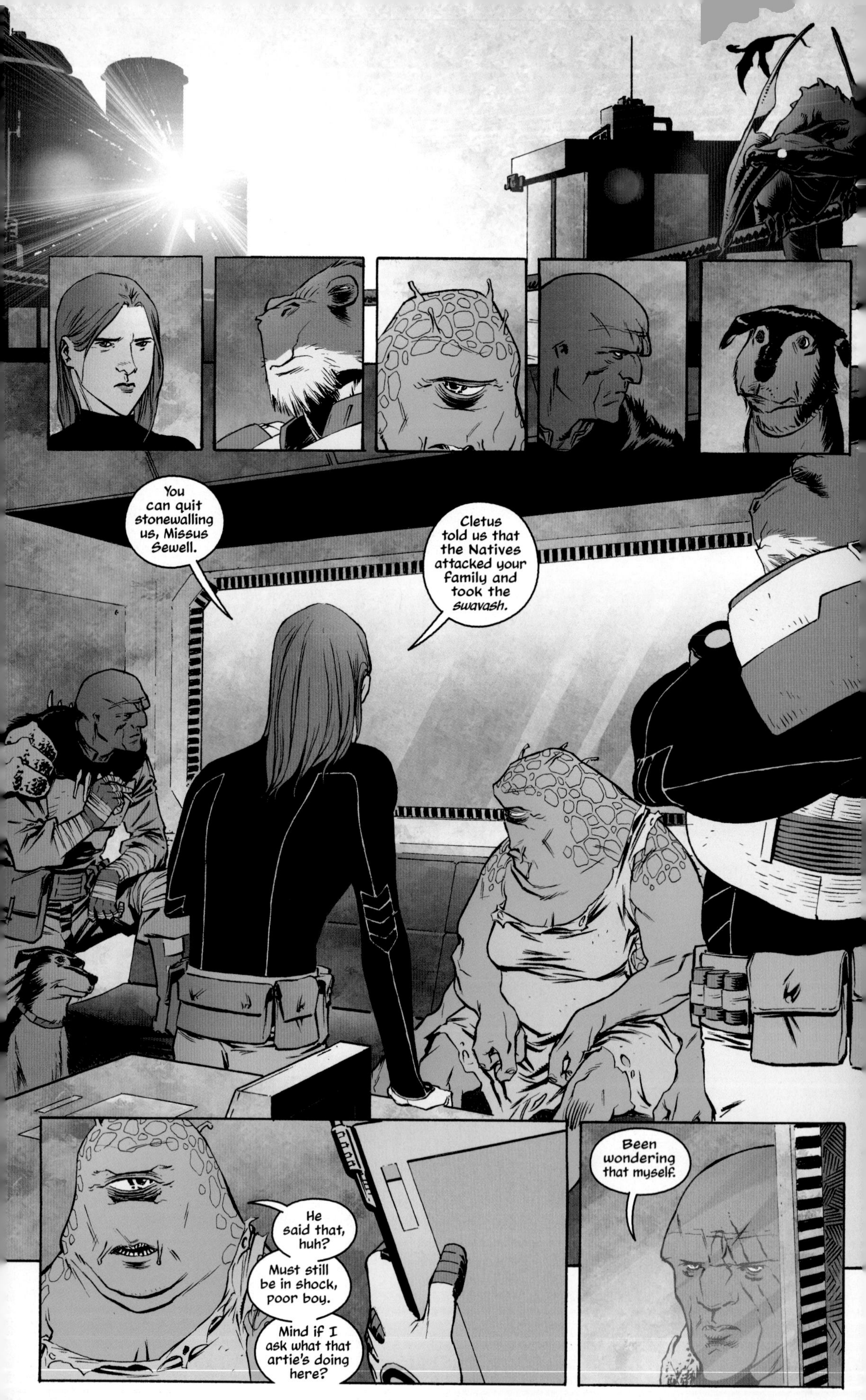
You can quit stonewalling us, Missus Sewell.
Cletus told us that the Natives attacked your family and took the *swavash*.
He said that, huh?
Must still be in shock, poor boy.
Mind if I ask what that artie's doing here?
Been wondering that myself.

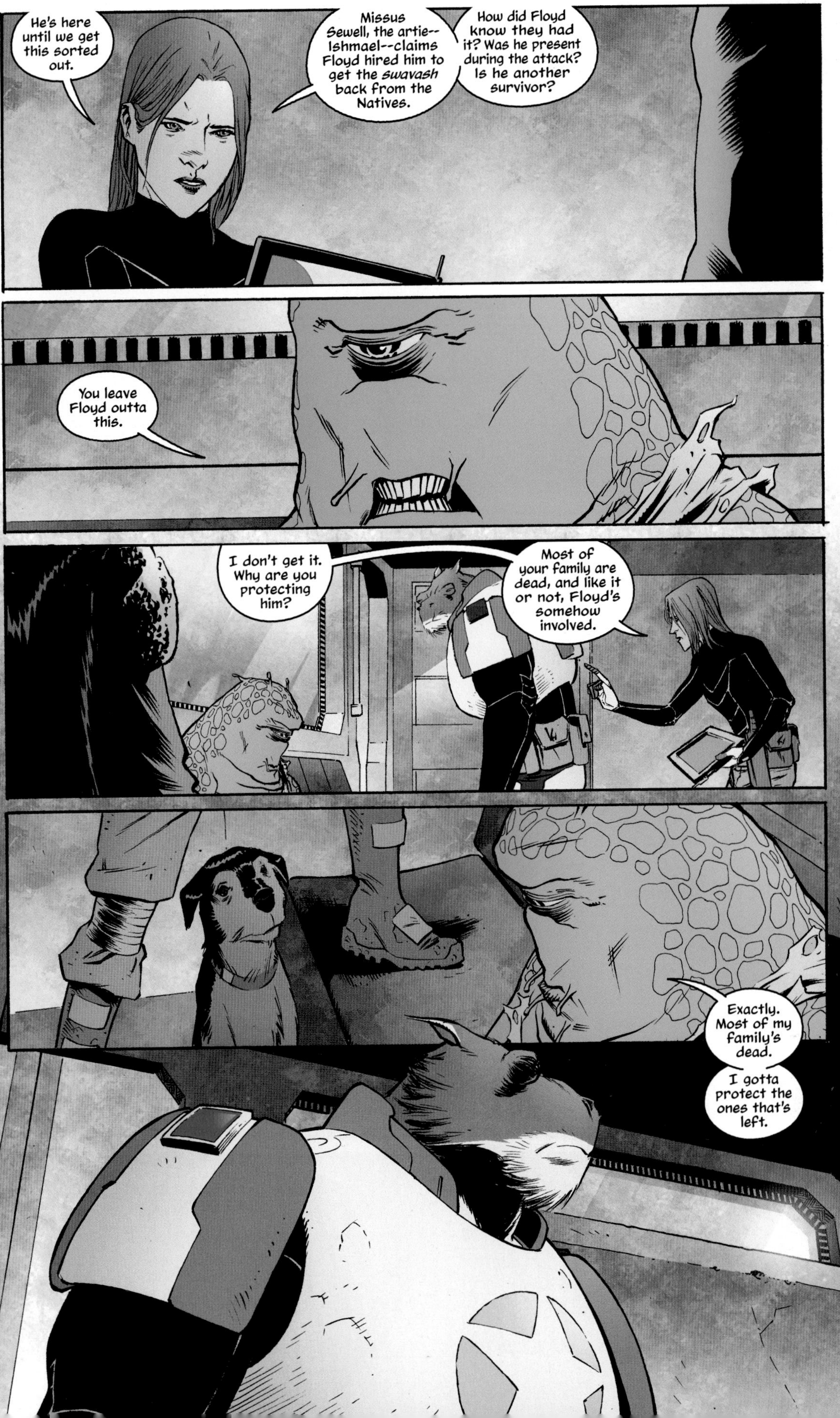
He's here until we get this sorted out.
Missus Sewell, the artie--Ishmael--claims Floyd hired him to get the *swavash* back from the Natives.
How did Floyd know they had it? Was he present during the attack? Is he another survivor?
You leave Floyd outta this.
I don't get it. Why are you protecting him?
Most of your family are dead, and like it or not, Floyd's somehow involved.
Exactly. Most of my family's dead.
I gotta protect the ones that's left.

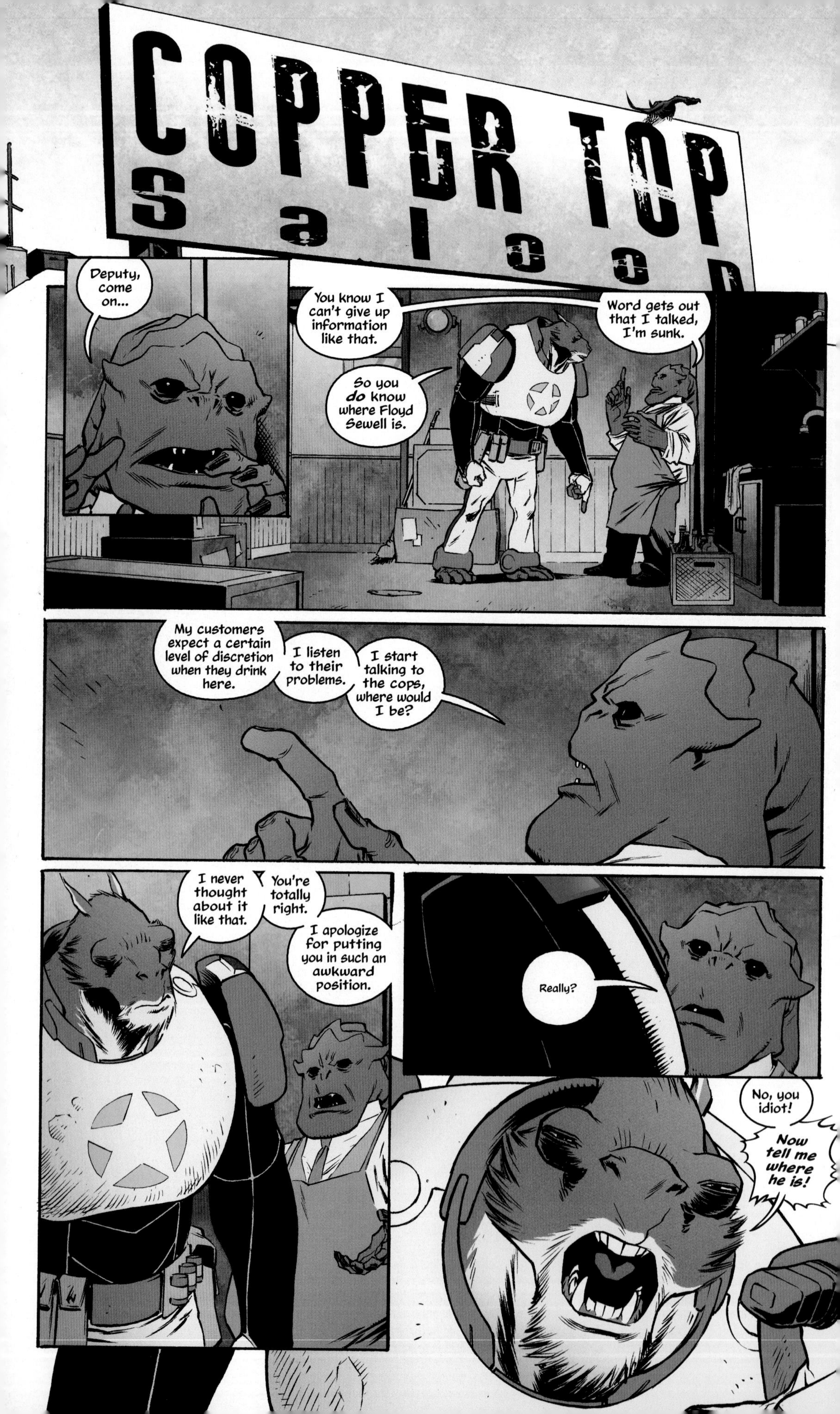
COPPER TOP
Saloon
Deputy, come on...
You know I can't give up information like that.
Word gets out that I talked, I'm sunk.
So you *do* know where Floyd Sewell is.
My customers expect a certain level of discretion when they drink here.
I listen to their problems.
I start talking to the cops, where would I be?
I never thought about it like that.
You're totally right.
I apologize for putting you in such an awkward position.
Really?
No, you idiot!
Now tell me where he is!

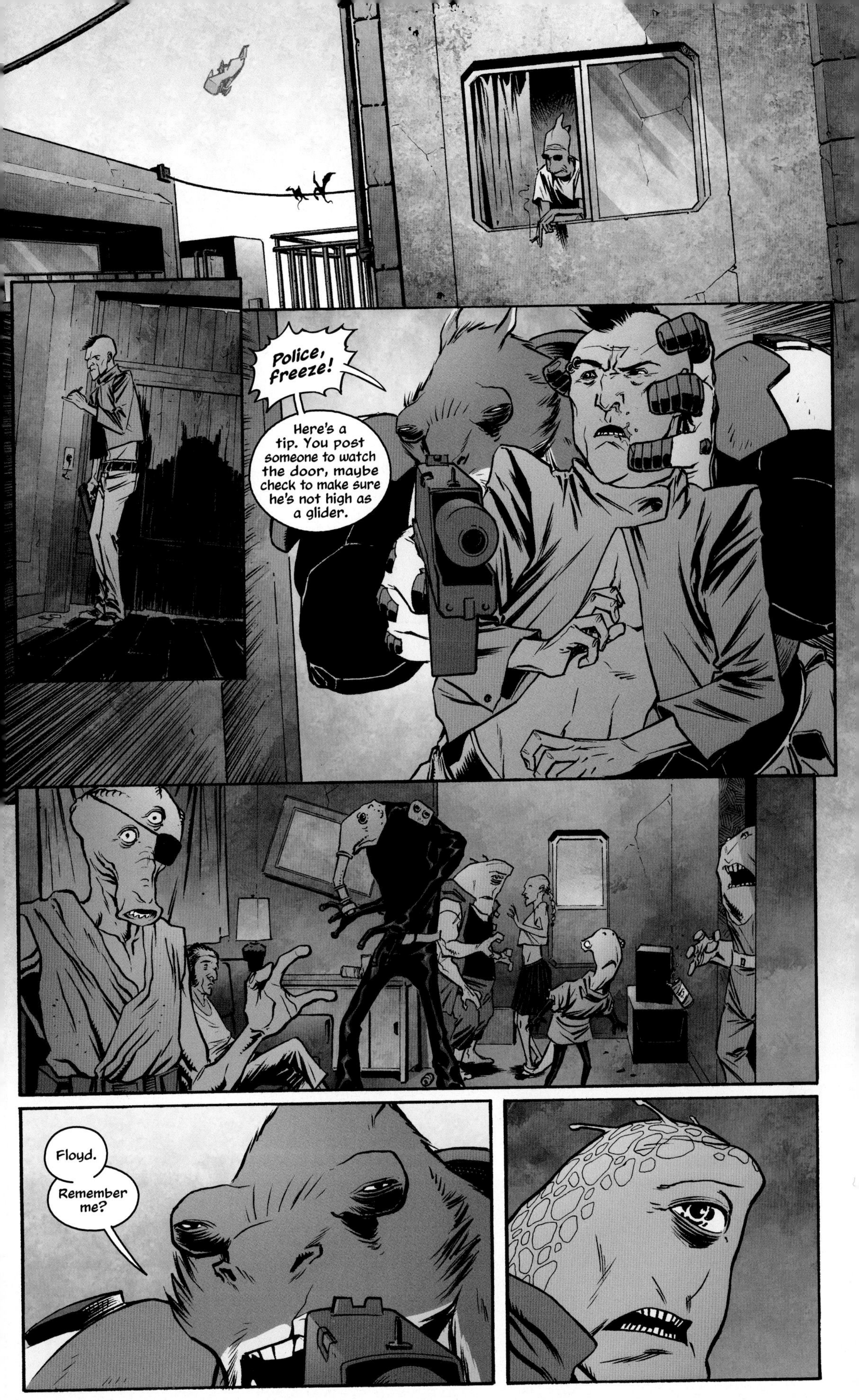
Police, freeze!
Here's a tip. You post someone to watch the door, maybe check to make sure he's not high as a glider.
Floyd.
Remember me?

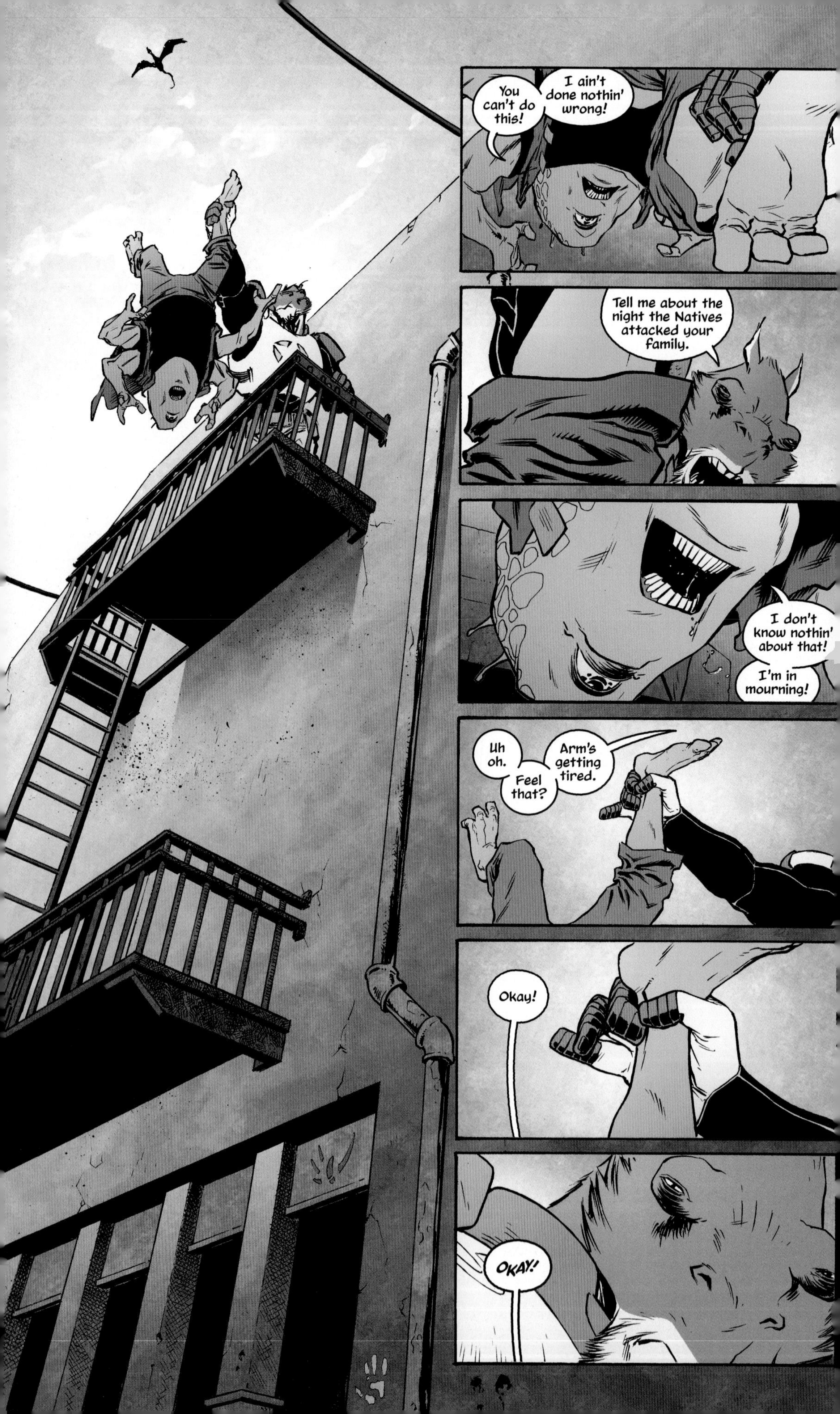
You can't do this!
I ain't done nothin' wrong!
Tell me about the night the Natives attacked your family.
I don't know nothin' about that!
I'm in mourning!
Uh oh.
Feel that?
Arm's getting tired.
Okay!
OKAY!

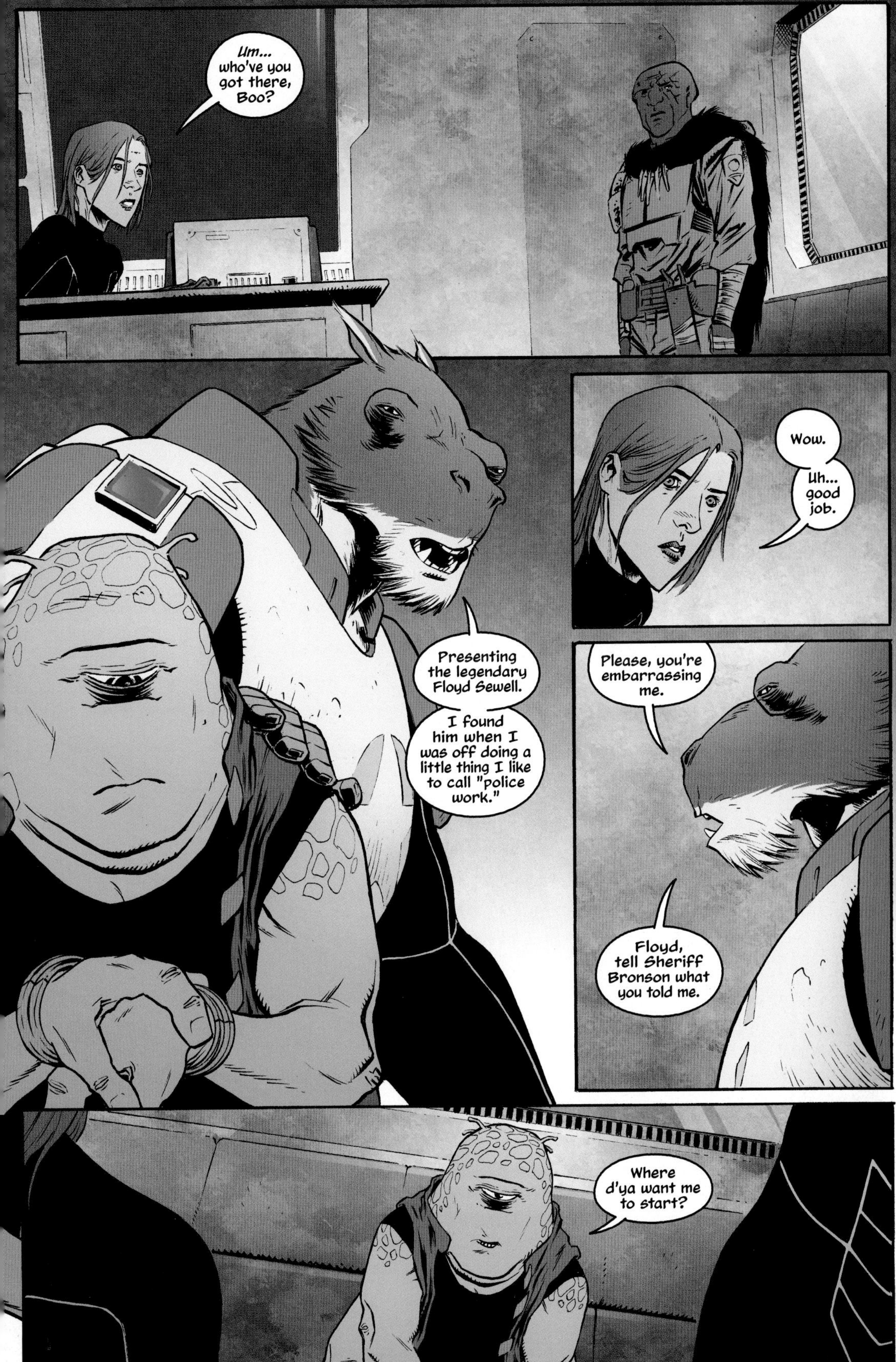
Um... who've you got there, Boo?
Presenting the legendary Floyd Sewell.
I found him when I was off doing a little thing I like to call "police work."
Wow.
Uh... good job.
Please, you're embarrassing me.
Floyd, tell Sheriff Bronson what you told me.
Where d'ya want me to start?

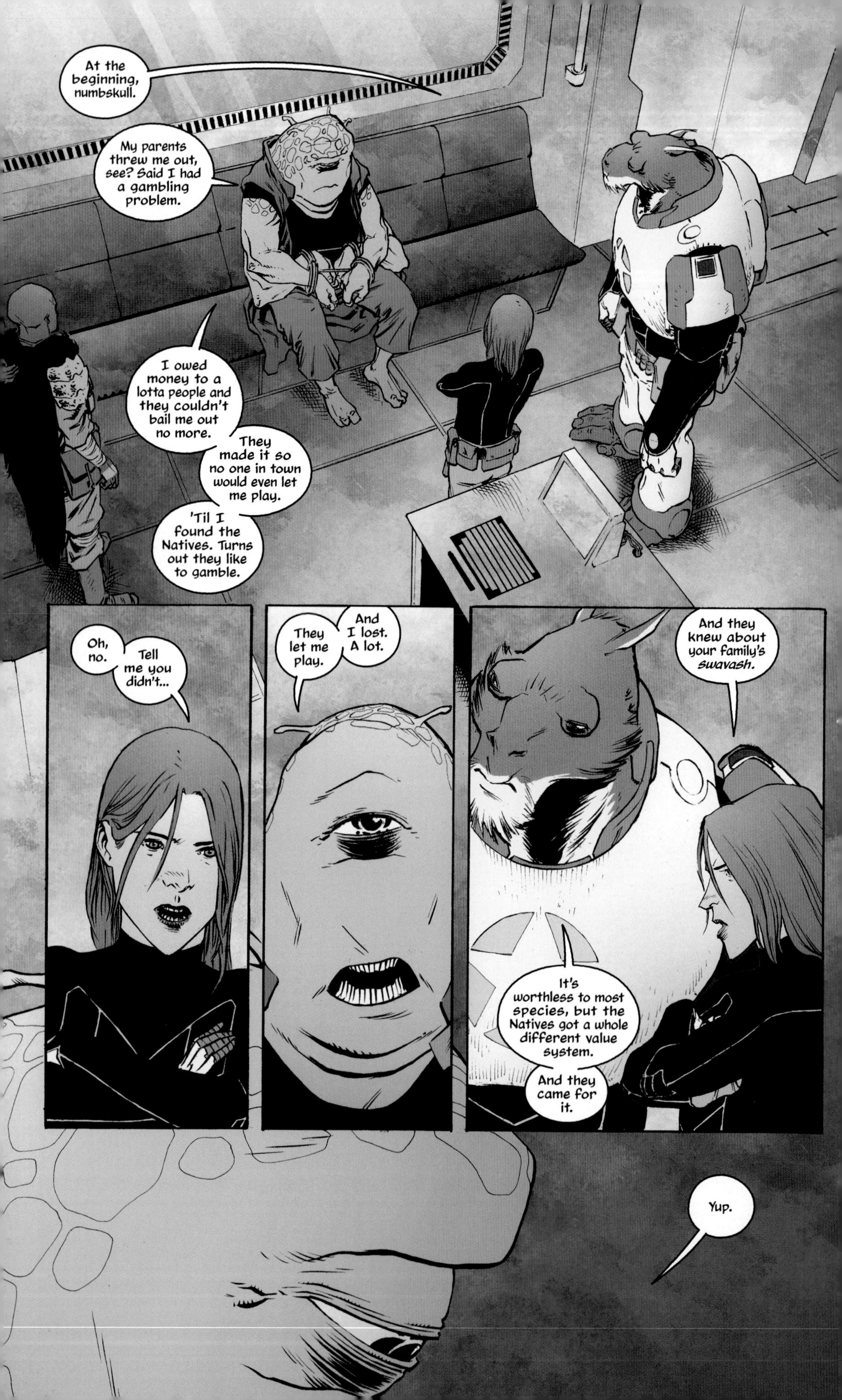
At the beginning, numbskull.
My parents threw me out, see? Said I had a gambling problem.
I owed money to a lotta people and they couldn't bail me out no more.
They made it so no one in town would even let me play.
'Til I found the Natives. Turns out they like to gamble.
Oh, no.
Tell me you didn't...
They let me play.
And I lost. A lot.
And they knew about your family's *swavash.*
It's worthless to most species, but the Natives got a whole different value system.
And they came for it.
Yup.

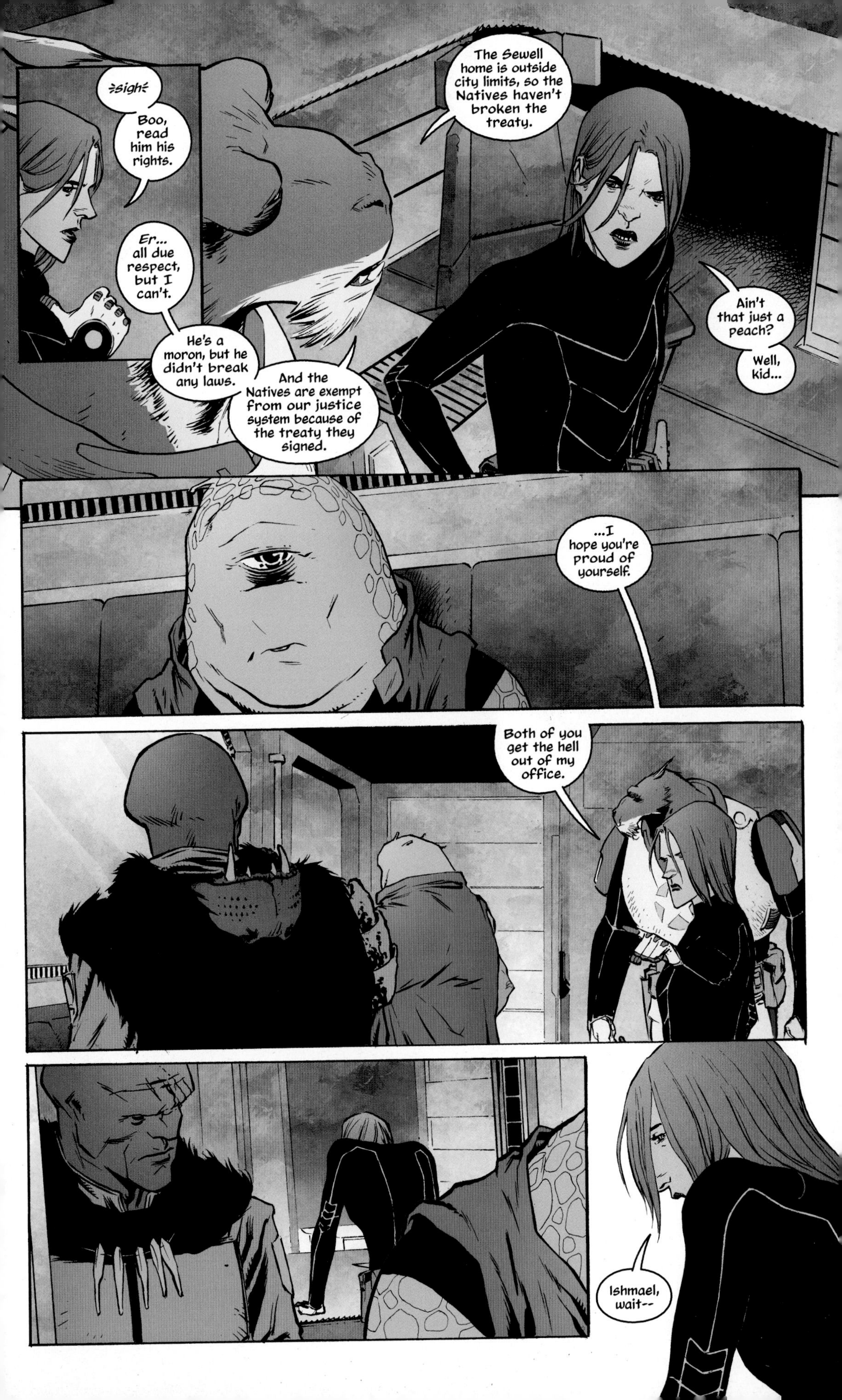

≈sigh≈
Boo, read him his rights.
Er... all due respect, but I can't.
He's a moron, but he didn't break any laws.
And the Natives are exempt from our justice system because of the treaty they signed.
The Sewell home is outside city limits, so the Natives haven't broken the treaty.
Ain't that just a peach?
Well, kid...
...I hope you're proud of yourself.
Both of you get the hell out of my office.
Ishmael, wait--

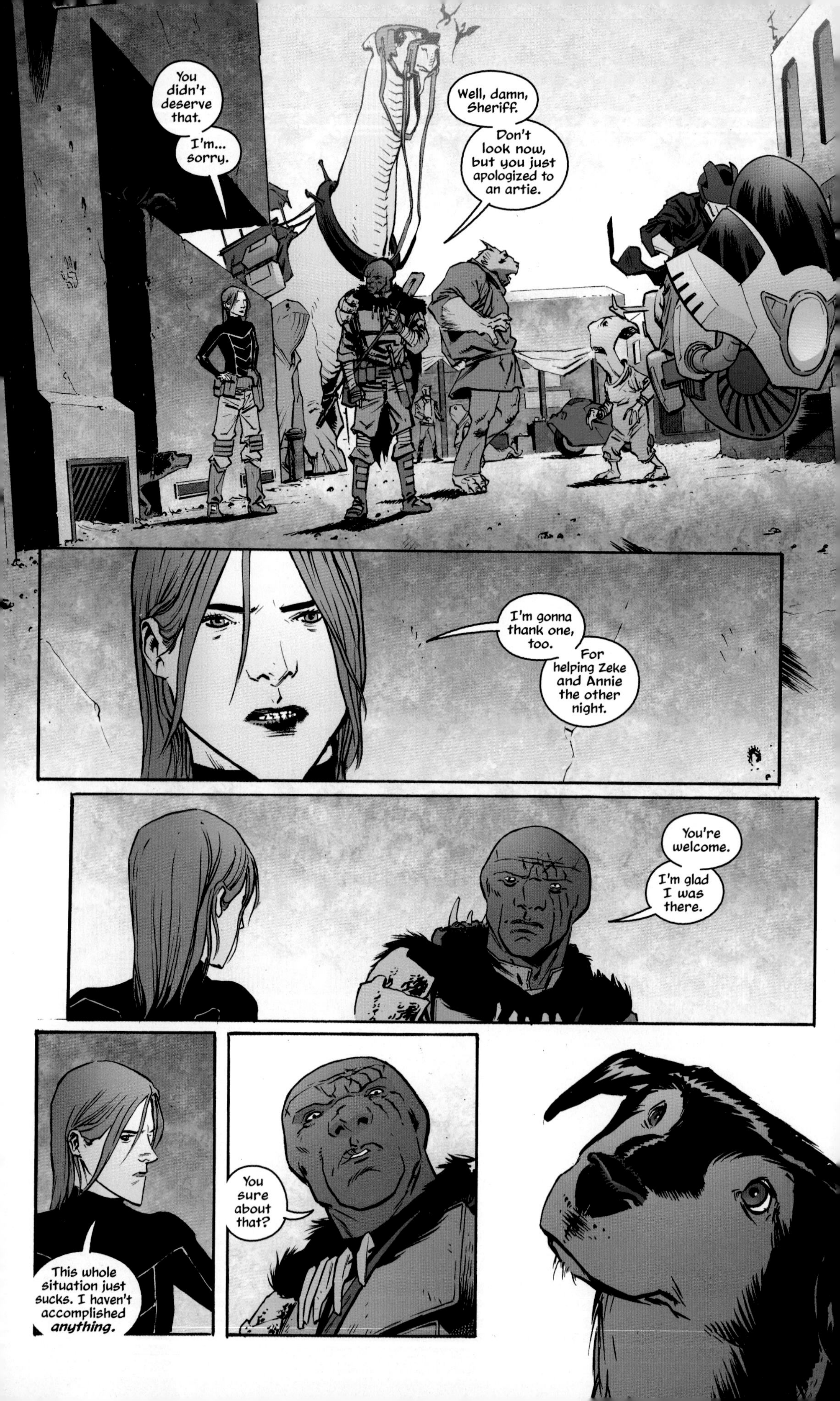
You didn't deserve that.
I'm... sorry.
Well, damn, Sheriff.
Don't look now, but you just apologized to an artie.
I'm gonna thank one, too.
For helping Zeke and Annie the other night.
You're welcome.
I'm glad I was there.
This whole situation just sucks. I haven't accomplished *anything*.
You sure about that?

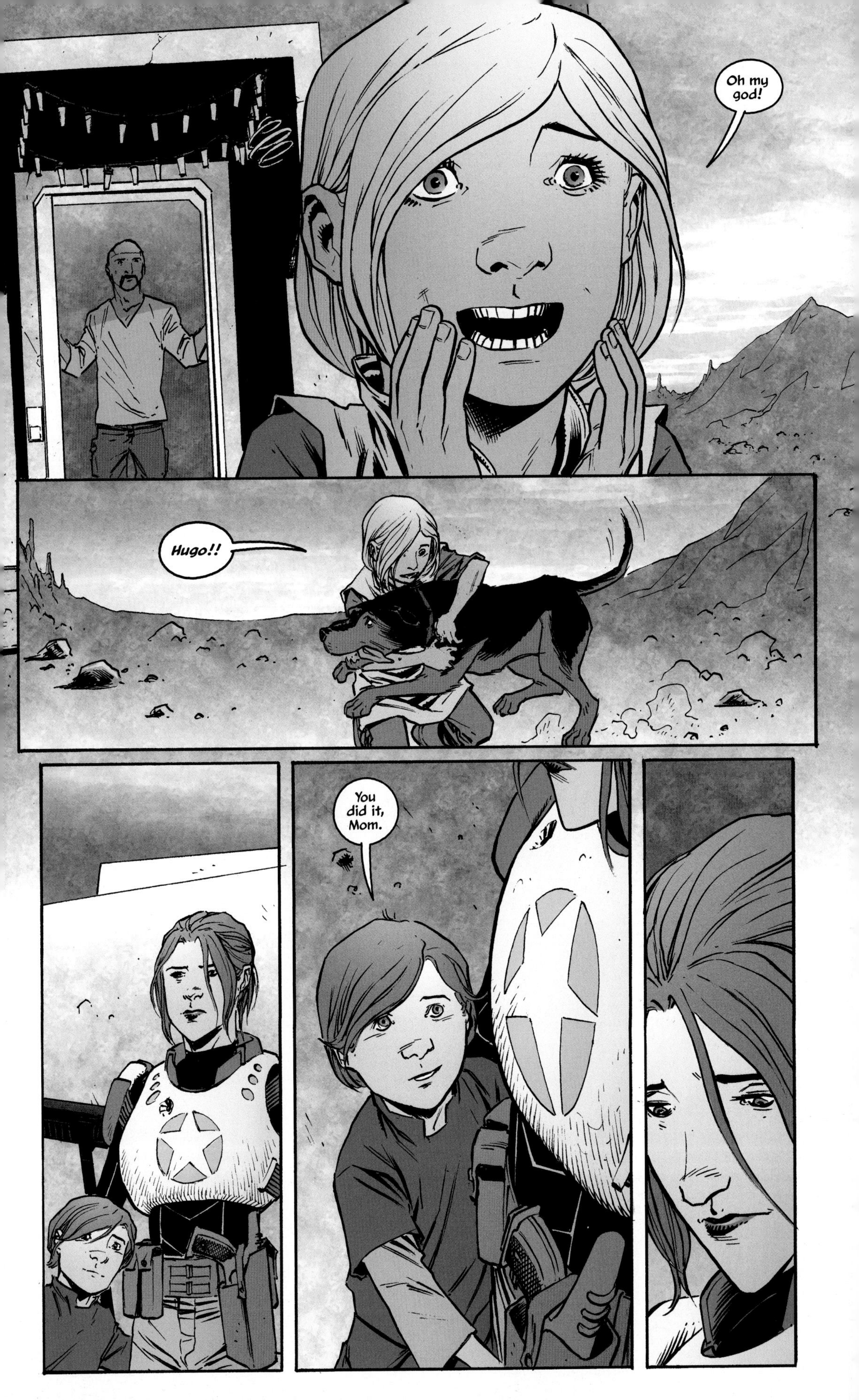
Oh my god!
Hugo!!
You did it, Mom.

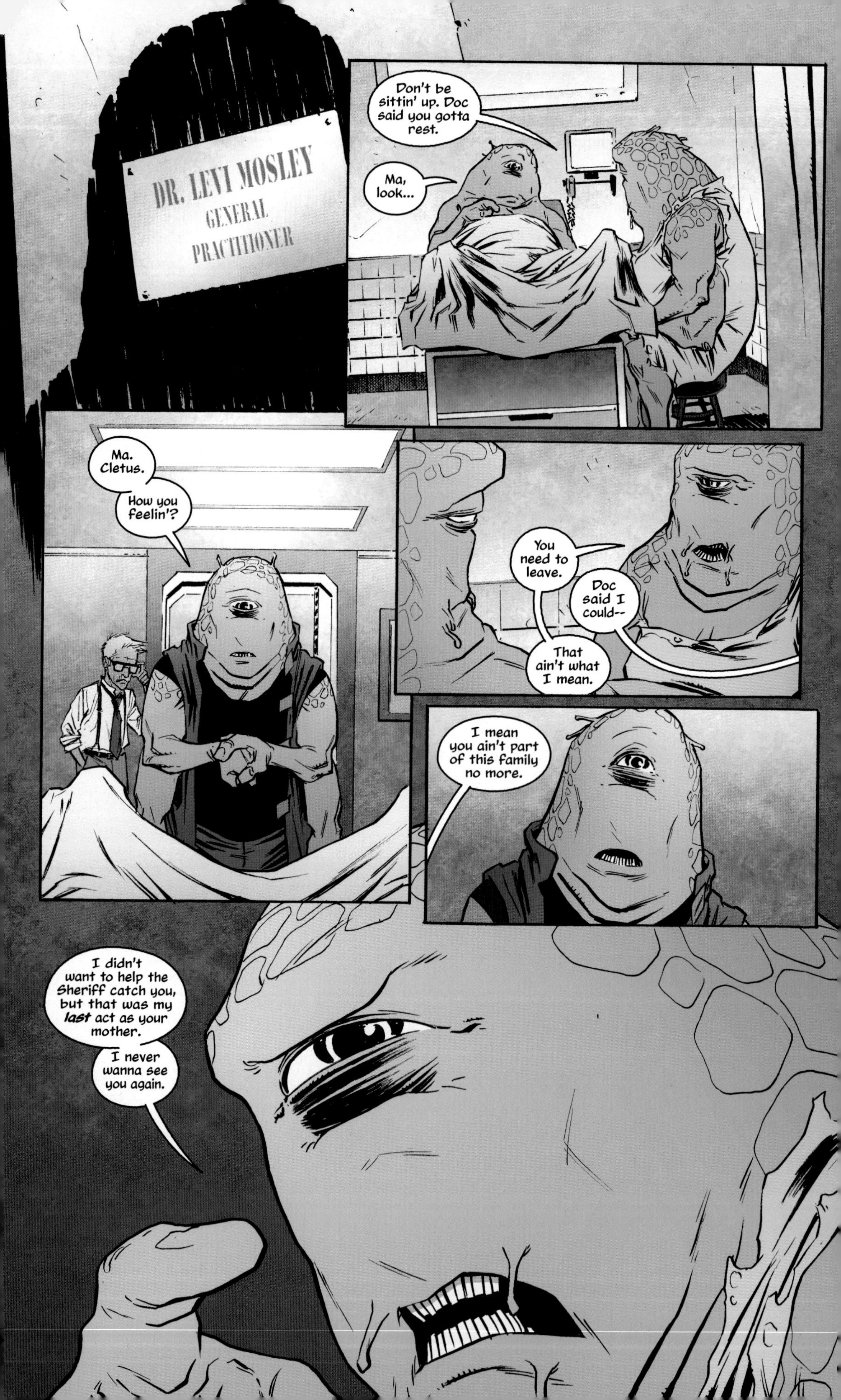

DR. LEVI MOSLEY
GENERAL
PRACTITIONER
Don't be sittin' up. Doc said you gotta rest.
Ma, look...
Ma. Cletus.
How you feelin'?
You need to leave.
Doc said I could--
That ain't what I mean.
I mean you ain't part of this family no more.
I didn't want to help the Sheriff catch you, but that was my *last* act as your mother.
I never wanna see you again.

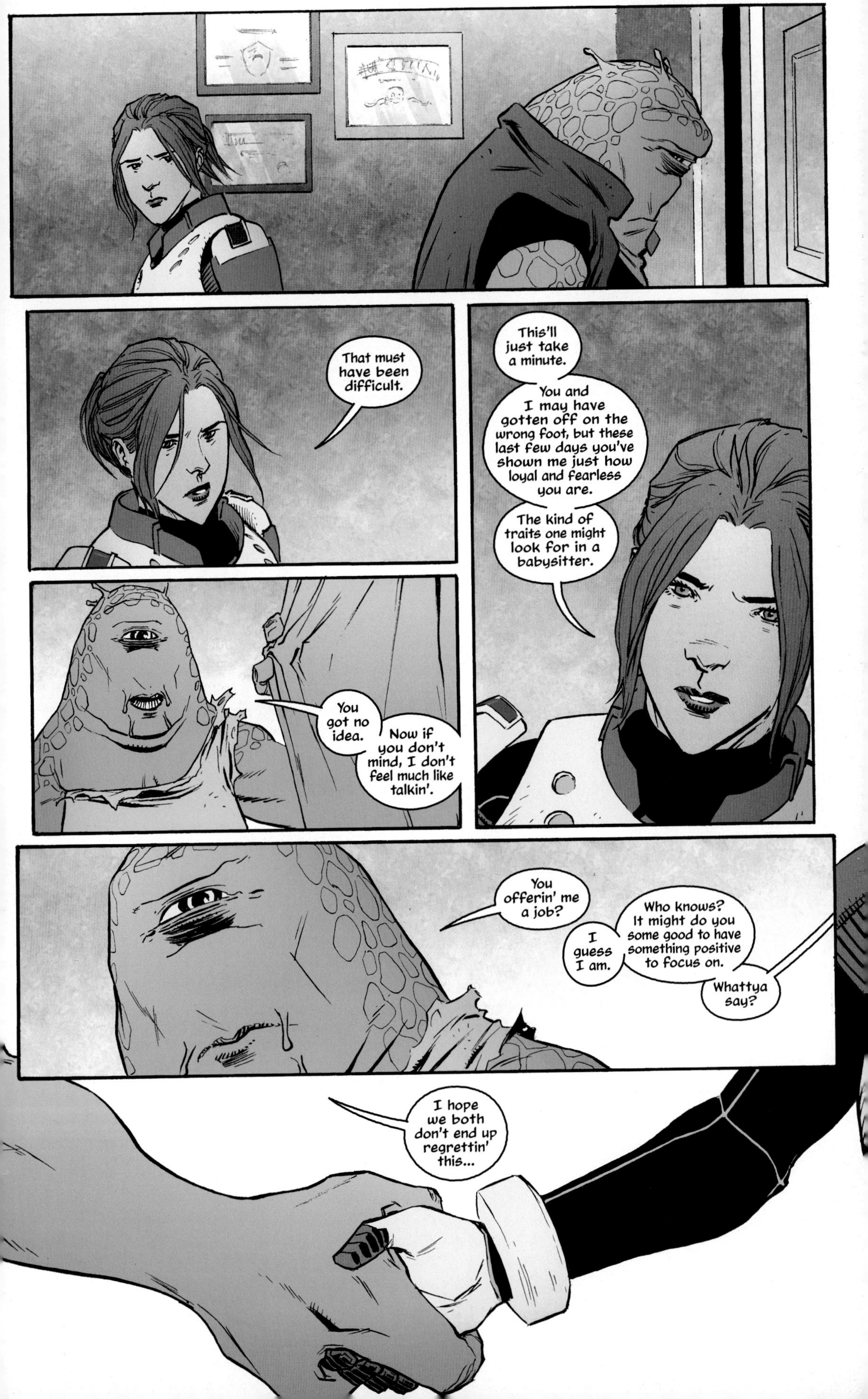
That must have been difficult.
This'll just take a minute.
You and I may have gotten off on the wrong foot, but these last few days you've shown me just how loyal and fearless you are.
The kind of traits one might look for in a babysitter.
You got no idea.
Now if you don't mind, I don't feel much like talkin'.
You offerin' me a job?
I guess I am.
Who knows? It might do you some good to have something positive to focus on.
Whattya say?
I hope we both don't end up regrettin' this...

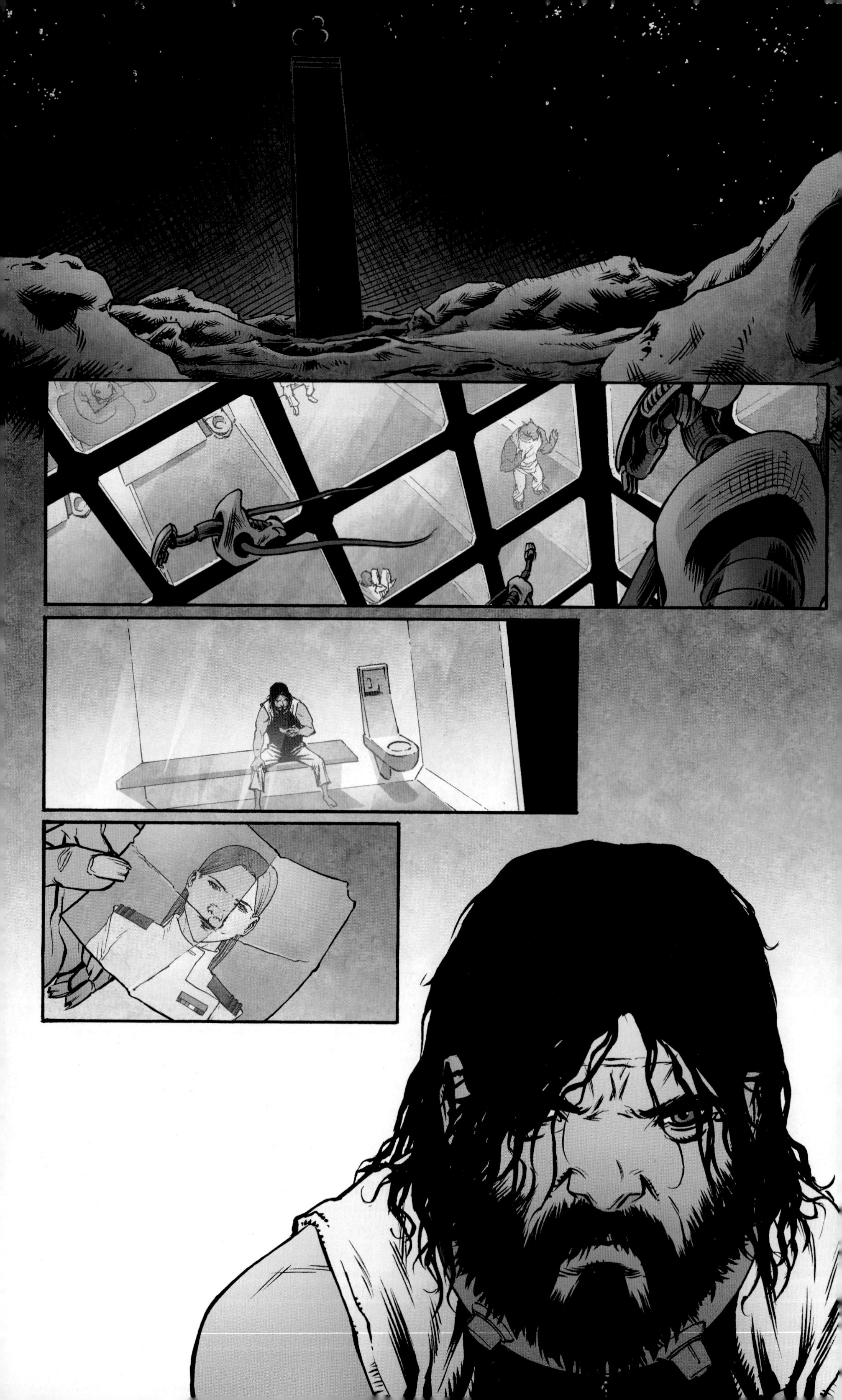